CHANDLER MOORE

REDEEMING ROYALTY

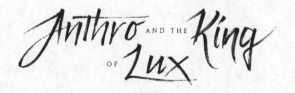
Anthro AND THE King OF Lux

Dedicated to:

My sister Lydia.
This book would not be the same without you.
Thank you for always listening.

CONTENTS

I	The Child's Mind	1
II	The Fields of Change	10
III	The Scarlet Stain	20
IV	The Glory of Humanity	30
V	The Horror of Humanity	40
VI	The Hope in History	48
VII	The Parchment	68
VIII	The Awakening	78
IX	The Reign of the Fittest	86
X	The Moral Doubt	106
XI	The Child's Dream	132
XII	The Depth of the Darkness	142
XIII	The Thief in the Night	149
XIV	The Two Brothers	163
XV	The Great Divide	174
XVI	The God of Suffering	192
XVII	The Call to the Sick	208
XVIII	The Three in One	224
XIX	The Revelation of God	235
XX	The Two Become One	246
XXI	The Chains of Freedom	256
XXII	The Last Confession	271
XXIII	Behold Your King	278

Chapter I

The Child's Mind

Under the dying shadows of a twisted oak sat a young boy with his back pressed firmly against the coarse bark. Beneath the overhanging claw of branches, thick mahogany curls further shaded vibrant emerald eyes. Behind these sat a growing mind embedded with thought well beyond its years. Gnarled and exposed roots snaked through the eroded banks of a winding stream. The flow of cool mountain runoff tossed together stone upon stone, gently vibrating the air as it etched its form ever wider. An earthy musk of rainfall hung in the air, the aroma rising from the thick wood just beyond the reach of the oak's outermost touch. Spots of sunshine penetrated the skeletal grip of wood above the child, casting an array of light and darkness across his face.

The boy's palm was held open with a sleek river stone resting upon it. His shimmering emeralds were transfixed upon the object. He stroked its smooth surface as one would a small pet. Suddenly, he wound up and sent it flying across the tranquil surface of an eddy before him. One skip. Two skips. Three. Four. Five. And no more as the polished granite sunk down to join its submerged brethren.

He watched the ripples as they spread out, noting the collisions between the opposing sets. Then, reaching out beside him, he seized another stone. He ran his fingers across it, his eyes closed to allow him to hone his sense of touch. This one was just as smooth as all of the others he had thrown, not one of which had achieved more than five skips. After moving the stone between each hand, he placed it squarely on his palm, opening his searching eyes to study it further. The stone had a deeper hue than his light olive skin, but it looked to be every bit as polished as it felt. The youth rested his head back against the living remnants of the hardwood and closed his eyes once more to contemplate.

Why can't I get a stone to skip more than five times? What are the possible reasons? This part of the water is calm, which makes for perfect skipping conditions—or so I'm told. The stones in this area sure look and feel smooth, which should mean that they can skip very well. But maybe they only appear that way. Could that be? If I were able to look at them under those powerful lenses that they have in the capital, maybe the rocks wouldn't actually be smooth. Maybe there are tiny bumps and scrapes that I can't see or feel.

I wonder…if that's true, then perhaps the rough hidden surface of the stone limits how many skips I get out of it. That's possible…right? Yes, I think that is a possibility, at the very least. So, what else? Maybe there is some kind of unwritten law in this kingdom that rocks can only skip across water a total of five times? That seems unlikely, especially as I know people who say they've been able to get more skips. Haven't I seen them do it? The unwritten law idea is not likely. What else could it be, then? Well, I guess I could be the problem and not the river or the stone, but…

"Hey! Anthro! Are you asleep?"

Anthro was jolted out of his speculations as two more youths approached him, moving down the bedimmed shoreline.

"No, just lost in thought." Anthro spoke as he sent the stone in his hand flying across the water.

Four skips…

"Well then, nothing out of the ordinary here," a slightly chubby boy with golden hair said with a chuckle, climbing off the bank and onto the oak's unveiled footing.

"That's right, Kalo, but did you find a better way to get into Mediocris's farm?" Anthro asked as he stood up and stretched his stiff joints, popping his right elbow. He subconsciously ran one of his hands along the wrinkles of bark and glanced up at the canopy of leaves in the forest before him. Legions of individual offshoots were capturing their last rays of vitality, so many of them already blurring together with the approaching nightfall.

"We did, but his dogs almost got us before we could get anything good," Paro said as the three children jumped along the tangle of roots and entered the deeper shade of the bordering forest. "I guess there is no way around them."

"The big brown one just about got a nip out of Paro's back-side!" Kalo said. Despite his larger size, Kalo was faster than most of the boys his age.

"Only because you took off the moment we heard them!" Paro replied while positioning himself in front of the group. "I'm every bit as fast as either of you if there are no head starts." While taking large steps away from them, he shot his friends a mischievous look through his black sheepdog hair. "I'll beat you both back to the gate!" With that, he took off along the narrow, wooded pathway that led back to their city.

"Apparently, *he's* allowed to get a head start," Kalo said to Anthro as they both started off to chase after their friend, the mystery of the stones left for another day.

* * * *

"You boys just made it back in time," exclaimed a decrepit old man. The elder was leaning against an unimposing spear cut simply from local timber. "You were about to be locked out for the night."

The boys were coming over the western bridge and up to the crudely fortified city gate with Kalo reigning victorious. The last pure rays of sunlight that could work their way through the forest the boys had come from were all but gone.

"We'd have found a way in," Kalo boasted as he put both of his hands against his sides, winded but not depleted.

"I suppose you all would have. Be mindful of how skilled you become at getting into places where you don't belong. One day you just might fail to get out." The man spoke neither threat nor jest.

"What he meant to say was, 'Sorry sir, it won't happen again, and thank you for waiting up for us.'" Anthro gave the man a slight bow as he spoke.

The gatekeeper returned the gesture with a mild bow of his own. "Now, there's a boy who knows how to address his elders. Gives me just a bit of hope for what may come from the whole lot of you."

"Suck-up," muttered Kalo as they made their way past the wrinkled guard and into the city of cracked cobblestone and patched brick.

Anthro held his tongue until the boys were well beyond the ears of the elderly militiaman. "I keep trying to tell you that it is not 'sucking up.' It's called 'working people.' Watch them, study them, and learn what makes them tick. Figure out what they like to hear and then give it to them. It will get you into, and out of, more places than just sneaking skills."

"Call it what you will…but it sure looks like…sucking up to me," Paro said from behind them, his breaths coming in heaves.

"Anyway, what were you…thinking about this time, Anthro?"

"I was wondering if those seemingly smooth rocks aren't as smooth as they look and, if that's true, whether it affects their skipping potential."

By habit, the boys turned off the main street of the city and onto a large side road that meandered its way toward the homes of the city's proletarian housing district. The familiar, pungent mixture of refuse and char filled their nostrils as they entered the hoard of apartment row houses.

"Simply life-altering meditation, Anthro," Kalo said. "Why do you waste your time with that kind of thinking? Do you really think you're going to change the world with that head of yours?"

"No," Anthro replied. "I just believe some things that appear obvious to us are worth a closer look. I'm trying to understand the world as it is, not change it."

"And that's your problem, buddy. You're stuck contemplating the rocks themselves, when you could be spending valuable time considering what to do with them instead."

"Do with them? Like what?" Anthro asked.

"Oh, I don't know. Distract dogs, smash windows, throw at enemies, or…" Kalo broke off suddenly.

As the trio turned onto Anthro's street, they saw a young girl coming toward them with a stack of wood much too large for her slight stature. The wood was piled so high that the girl was struggling to see over it.

Kalo, grinning maliciously, twisted around to ensure that the street behind them was as vacant as the one before them. He crept forward while signaling Paro to follow. The two boys hustled ahead of Anthro and made their way over to the girl, crouched well beneath the bounds of her restricted vision. Then, to Anthro's horror, Paro stuck one of his legs out as Kalo gave the girl a strong shove in the back.

The girl stumbled forward, the pile of wood collapsing in her petite arms as she tried to recover. It was to no avail. She fell hard against the stone roadway as a wedged branch scraped across her face. A sharp red line was etched into her pale, freckled skin from temple to chin. Kalo erupted with laughter and Paro followed suit.

Anthro froze, and time slowed along with him. His mouth sat agape, his fists were clenched, and his eyes were wide and transfixed upon the girl. The boys had always enjoyed their various neighborhood scraps and were often the instigators, but this was much different. This was a younger and defenseless target. The others had fought back; she had crumbled. Their frail victim sat bent upon her knees, her hands supporting the weight of her curled upper body. Wavy auburn hair covered her face like a veil.

He watched a droplet of blood form upon her temple. The deep red orb glistened like a tear before flowing down the curves just below her eyes and resting upon her upper lip. Red tear after red tear followed after this forerunner. Just one crystal bead fell from her eyes, following its own path but meeting the small red pool that had gathered upon her lip. The crystal and crimson united together, becoming one tainted drop, and fell upon the cold stone below.

Anthro's stomach turned within him. His fists clenched ever tighter and his faced flushed. A bead of sweat formed upon his brow. The salty droplet raced down his warm cheek, leaving a remnant of its icy touch in its wake. He wanted to help. He wanted to fight back for her. But he could not move. Kalo looked toward him expectantly, and as their eyes met, Anthro— despite all his inner protests—slowly joined in their laughter at the girl's suffering.

As he made his way past the fallen girl to join his waiting friends, she was still unmoved from her position; a broken statue of pain and inscrutability. Her face was set toward the ground, eyes careful to avoid his. Could he bear the shame if their eyes met? Despite her scraped knees and the bleeding scratch across her pale cheek, her downcast face showed no emotion, no recognition of the pain, the internal hidden within her somber, vacant expression. Her defeated posture and the one crystal droplet that had fallen from her eyes were the only visible manifestations of her inward feelings.

Anthro, still masquerading a half-grin on his face, tried to see into the girl's eyes despite his hesitation. He knew that he was guilty, perhaps unforgivably so, but somehow he thought that if he could but look into her eyes and she into his, she would see that it was all an act. But even then he knew that a mere look of pity and apology could not atone for his cowardice. His conscience was screaming at him to go to her, to help her, to bring some healing to her misery, to turn on his friends if need be—and yet his fear of man, or boy, overpowered him.

Anthro knew this girl. Her name was Keta and she was a year or two younger than himself. They had never spoken before, but he had watched her from the rooftop of his building, analyzing her young life as he did with everyone on his street. No siblings and no father as far as he could tell, though there was a man who would come into her home at times, usually late in the evening. He never stayed long and Keta always seemed to try to avoid him.

It was clear that Keta helped take care of an old woman who lived at the end of the block. He did not know whether she was related to her, but Anthro was positive that the aging woman was to be the recipient of this woodpile. This was a usual weekly delivery that involved several trips. Her actions were small, yet mighty for one so small and of such limited resources—acts of a charitable heart within a lonely child.

The boys had poked fun at her in the past, as was their habit whenever smaller children were around, but never before had anything violent or physical been done to her or those younger victims. That had always been reserved for kids who could at least attempt to stand their ground. Even within the stale air, Anthro could sense the sudden shift that had occurred among his friends, the coming of age. All these years they had only been testing the waters, seeing just how far they could go and how much they could get away with. And all the while, they had been developing an appetite for powerless prey. Having now wet the tongue, they would begin to consume. With the nausea intensifying, Anthro walked on.

After reaching his stoop and parting with his friends, he paused—waiting for them to move out of sight—and then looked back down the street. On a flickering edge of shadows and firelight, she was still kneeling in the distance like a forgotten phantom. He took a step toward her, physically extending a hand in her direction, overwhelmed by shame and guilt. Powerful and contradictory emotions and ideas swirled within him, demanding him to help. They bid him to flee, yet commanded him to redeem. They compelled him to let be, but required him to intervene. He had to run to her. He had to hide from her. At both ends, he found only fear.

Hesitantly, Anthro turned away and started up the lifeless stairs. He took only five steps before bending over the railing and vomiting. After wiping his mouth, he fled inside.

That night, long after his mother had gone to sleep, he stared at the ceiling of his bedroom. After a dinner of little appetite, he had walked out to the roof of their small, three-story home and looked down to where the girl had been to find that she was gone. The fiery streetlights were bright enough to reveal several sticks that remained scattered where Keta had fallen. The majority of them had been picked up and eventually, Anthro assumed, made it to their intended destination. His peaceful thoughts on river stones seemed as if they had occurred in a distant life, not mere hours ago.

How could I let them treat her like that? Because I'm a spineless coward. How can I even be friends with kids who take that much pleasure in pushing around a small girl? Because I have no one else. Do I need anyone else? And what makes me feel so bad? Kalo and Paro don't seem to care, why do I care? Do I care?

Her face...the blood. Will it scar? I hope it heals. It needs to heal. Why?! Why didn't I do anything?! Wait...I definitely did something. Doing nothing was an action, wasn't it? Not helping her is the most cowardly act I can think of. What I saw was wrong. What I didn't do was wrong! What I did was wrong! What can make it right?

Anthro entered a restless sleep. The day's events and feelings had clawed their way through every branch of his subconscious. An unmoving image of broken innocence hung over him throughout the night, haunting his occasional dreams with an edge of nightmare.

Chapter II

The Fields of Change

Anthro sat upon a makeshift mirador, balancing his weight on the short parapet wall, his eyes ever scanning, his mind ever churning as he overlooked the cobblestone street below. Years of using this perch had made him confident as his feet dangled over the fringe of fractured mortar. Overcast skies meandered above him, the falling early spring sun creating visibility while hiding itself from sight. Anthro, his thoughts a hazy mimicry of the air overhead, had his vision homed in on the far end of the block.

There she was again. Her body bore the healthy tone of growing youth, thin but no longer frail. Auburn waves of light golden-copper surrounded her freckled cheeks and draped well below her bony shoulder blades.

Keta strolled lazily to the first floor of the leading apartment on the road and stood at its rickety stoop, reaching out and touching the carved wooden handrails. As she ran her hands up and down the smooth birchwood, Keta longed for the gentle touch of the woman who would never again climb these small steps.

Her sadness was of such volume that even at this distance it was visible in both her posture and mannerisms. She lingered at the stoop, seemingly without purpose, like a stray dog seeking shelter with the homeless. Eventually, she continued her journey home, always careful to avoid that stare from aloft.

With considerable finesse, she had avoided meeting his gaze over the course of the last few years and had evaded any rendezvous with his companions. She was careful to observe the boys' growth from playground hectoring to more advanced forms of malfeasance. Not all of them had grown in impropriety, though; there was one, the watchful one, who had seemed to distance himself from the other two—but not far enough to warrant her trust, nor even her glance.

Anthro watched Keta disappear into the dim light of her home's entrance, his attention wandering through the fragmented memories of his father and the questions that had firmly rooted themselves within his young mind in the days following his death. Confusion, hurt, and sorrow had all been present that week, but the perception that had caused him the most lasting trouble was just how ephemeral his father's existence had been. He died, but the city clock tower just kept moving. Anthro had been sent back to school the very next day. His mother had taken a second job to support the family finances as quickly as his father's employer had replaced him. And Anthro, his father's only heir, would only ever know so little about the man. Everyone was so replaceable, so forgettable.

These thoughts, whenever they arrived, filled him with a strange feeling that he could only bear for so long before needing some distraction. He would never run at their first appearance; what if they were important concepts to consider? But he could never analyze these ideas from a mind and heart driven merely by cerebral stimulation. No, he felt their substance, feared their power. Therefore, he had made it a habit to explore them from fresh angles with each new arrival, but never allowed himself to dwell on them for too long without seeking respite: a jaunt in the nearby woods, a dive in the river, an afternoon spent laying in a grassy field, with warm sun rays thawing more than just skin, a surveyed sunset over that field of—

Now, there's an idea. I wonder, though: Would it matter? Would she care? Could it possibly make things worse? How could it? She won't even look at me, after all this time. Why should I even bother? She's punished me enough. I know my mistake; why can't she just get over it? Why do I care? I don't care. Stupid idea anyway.

He forced his mind past that interruption and on toward other matters. Considerations of his recent educational lessons were always a good diversion. But then, out of nowhere, an image of a small smile on a pale, lightly freckled face.

No, it won't matter. It's dumb.

He moved his contemplation on to his recent fishing adventures—the trout were plentiful this year—but then his thoughts drifted once more. He imagined a pair of dispirited azure eyes finally meeting his own, a glimmer of foreign hope shining in them as if, for a moment, this life had not been her lot; as if she had found a brief taste of something better from a world her dreams often spoke of but her eyes never saw.

What do I have to lose? My pride? Ha! What do I have to be proud of? Am I afraid of her rejecting my peace offering? Afraid of being made fun of by my friends if I'm seen? I don't know. But fear... that stopped me from acting last time. Not again.

* * * *

The sun was still high as Anthro made his way out beyond the confinement of the city walls and into the forest of limitless adventure that he often traversed. He knew its twisting trails well, and could describe every similar tree as a distinct and obvious landmark. As he walked, he carried an empty fishing tackle box along with him. It would be used to carry something else this time.

Within minutes of entering the timbered countryside, he felt his muddled psyche calming. The glamour of this wild garden always had this effect. He soaked it in as he journeyed on. Beads of sweat dripped down his back and his heart beat with vigor, but after nearly an hour he had made it to his terminus.

A myriad of saffron blooms swayed in the breeze, dancing to the dynamic flow of the air. Sunlit dots of dazzling red, manicured with specks of a deeper magenta, were poking their way into the golden sea before him. The bright star of the day cast brilliant light upon the open glade, sharpening the quivering concoction of color. The blue celestial canvas above provided the perfect backdrop for this tapestry of nature, this harmony of wind and plant, of sun and sky.

Anthro stopped on the edge of the forested path and watched as the valley crosswinds whipped through the glade, performing a whispering, choreographed jig among the multitude of petals. Nature sang her best song and he beheld her beauty.

He leaned his back against the juvenile bark of a nearby elm. The slender tree rocked slightly in the breeze, the gentle movement and esoteric sounds of the swaying branches adding to the euphoria of the environmental theater. Anthro felt something in that moment. It seemed like a new feeling, but at the same time one that was very old: a desire that had always been with him, though distant and mysterious. Now he could sense it being drawn to the surface of his thoughts, yet somehow even upon its unbridled manifestation it remained but a dim reflection. He could not discern whether this arose from within his conscience or from somewhere else. The feeling almost startled him, yet it did not diminish the wonder of the experience he was having.

This sensation, it was a sudden and strong urge to thank someone or something. Odd, he knew, but he was not afraid of strange thoughts. As he gazed upon the masterpiece before him, he wanted to thank a hidden composer for creating such a powerful work of art, such a clear depiction of elegance, such a beautiful song.

He had taken art classes in his educational programs, but why did this field before him produce a wonder that no amount of aesthetic education could ever hope to match? And who could he thank: the flowers, the wind, or perhaps nature itself? They were all mindless and he was rational. He knew that much—and to thank something that had no capacity for rational thought or emotion would not suffice.

This idea of thanksgiving felt bizarre. It produced a desire to express while simultaneously creating a sense of shyness. Nevertheless, the urge was overwhelming—and exhilarating. How he wanted to sing a piece of praise and to direct that chorus of exultation toward a magnificent artist or poet higher than himself: a creative being of immense beauty and tremendous power, a wonderful songster of unlimited imagination.

In this moment, with this new thought budding within him, he felt a twinge of sadness arise from the soil of his heart. This desire to praise left him wanting. An anonymous artist could not be thanked in the same way that a known artist could, and surely a non-existent artist could not be thanked in any meaningful sense of the word.

Beauty. Awe. Wonder. Splendor. Majesty. His senses screamed of glory. A glory outside of himself. A glory greater than himself. He sighed softly and rested, falling against the tree to his usual meditative position, this time with his eyes and heart wide open.

* * * *

As shadows began to advance upon the meadow, Anthro awoke from his mental rest and began the task of gathering the best flowers the field had to offer. With hands unaccustomed to nimble work, he slowly placed them in his tackle box and began the trek back toward the city.

As he came across the small bridge that led to the gate, he stopped to appreciate the construction that had taken the last four years to complete. The aged timber entrance had been systematically replaced with tall stone walls and an impressive gatehouse designed to withstand even a mild siege. Two prominent towers stood on either side of the arched entryway. A formidable iron portcullis was lowered within it every evening. Even the remaining wooden walls and exterior defenses surrounding the rest of the city had been greatly fortified.

No longer did a couple ragtag militia stand guard; now fine soldiers of Tenebris manned the gates and were scattered along the walls. There were bowmen at the high points, ready to rain down a barrage of arrows toward any unwelcome guest. Burly pikemen stood near the main gate, strong men who could form a wall of death at the sound of a trumpet. Anthro also knew that skilled swordsmen, masters of war garbed in stunning steel arrays, were in the city; knights, the pride of the Army of Tenebris.

The new military presence captured the imaginations of the adolescent boys of the city. Proud thoughts of honor and glory dominated their minds and produced war games of all sorts. Their pictures of war were purely romantic. They were always the victors, the champions, the heroes. They were always the survivors; injured, of course, but never mauled, never handicapped. War. They were captivated by its magnitude, ignorant of its true horror.

The adults of the City of Mori were just as imaginative, though much more realistic and far more pessimistic. War in this kingdom, the Kingdom of Tenebris, was nothing new. In fact, those former wooden walls surrounding Mori had only been a cheap replacement for what had been destroyed in the last war to rage across the kingdom. How quickly the daily routines of life could make one forget all about the gory horrors of the not-so-distant past. Yet war was inescapable in Tenebris. Young blood was embedded in the soil of every past age; this passing one was proving no different. Peace was a dream, a hope never fully realized. When it finally seemed a reality, the illusion would be crushed by the force of a greater war and the loss of more life. Such a story is the endless trajectory for any kingdom of humankind.

Even with Anthro's critical mentality, he could not escape the fascination of this latest threat of war. He took in the scene, briefly imagining a fiery siege and a harrowing mission. Finally, he made his way down the road and back into Mori, knowing that today he had a real mission, though of a much smaller scale.

*   *   *   *

Anthro crouched near the corner of the street in the fading light, taking refuge in a narrow alley. Several people had passed by, but that was minutes ago. He peered out once again, looking up and down both streets, searching windows—meticulously ensuring that his actions would be unobserved. Still fearful, but for once not failing to act despite fear's persistent presence. The street seemed as clear as he could hope for.

He made his way quickly to the stoop with his tackle box in one hand and a delicate wooden vase—which had taken a serious toll on his savings—wrapped in the other arm. He set the vase down on the top step, already having filled it with fresh water. He opened his tackle box, gently tucking the wild bouquet into the vase. After placing the combination of crafted wood and captured flower in the center of the landing, he took a couple steps back to view the arrangement. Not right. A little adjustment to the left.

That's it. I hope she sees them with sunlight shining on the flowers; that will make them look better. More like they were when I saw them. I hope they make her happy. That's more important than her forgiveness, but I still want that too. Does a little bit of nature help everyone? I guess I'll find out soon enough.

He took one more moment to appreciate the flowers himself, remembering the song, and then scurried off to his home unseen.

Anthro awoke early and made his way to his observation perch. He would not chance missing this. After an hour or so, the street began to fill, crowds moving to and fro seeking entertainment and leisure on a day of the week when few labored.

Two hours and still no Keta. All those who passed by paid no regard to the lonely floral arrangement. They were always on the move, never wanting to miss out, but never seeing.

A little before the three-hour mark, Keta appeared. As usual, she was alone. The sun was high in the air and light filled the streets, iridescence falling where it was needed most. Anthro's heart began to race, and his cheeks were suddenly burning. This was not a crush—not in the slightest—but still his emotions raged and he was not completely sure why.

She made her way down the street, habitually not looking toward the tops of the apartments, and was just about to round the bend when she stopped abruptly, nearly causing those behind her to trip.

Slowly, timidly, like an injured cat being offered a crumb, she approached it. A cheap wooden vase holding a burst of color; splendid, wonderful, but why here? Why on the stoop of a dead woman's apartment? A woman known by so few and cared for by none but Keta. Was it a mistake? A silent tear brushed her lightly freckled cheek.

Keta knelt down, her hands cradling the smooth rhythmic sides of the vase, and closed her eyes, inhaling the sweet perfume. She knelt there, oblivious to those on the street, lost in her own world, unaccustomed to this feeling. She reached out with her slender fingers and smudged nails, touching the golden petals of the most prolific daffodil of the bunch.

Though the muscles of her cheeks were not used to the action, a coy half-smile slowly formed upon her face. Happiness: Such a foreign feeling in her life. Such a medicine for her being, yet so allusive: a wisp of vapor—visible, yet unable to be grasped. Now in this moment, it was present—almost tangible. This feeling found here on the doorstep of a woman who, for the majority of Keta's life, could not even remember her name. On this humble stoop, still within the week of the death of the only human being in the world whom Keta could honestly say that she loved, she felt happy. She smiled; a genuine smile, imperfect but perfect.

Who? A brief thought burst in Keta's mind. Her head jerked; somehow, she knew. Balanced on a third-story parapet he sat, gazing in her direction, as he always did.

Anthro stared back. For years, those eyes had rejected him, tormented him, and convicted him. Now, for what seemed like the first time in eons—lens focused upon lens—a quartet of pupils contracted by light while beholding the light of another. Was he imagining that he could see the blue in her eyes from this distance? Maybe, but her smile—that, he had not imagined. Though it had slowly faded as their eyes met, he knew it had been there, if only for a moment. Now they beheld one another, still from a distance but finally seeing; Anthro speaking with his eyes what he longed to confess with his mouth. Keta felt unsure and confused, but wonderfully comforted by a different touch of kindness. Maybe that was still possible in this world of hers.

The meeting of their eyes: neither of them knew the length of the trance. Finally, Keta broke away with much to consider and a lingering happiness. She ran her hand softly over the tops of the flowers, feeling their delicate petals once more before standing and making her way around to the next street.

Anthro wondered. He hoped. He thought.

Chapter III

The Scarlet Stain

Golden leaves cavorted across the cobblestone paths of Mori. The numerous hardwoods that grew within the city's walls were adorned by a spectacular decay of chlorophyll, revealing pigments of diverse marvels otherwise held captive by a dominance of greedy green.

"Did you hear that there was another skirmish outside the city yesterday?" Keta, now a blossoming teenager with thick auburn curls, spoke with the hushed voice of falling leaves.

"I did. Third one in a month. It's odd. You would think they'd either try to attack or just move on. Why do they keep sending such small groups that are destined to be annihilated?" Although spoken as heavy words, they were softly drummed by a muscular youth on the cusp of adulthood, with dark skin and a scalp that was shaved perfectly clean.

"They're trying to find weaknesses in the city's defenses." Anthro's voice took on Keta's hushed tone, though their topic of discussion was no secret. "I guarantee it. Think about it, Aradis. The first skirmish was to the north, second to the south, and now this last one on the western edge of Mori. I bet they are intentionally provoking just enough response on each side of the city to see what kind of counter is given. Most likely they expect a similar response and tactic to be used if their forces launch a larger attack against that area. The sacrifice of a few small groups would be worth it if some kind of deficiency in our defenses was found."

"But they waited too long!" Aradis exclaimed, his tone taking on its usual animated quality as he broke the muted hush of the conversation. "The Eagle Battalion should be here tonight! They're the ones who retook Victus with only minimal losses. I heard that only three of their men fell as they laid waste to a cohort of over 200 enemies within the city."

"Victus is just a small border town, not a real city," Anthro stated. "No outer walls or robust defenses. Retaking it doesn't overly impress me." He hesitated. "Though if those numbers are even remotely accurate, that is something to boast about."

"Still, I'll be glad to have them here!" Keta said. "I think it will help bring down the tension in Mori a bit."

As the last stubborn leaf of autumn refuses to yield to the onslaught of wintertide forces, so Keta was still clinging to a tendril of hope against an inevitable war. There was only frost on the horizon; nevertheless, she held on.

"I agree. I'll be happy to have them here as well. I just don't want anyone to forget that even the best of them are merely human." Anthro eyed Aradis.

"Let a man dream! I'll be there one day. Maybe you too, Anthro." Aradis never missed an opportunity to attempt to capture his friend's heart with the honor of avoiding a draft by volunteering to serve in the army. Both of them were nearing the completion of their educational requirements. If the war continued to escalate, they were presumably going to be drafted into the army to serve a mandatory three years before being allowed to pursue a non-military career. The best way to avoid a draft, according to Aradis, was simply to join the cause willingly.

"We'll see," Anthro said. "Honestly, I just wish the Kingdom of Psychios would get on with it. Why isn't there a full invasion force across our borders yet? Do they want a war with Tenebris or not?"

The rustic, free-standing bell tower under which they were seated sounded four times with enough might to stir the crisp ground beneath them. Another draft of wind blew in as if scheduled with the chime of the hour, bringing with it an array of gyrating colors from above.

"Oh, don't talk like that Anthro," Keta replied. "I'm not in favor of escalation, no matter how it turns out. I'd take a couple of random battles here and there over an open war. I've been reading about the historic wars ever since Psychios infantry started attacking Tenebris trade caravans. The number of people who die is just staggering, and it's not just from the direct fighting. There's starvation, disease, internal betrayal, and everything in between. It's hard to fathom the amount of death involved." The last vibrating echo from the bronze bell overhead faded within a fresh gust of chilled wind.

"Whether or not you are able to fathom it, death might be coming to Mori. And that's why we've got to live it up while we can! Right, Keta?" Aradis gave her slender form a playful and gentle shove, his stalwart arms pushing her just a bit harder than he had intended. Keta was used to his inability to control his own force and always knew a bruise or two was to be expected whenever she was in his company—which, by choice, was quite often.

"You boys have fun," Keta retorted as shadows quickly lengthened around them. "I just can't understand that kind of thinking." It was not meant as a rebuke; she was genuinely unable to see things from Aradis's perspective. "Forgetting reality for a couple of hours doesn't change things."

"Forgetting reality?" Aradis said. "I'm *embracing* it! If I'm going to die tomorrow, I may as well enjoy today!" Aradis turned and threw his hefty oversized arm around Anthro's shoulder, forcing him into a slouch to bear the weight. "Looks like it's just you and me as usual, my friend."

"See what you're doing to me, Keta, leaving me alone with this guy?" Anthro glared at her as he tried valiantly to release himself from Aradis's grip. Without his willingness to comply, winter would come before Anthro could escape.

"You've no one to blame but yourself. You could always ditch him and come to Chera's to help out. The kids have been nervous with all the war talk—they hear everything—but it'd probably help having a man around for once." Keta had long served alongside Chera, the city orphanage's matron, whenever she had the chance to give the time. Even when such time was a prized commodity, she usually found some way to maneuver her schedule in order to spend an afternoon with the children in any given week.

"Aradis, you're suddenly looking like a pretty good option," Anthro teased, finally breaking free of the relaxing death clench.

"About time you started coming to your senses." Aradis gave Keta a shining white grin. "Well, Keta, tell the kids we said hello." He cheerfully started down the street and yelled with more thunder than the bell tower, "Tonight, Anthro and I are going to eat, drink, and be merry, for tomorrow we die!"

Before Keta could reply, Aradis was beyond a distance she was willing to shout toward. She turned to Anthro, who had not yet chased down his friend. "I'm sure the children will love the message. You two stay safe. The rest of the city is more nervous than you are." The shadows disappeared as all became one matted blur found within the hazy light of dusk.

"Don't worry about us. With my brains and his brawn, what

couldn't we handle?" Anthro jested with partial truth. "For the record, I do think what you do at Chera's is great. You always find some way to help people." He finished his words with a smile. The more he had gotten to know Keta over the years, the more he discerned her unceasing service for others. A servant's heart, a motherly demeanor, and a clever mind were all attributes that kept their friendship balanced and engaging.

"Thank you." Keta returned the smile, her dimples persistently asymmetric, as if a childhood devoid of necessary laughter had caused even her grin to reflect that gnarled past. "And 'for the record', we really could use your help at the orphanage. The kids would enjoy having you spend some time with them."

"Maybe one day. A man helping at an orphanage—actually involved with the kids, not just making repairs and whatnot—just feels odd even thinking about it."

"You of all people should know that your feelings don't always match with what is right. Those kids, especially the boys, need men in their lives and you feeling odd about it has nothing to do with the fact that they have that need." Keta stated this firmly while looking into his scattered eyes. She was not trying to give him a lecture—then again, maybe she was.

Anthro returned the gaze. Her focused stare always called him back. He was used to Keta trying to challenge him to do more with his life. He liked having her influence, even if he rarely took her advice. He was finding himself to be a man of much thought and far less action. Did that matter? He decided to think about it later. "You—"

"*Anthro!*" Aradis screamed from the far end of the street, cutting him off.

"Well, that's my call. I'll see you, Keta. You stay safe too." Anthro gave her a wave as he turned to trot down the road and catch up to the ever-impatient Aradis.

"I'm still more worried about the both of you," Keta said to herself as she swung in the opposite direction toward the orphanage, her only remaining company the band of stray leaves that sailed through the brisk air, each one a traveling ghostly form in the fading twilight.

* * * *

The night was nearly spent, the air a thick mass of chilly atmosphere nestled in the settled stillness that follows after a front. Anthro felt a fading zeal of inebriation as he tramped back home alone. As usual, he had not overdone the drinking as Aradis had. Anthro had left his friend passed out at the party house, but tonight he felt like ending the evening—or beginning the day—beneath his own sheets. Alcohol, and nearly any other depressant or stimulant, was in hearty supply throughout Tenebris, and a consumer's age mattered little in obtaining even large quantities of a given substance. Drinking was a favorite pastime for most citizens of Mori and Anthro felt right at home with that, although he typically showed a bit more restraint than the average man his age; he always liked to keep his wits about him to at least a mild degree.

As he walked the narrowing path alone he let his mind drift toward the woman he had spent most of the evening with. What was her name again? Katharsia? Maybe. Whatever her name, the lady was more than just a comely figure. She could hold an intelligent conversation as well as her wine, and although their sensual interactions had not gone as far as Anthro would have liked them to, he was confident that with another meeting or two that would change. The thoughts of her were a welcomed distraction against the benumbing temperatures that surrounded his thin cloak. The invading polar air was more frigid than had been expected with this much color still present in the foliage.

A small snap to his left drew him away from his inner fantasies. That was the second time he had heard it. The lingering effects of the alcohol wore off suddenly, replaced with an influx of adrenaline. The calm of the night had carried the vexing crack further the second time, and with it came greater clarity. Anthro, without breaking stride, focused his hearing in the general direction. With the increased focus, the soft sounds of the night became distinguishable from one another, and one set of them did not belong.

Footsteps. Definitely footsteps. No more than fifteen feet behind, hidden beyond evergreen bushes of black. Anthro was sure of the origin of the sounds and even if he could not determine more details, he knew that without a doubt he was being watched through the thicket—or more precisely, stalked. He considered grabbing his small pocket knife, but he could not let the attacker know that he was aware of his presence. The footsteps were ten feet away and closing in.

Keep moving. Same rhythm.

No moon. A couple of stars and one or two remaining candles off in the distance were the only lights to be seen. He had taken a shortcut connecting two districts within the city walls, but this was a vulnerable place: the worst possible location for him, the best for an assailant. Scattered trees, a diminished road nearing a small footbridge, and that painfully thick brush were his only surroundings. Darkness filled every void, both above and around him.

Run. No. Knife? No, I already thought of that. Keep walking, don't change speeds. He's going to come from the left—that's what I'd do, just as the path nears the bridge. Be ready. If there is a weapon, disarm, then run. If no weapon, disorient, then run. Confirm there is only one of them before turning your back. If I can disarm him, why not get the weapon and fight? No, too many contingencies. Am I ready to kill? Here he comes!

Anthro exhaled deeply with a visible collision between the warm breath in his lungs and the outside atmosphere. Between a brief gap in the scrub, his attacker charged forward. The raspy pant of the assailant drew forth an animalistic energy within Anthro. The soft crunch of the underbrush became deafening. The air now carried forth a pungent scent of sweat and earth. Darkness itself diminished, revealing with a moonless shine the glimmer of dual edges, the unmistakable sheen of sharpened steel.

The beast that was awakening within Anthro roared, moving him toward the man, stealing the attacker's confidence. Here in the dead of night there would be no flight. Anthro twisted his body around in a fervor of strength, seizing his opponent's right wrist like a constrictor and clamping shut the blood vessels within from the force of the grip. This brute within merged together with years of wrestling matches against Aradis as he continued his maneuver with a level of skill unforeseen. His enemy's stinging edge drew close but its trajectory promised that it was swung only in vain. Anthro carried through with his motion, slamming the full power of his elbow into the rear of the would-be mugger's skull. The thud of bone upon bone sounded as if a hammer had fallen upon its anvil. All the while he had shifted his other hand free of his opponent's wrist and onto the handle of the weapon. Pain shot like lightning down his entire arm from the collision, but he had it!

Anthro had total control of the blade, feeling the frigid steel hilt as he tightened his hold upon it. Now was the time to flee. What more did he need to do? The attacker had been driven to his knees and was twisting around at the waist, his arms flailing wildly, desperately trying to face Anthro despite his sure concussion. A helpless foe. Victory won. Nothing left to do but run. But then the animal within spoke as if untamable. Power. Anger. Hate. Had these always been within him? Anthro was hardly aware of their presence, oblivious to this present form of intoxication. The passion of the moment had its own relentless grip on him. Bloodlust. Revenge. Justice?

Anthro thrust back and then drove forward with all the force he could muster. Sharpened metal cut through flesh and sinew, ripped between ribs, and severed vital organs. He drove the blade straight through the man, right down to the cross guard. Blood splattered across his right hand, pitch black and red hot in the night.

His enemy's eyes rolled back, replaced with phantom orbs of empty vitality that were chillingly visible in the darkness. Had death taken him that quickly? A gurgle of screams was drowned within, his cries restrained as his life was extinguished in mere seconds. In a sudden daze, Anthro relinquished his grip on the sword, leaving it impaled in the corpse as the body crumbled in on itself. He turned away and ran as if pursued by a full host of enemy spirits, refusing to look back. But what was that on his hand? Far too hot to be blood, surely?

Still panicked, Anthro made it to the next district, not sure if he should welcome its emptiness or despise it. There was a small fountain just past the vacant entrance. He washed his hands thoroughly, scrubbing his right hand with extra force. Even though the man's blood had rinsed off quickly, his hand still blazed as if lit with supernatural fire. The invisible inferno was raging across the majority of his hand and wrist.

An itch. An ache. A burn. A stain. He was not physically injured; that much Anthro knew. Was he just imagining the pain in his head? Perhaps he was delirious and in shock? Anthro could not see it, but he could feel every inch of it, and slowly he became convinced that it was simply too powerful to be mere fantasy or delusion. Every last bit of where the blood had settled seared him with a fiery intensity that he could not even begin to explain. Violence. Death. Murder? From Anthro's burning limb the blood released the death cry that the assailant had been denied.

* * * *

"Run!" Anthro screamed in the solitude of his chamber, his body covered in a cold dripping sweat, heart pounding, adrenaline exciting all of his senses.

But it was just a dream. Just a dream. No, a nightmare. The third one this week. Twelfth one in the thirty-two days since he had killed the man. Why did he keep thinking about it? It was not his fault. The man had attacked him! Anthro had not gone looking for trouble.

I killed him, but it was self-defense. It was definitely self-defense. He had a sword! Well, I had the sword . . . but it was his and he tried to use it first! But I didn't have to kill . . . no, he deserved it! If I had let him go, he would have just attacked someone else who couldn't have defended themselves. He got what was coming to him. What was in his blood, though? I can't stand this burning. It's a constant reminder of that night. I keep thinking the pain is gone and then there it is again. When it's quiet. When I'm all alone. This miserable stain. It's not my fault. What I did benefited society. It was for the good of Mori. It even protected the helpless! It's not my fault.

Then why haven't I mentioned it to anyone? Why do I hide what I claim is innocent? I haven't even told Aradis or Keta. Shame? Guilt? Fear? Cowardice? Doubt? Uncertainty? This burning will drive me mad. Ignore it? Suppress it? Maybe. More time. I need more time before I make a move.

As Anthro lay back down for another sleepless slumber, the searing in his hand slowly faded once more. But it was still present. It was always present.

Chapter IV

The Glory of Humanity

Above the expansive hoard of human habitation, bright sunlight dominated the sky. Within the perimeter of the bulwarks, the air was alive, infused with excitement and wonder. Below, wandering the spiraling labyrinth of construction and commerce, was Anthro. His mind raced wildly as his eyes surveyed the splendor of Babylonem, capital city of Tenebris. *We built this. We built this!* This thought recurred again and again as he aimlessly journeyed within the boundaries of its high, noble walls. Here, human achievement had approached perfection. At last, societal imagination had neared its limit. As if the outer barriers were enveloping him in a seductive embrace, Anthro let the city take its hold of him.

Everything before him, around him, and behind him was distinctly crafted as if even the simplest of dwellings was of such quality that it alone would be a wonder for the world to behold. Yet, the entire megalopolis was one great composition. Each individual edifice was a unique work of art and every supporting member sculpted as a portrait of robust individuality. Nonetheless, no piece stood alone. All came together as a cohesive totality. The very uniqueness of one element was the essential complement of the next. Here was the nucleus of Anthro's nation. Here was the heart of Tenebris. Here was Babylonem, the zenith of all civilization.

Guarding every entryway stood begemmed archways reflecting a blaze of varied lights in a myriad of directions, a spectacle of color and charm. Painted metals and stained masonry manicured the horizons of each new courtyard. No building was the same as another; not one was out of place. Even the roadways utilized natural stones of varying hues and tones, carrying Anthro through the endless maze of boutiques and bazaars. What amazed him most was not simply the architectonics before him, but the stunning unity that was achieved amidst such dynamic diversity. How had humanity created such adroit and splendid beauty? He could only believe that if other kingdoms in this world knew of the glory that adorned Babylonem, those lands would never rest—would never cease to assail her—until they had won this crown of humanity for themselves. The amount of integrated engineering, the endless raw materials, and the human exertion required for such an urban expanse was simply unfathomable.

What was more, the crowds within Babylonem matched the city's splendor in all its grandeur, pomp, and nobility. Were these even human beings before him? It was as if the men had spent every waking hour seeking only to perfect the body in both health and stature. And the women, each one a siren of seduction, a damsel of decadence, an empress of elegant expression; could such allure ever be adequately recounted?

His eyes drifted toward one such woman as she casually leaned underneath the shimmering shade of a stained-glass footbridge. Buildings for trade and feasting were linked by the span. Painted sunlight danced across the woman's hourglass form. Anthro neared closer to her as she gazed at the colors above and the endless stream of the crowds beyond. Even as he approached her, he could not avert his stare. The spectrum of light reddened her lush lips and heightened the glow of her smooth cheeks. Upon her slender fingers sat fat rings of amethyst, emerald, and diamond. Around her neck and over her round breasts rested a string of pure white pearls. She was like nothing he had ever seen. She was like everything he was seeing. She tilted her chin toward him, as if feeling the pull of his fixated trance. Seven colors shown in her eyes as they met his emeralds. The corner of her lip curled upward. With a will of their own his feet kept moving forward, his face flushing with heat and his eyes unable to hold onto their temptation.

With drunken steps Anthro carried on, only to be intoxicated further with each new encounter. The only restraint from complete indulgence was the subtle hunger for more before the initial taste. Eventually, as if carried in on a foreign wind, a soft whisper of misgiving ruffled within his ears. A suppressed thought given life from a different perspective. What would Keta make of all this? How starkly she would stand out amongst the women here, surely in body, but perhaps also in heart? Where would she be able to express her passion for serving the poor and destitute? Where would she find someone in need? Could poverty even exist in such a rampant state of decadence? It seemed ridiculous to imagine. Yet, with the thought now present in his mind, every now and then he would glimpse a shadow or a figure censored behind the crowds. No sooner had he seen the specter than it disappeared as if a noonday sun had shone brightly upon it, revealing nothing but the dominant foreground of opulence. What wandered under the surface of this utopia? Was there more to see here than just radiant light and luxury?

Perhaps, but who could not remain impressed with what humanity had accomplished here? And not just mere men, but Anthro's fellow countrymen. For these were *his* streets. These were his brothers, sisters, and soon-to-be lovers. This was his city, his capital, *his* kingdom. Anthro, soldier of Tenebris. Anthro, defender and hero of Babylonem. In distant lands and in the heart of the capital the barbs would sing tales of Anthro of Mori. The minstrels would all give poetic praise to Anthro and Aradis, the two noble knights from Mori who volunteered to serve in the great armies of Tenebris.

A commitment that had once been laced with hesitation was now inflamed with fervor. Aradis had spurred on the mutual decision, avoiding a draft by joining freely. Now, after ten months of military training, they had made it to the capital with equal ambition and zeal. Here they would be formally inducted into the ranks of the Army of Tenebris by none other than the King of Tenebris himself. The king, much beloved by both soldier and civilian, had a personal interest in each and every one of his infantrymen and saw it fitting to have them begin their service with his personal blessing.

The army had made significant progress since their efforts against the scattered raids by the Psychios military three years before. They had driven every last enemy out of their borders and were now, despite the newly signed peace agreements, preparing for a grand offensive that would ultimately seek to extend the nation's borders in all directions. For too long, the people of Tenebris had endured mistreatment by these inferior and unstable nations; for too long, the world was ignorant of Tenebris's blatant superiority. It was time, for the good of the world, to enlighten those lesser nations. Nationalistic ideologies spread like wildfire within this nation that progressed daily in a rising arrogance of its own professed preeminence. The world would soon learn the might and the right of the people of Tenebris.

* * * *

Anthro stood shoulder to shoulder with his regiment, garbed in splendid dark silver armor that was fenced with royal blue and worn by the common foot soldiers of Tenebris. On his left side sat a scabbard decorated with black grapevine engravings that covered a three-foot sword of fine steel. A short cross-shaped, leather-wrapped hilt protruded beyond the scabbard and his left hand held firmly to this oxhide-covered haft. His right hand supported a sizable elliptical shield that stood haughtily by his side. It was a standard position of formal rest for servicemen.

The shield, like Anthro's armor, was a dusky metallic silver. Etched eloquently upon it in midnight blue and black was the Crest of Tenebris. The emblem was uniquely designed and consisted of an intricate fruit tree that made up the majority of the background. In the foreground, placed over the distant tree, was an oversized fruit of apple-like appearance that had been eaten down to the core, a serpent coiled menacingly around it. The limbless dragon's tail twisted all the way to the top, its dreadful maw situated at the bottom. The serpent had its mouth open as though returning from what must have been a fearsome strike, its hollow fangs guaranteeing a lasting pain far greater than any pleasure the fruit might have provided.

The design was stunning yet discomforting. Staring at it for an extended period of time gave the viewer the impression that the snake had come to life. It was an eerie optical illusion that sent a chill down anyone's spine, making it appear that the snake had its oblong pupils set directly upon them as though it sought nothing less than to devour them whole. The meaning of the crest had long been lost in the ancient history of the kingdom, but still the symbol remained as if it were some secret message concealed within the mysteries of ages no longer known.

With great discipline and eager expectations, Anthro and 499 of his comrades stood eagerly awaiting the king. A large crowd of citizens surrounded them, for the king was much beloved by his subjects. The people rarely missed an opportunity to see him and they never failed to listen on any occasion to hear him speak. There was something about the king's voice—or perhaps it was the message more than it was the actual diction—that captured the people's hearts time and time again. Whenever the hour seemed bleak and the people started to question their ruler, he would, without fail, assail any doubts about his wise reign. The mysterious king had been ruling Tenebris for longer than most of the citizens had been alive, though one would not guess that by looking at his only slightly aged appearance.

"Crow Battalion, attention!" A burly and scarred lieutenant colonel in charge of Anthro's battalion shouted this as the king's herald made his way onto the platform that lay before the infantry and the crowds.

"Thank you, Lieutenant Colonel. Ladies and gentlemen, proud soldiers of Tenebris, it is my honor and privilege to greet you this day and to bring your eyes to this stage where your king shall soon stand." The herald was a wiry middle-aged man in sleek cerulean robes. "For ages, our great king has served not only this city, but the entire country of Tenebris with unwavering loyalty and faithfulness toward all his subjects. His protracted reign is surely sustained by his love for his people. What other king has served his people so truly? What other king of this realm has brought such prosperity to so many?" He paused as if allowing any other kings to be named.

"Of course, there is no other! The kings of other nations hoard their wealth, but not ours! The so-called mighty rulers of other lands exploit their people and drain their resources to fatten their own kin, but not ours! Who is like our king? I tell you, though you already know; there is none! He supplies all your needs; he gives you both riches and physical blessings beyond the wildest imaginations of any foreign people. It is this king of worldly prosperity who will be before you! It is this king who now and forever gives you the best life that you can fathom and yet demands so little from you! Who is like this king? There is none! And with that reminder, I present to you the ruler of this world, the king of health and wealth, the mighty King of Tenebris, our great King Beelzebul!" The herald gave a quick bow and then scurried off the stage.

The crowds erupted with applause and the soldiers pounded their gauntlets onto their shields as King Beelzebul made his way to the front of the podium with an outstretched waving arm. Upon reaching the center he stood for a moment, absorbing the praise, and then raised both arms, asking for silence. The audience obeyed and he briefly stood before them with a wide toothy grin plastered on his visage. No matter the day or the speech to be made, King Beelzebul was never without a grand pearly white smile that further convinced the people of his loyalty. How could they be so fortunate to have a king this wonderful? He never ridiculed his people and he certainly never scorned them; quite the contrary, he was always full of praise, overflowing with kind words and filled to the brim with great promises. What more could the people ask for? There were only good feelings around this monarch—always tickled ears, fulfilled desires, and reassured hearts.

"My people, my new soldiers, you are too good to me! Surely, it is I who am blessed to have a wonderful city and nation of men and women such as yourselves. A king is only as good as his people, and if there is one thing that I know, it is that my people are good." His forged smile was unmoving and his thick, golden crown gleamed upon his scalp. His aristocratic robes, made of the rarest and most expensive fabrics, swayed lightly in the breeze. The king must be an example for the people to aspire to; any attire that consisted of less extravagance would simply fail to give them the proper motivation to seek greater riches themselves.

"Look at you all. Never in all my years of rule have I stood before such wealth and luxury. Surely these riches and this beauty are a testament to your virtue. Adornment of such external splendor speaks to the purity that must be within you. You, my people, are blessed!"

As usual, the crowds were captivated. King Beelzebul's messages were all typically of this fashion, but the crowds never wearied of their substance. Some messages never grew old in Tenebris, no matter how many times they were recast.

"Is it not this greatness that has warranted this occasion today? You men before me, you will be the harbingers of our glory to every distant land. The armies of Tenebris swell, for the time is ripe to spread our riches and grandeur." Rapturous applause rang out. "We are not a selfish people. We will not just sit idle in our affluence while other nations wallow in their rags." The crowds erupted in even more thunderous praise. King Beelzebul's smile never wavered. "Some will certainly claim that it is an aggressive act on our part, but it must be remembered that we were the ones first attacked just three short years ago. We have sought peace with the rulers of the other nations, but none can be found despite our most concerted efforts. The people of other lands suffer, their resources lie unattended and underutilized as incompetent and immoral rulers squander what could be rich lands. We shall save them! Do not fear that your wealth will diminish, for we shall not take from you. We shall only teach them our ways, and, without question, they will thank us generously. Tenebris shall be known! Tenebris shall be honored! Tenebris shall be victorious!"

The king's blue eyes had a steely gleam in them, which for the slightest moment looked sinister, but the expression vanished quickly. If it had ever really been there, that friendly grin seemed to say otherwise.

"You men before me—I have but a few final words of encouragement for such fine soldiers as yourselves. Remember this, my beloved servants, my most wonderful people: the more you serve, the more you will obtain. The more you give, the more I will reward. The more work you do, the more you will shower in the luxuries of this present world and find what it truly means to have an abundant and meaningful life. Now I give you my blessing, as King of Tenebris, to go and spread our prosperity to the farthest reaches of the earth!"

Beelzebul had spoken, the crowds had heard, and the message once again had struck home. In the early years, it had been necessary to speak from a more idealistic lens, yet luxury had seeped into the majority of Tenebris. Beelzebul knew well that the decadent were ruled more by the material than the transcendent. It was the savages and brutes who fought for glory and cause. It was the prosperous and rich who fought for themselves. Both were slaves in their own way, but the brutes of a far worse kind.

Freedom of the self is not in contradiction to one's slavery, for the self can be a powerful master. Those who wish to see the flourishing of the human race must move it from the shackles of the transcendent to the bonds of the immanent. He who wishes to rule humanity must set them free through the path of the material. Only with wine in every stomach, only with honey on each hand, only with the mastery of the material can the path of the transcendent even begin to be trod. This is the error of the brutes: they reverse the order.

Yet the rich are not innocent. They lack the resolve to take all that is within their grasp. They restrain and weaken their own commitments to themselves by playing with hollow ideals. Thus, they are never filled. Thus, they never begin to awaken. Thus, society remains stagnant. Thus, all remain in bondage. All this Beelzebul knew well, but he was determined to provide the way forward. He would provide the resolve to realize the collective material potential of humanity, and then—and only then—would each slave be ready to begin the journey toward lasting freedom.

Chapter V

The Horror of Humanity

Birds of prey circled above, dancing in a flight of death as they moved closer to the field of torn human flesh. Blood. Gore. Screams. Carrion and rot. Death. Death everywhere. Men pleading for death. Men begging not to die. Death taking them. Death leaving them.

This is war? This is nightmare incarnate. The torment of every fear drawn deeply from the well of human despondency and laid out for all to see its naked misery. How are there songs about such things? Laments I can fathom, but songs! How do the young—how did I—fantasize about this? This! What did I expect? I signed up for this, but did I really understand? Could anyone really understand? Can I ever forget? Can I ever unsee?

What is this? Is this blood and gore the food for the fat of Babylonem, the hidden forage of a beast of carnal pleasure? What is the head of this fiery dragon of death? Is it belief? Unbelief? Ideas? Nature? Or perhaps the dragon lies deep in each man despite any of these things? The nature of man. The nature of the dragon. Two beasts of unfathomable destruction and woe. A dance of flesh and blood, with violence and hatred, between humans and being.

"Anthro!" Aradis was covered in the filth of battle, blood slowly oozing from a moderate laceration on his left arm and mixing with coagulated crimson grime from those he had slain.

"I wasn't sure if you had made it. I saw that flanking cavalry come on your platoon. It looked rough from where I was. Where is your platoon leader? Hey? Anthro? Are you okay?"

Why was this so easy in the moment? My sword moved with no hesitation. There was no time for questions, just reaction. I suppose I'm good at that. How many eyes rolled back into darkness to never see the day again? How many lungs pierced through to never again fill with the breath of life? How many men did I just kill? My hand, the burning . . . my hand . . . the ghostly fire returns.

"Anthro! Are you hurt? Did your hand get injured?" Aradis eyed him nervously, unfazed by the twisted bodies that surrounded them and the fading echoes of the dying.

"Aradis . . . I'm . . . I'm glad to see a friendly face," Anthro replied. An injured horse with a wide gash across its ribs was whining on its side next to them.

"Glad to see yours as well. It doesn't look like many in your platoon made it."

"A few of them did. I figured we were heading into that ambush from the start, but Lieutenant Aphron didn't want to hear it. Almost killed me when I brought it up." He looked below the side of the hill the cavalry had come across and saw the lieutenant's body lying there, nearly severed in half. "The fool. Thankfully, I was able to whisper to about ten others to get to this upper ridge in time and use the rocks and the height to our advantage. I think six of us made it. The others are somewhere finishing off Kosian soldiers..." Anthro stopped mid-sentence.

Aradis had walked up to the wounded horse and had run his spear through its throat to finish it off. Never had an act of mercy looked so wretched and heartless.

Just then a mounted officer in full battle array rode up to Anthro and Aradis. "Men, well done. Much glory was wrought for Tenebris this day."

You call this glory? Anthro thought as the battle-hardened colonel spoke.

"Is one of you Anthro?" The man spoke with a deep voice that matched his grizzly appearance. The four-foot, freshly ensanguined bastard sword, which he held effortlessly in his left hand, was a fair complement to his burly physical features.

"I am, sir," Anthro replied, speaking with more of his usual confidence. He was always able to think and act more clearly when under authority.

"Do you wish to lose your head?" The colonel grumbled, slow but fierce.

"I'm not sure that I understand, Colonel." Anthro was taken aback. He noticed Aradis raise his spear an inch.

"I've talked to three men confirming that you defied your platoon leader's orders—or, should I say, your late platoon leader." The man's sword was raised toward the sky, an unmoving symbol of death. As he spoke, several more Tenebris cavalry were bearing down on where they stood. "It doesn't take a tactical genius to figure out that your position was vulnerable and adjustments were needed. It does take a man with a death wish to defy his orders in the heat of combat."

The static sword swung down with daunting speed toward Anthro, yet not to strike. The movement was too quick for him to react, but Aradis flinched and his spear lurched toward the colonel. If the man noticed, he gave no indication. The tip of his blade was now pointing directly at Anthro's chest.

"Free thinkers make horrible soldiers. Yet, with some limits, they tend to make good officers. Due to the rigid stupidity of your former second lieutenant, your platoon is in need of a new officer. Therefore, I repeat my question: Do you want to lose your head?"

"No sir," Anthro said, "and that is precisely why I chose to defy orders that were guaranteed to cause just that for myself and the men surrounding me."

"Well said, Second Lieutenant. I can't have my officers being so bound to orders that they are willing to die for them in the face of better options." The colonel lowered his sword as the cavalry arrived. "And son," he added, his violent eyes shooting toward Aradis with cold fire in them, "if you'd like to keep *your* head, I'd suggest never pointing a weapon my way again. You're fortunate you didn't test my steel against that stick. You'd have been unhappy with the result." Without another word, the colonel rode off.

Aradis spoke first as he eyed Anthro. "Second Lieutenant." A small smile spread across his face.

Anthro was yet again at a loss for words. The day had been long, his mind was filled with images of death, horror, and suffering, but somehow there was, somewhere deep within, a tingling sense of—pride?

*　*　*　*

Aprilis 22
2209 - Jamnondum

Dear Keta,

It's late. Clouds of darkness cover the sky; the full moon fights to be seen, but will it avail? I received your last letter—that is, I assume it was the last one. It was dated "Ianuarii 12." If anyone is right for that position, it's you. Working with them is probably similar to working with all the children you've spent time with, is it not?

I hadn't heard of any of those rumors you speak of. I would think that if there was anything even close to that actually happening, at least some of Tenebris's soldiers would hear about it (or even be involved in it). I'll start

43

keeping an ear out, but I don't believe it; it can't be more than a rumor. You know how people are.

Although, I do wonder what I wouldn't believe these days. We took another town a few days ago and I've been promoted again. Aradis is moving up the ranks a little as well. In all honesty—and I don't mean to scare you—I still can't believe we are alive. Keta, war is . . . it makes me think about what I am, what we all are. What is humanity, knowing that we can do this to ourselves? What am I, knowing what I have done to my brethren of flesh and thought?

Spear and Lance. Bow with Arrow. Sword on Shield. Man or Man. Death and Death. The ground is never satiated with its lust for human blood. The crow never tires of our rot . . . I've said enough (or too much) but sometimes I intentionally try to remind myself of how miserable the whole affair is.

Keta, I am afraid. I don't like admitting that. You were right to notice it when I was back in Mori on reprieve, but you were wrong as to why. I do not fear dying. The process looks brutal, but it is a fate that awaits every man and I've given it to so many. How could I not accept it myself? No, it is not dying that I fear. I think I fear death itself. Does that make me a coward or a fool? I've been watching the eyes of the dying. There is something in them that scares me, but there is nothing beyond death, so why fear? What is it that causes the doubt, that whisper of fear behind the eyes of breathless men? We are but dust and to the dust we shall return. Yet . . . no, I have to think more before I speak foolishly. But consider the thought: if death is nothing to us, then life is nothing to us. Death voids life. Death rips away meaning. Death breeds only vanity. To chase meaning in a world ruled by death is to chase after the wind, to grope at a vapor, to seek warmth from ice. Death is the incurable sting that conquers man's hopes, ambitions, and dreams. It is the great equalizer. It takes both rich and poor. Foolish and brilliant. Young and old. If none can escape it, then the grave defeats humanity in the end, making life nothing but a battle already lost to death.

Keta, there is one more aspect of this that I know I'm afraid of and this is why I write this letter. I am not sure what to do and it torments me. I hope that you will forgive my bluntness (does it grow with each letter?). Keta, I'm afraid that I'll stop caring about death. I've felt it. It is like a hardening that seeps into my mind, that at first is but an embryo. Yet it grows. It feeds. Quickly, silently. Before I know it, it has all but taken over. The embryo creates a beast, a monster; it creates something no longer rightly called human.

I could let it take over. It would make things easier. It might make me a better soldier. I believe, willingly or ignorantly, that most men around me have succumbed to it. Yet I fight it; my writing you is me fighting it. Am I the only one who does? Keta, it all feels linked. I am terrified that I will stop caring about humans dying. But how many can my blade pierce without the beast taking over? How can I think that we are but dust and only dust, and watch so many return to the dirt, and still think that we have intrinsic value? What incongruity! What hypocrisy! The two cannot rightly coexist.

I know that you have some different views on souls and spirits than me (and from most of the educated men and women in all of Tenebris, in all honesty), but entertain my mindset if you will. Something in me (my conscience?) tells me to fight it. But why? Why does human death feel so unnatural? To really think of what a human is—all that is in us—and to watch that sink into the dust to never return is wrong. If humanity is anything of worth, then it must be wrong.

Death. I don't think I'm afraid of it myself, but I fear for those I kill. For those I've watched return to the dust . . . that's what I am afraid of, and I am afraid to stop caring, to stop fearing. I'm haunted by what I'd be capable of if I stopped caring. I've seen the men who have no restraint, Keta. I've seen what men like that do. I don't want to be one of them. I've had my brawls and I have my vices, but this one feels deeper. I believe that nature is all that there is, and yet this sinking feeling, this haunting thought, that death itself is against our nature. What a contradiction! What a fool I am.

It is not just a feeling though. Humans . . . I've studied humankind, I've dwelled upon humanity. Keta, we are set apart. We are masters of nature. We subdue nature as if that is what we were designed to do, as if that is a very part of what it means to be human. Yet nature wars against us and we against it.

So much balance in this world; nearly everything I've seen or studied in nature is wonderfully balanced. All but humanity—and everything that man has touched. Humans—we are above nature. We are below nature. We rule it as it conquers us. We shine as unfathomable stars of our planet, as though we were chosen among all the beings of this world to rule over it, and yet the humble worm is filled with the death of us. The world is ours. The world will never be ours.

You told me you wanted to know what was troubling me, so there you have it. Now what do I do with it?

I won't end on that, though. I don't want the darkness to win. The moon is shining just a bit brighter now. Will the veil ever lift? Keta, I've seen and talked to some amazing people. The diversity mixed with the similarities never ceases to create a sense of wonder in me. Culture, art, music, history, creativity, language—always challenging my thoughts that humanity is nothing. The glory of man contrasting the shame, holding my mind captive against a conviction. Beauty clashing against a torrent of oblivion. Majestic speculation screaming against a shroud of eternal worthlessness.

As soon as the battles are done and the towns settle, I talk to as many as are willing. Keta, this world is fascinating. I always find the town's thinkers and pick their brains. You should hear their stories and ideas! I hope you get to see more of this world one day. Maybe in a time of peace. Peace? What a distant hope. What a universal hope.

I hunger for a better world. There is a dormant lust for it within me. A seed planted deep in my heart which water of this land will not benefit. This seed needs water from a foreign cistern to sprout. This craving is like the pining of long-lost lovers who have been torn apart, their love a distant memory that haunts them, comforts them, and gives them hope for the future as they weep for their past. Do you ever feel it? Do you ever wish to see a light dawn in the east never to fade, never to grow weary as it sings a melody of

46

new creation? A song of eternal, life-giving flame from a self-sustaining ember that is not subject to the slavery from the corruption of man that binds this present world? Keta, do you ever wish that you could see it all made new?

I do. Deep down, I want more out of this world than I see it offer. I want this world; I don't want to be rid of it. Nonetheless, I want it to be more than it is (or more than it appears to be). Is it rational to pursue such a mysterious longing, such a profound yearning buried in the heart of man? Where there is such desire, could there be actual satisfaction?

If it is only a wish, then I do not want it; of that, I am certain. I will embrace cold reality before lukewarm dreams unsubstantiated by any grounding of truth. Maybe it's out there. Maybe there is one true myth in this world of flesh and bone, dust and clay, steel and stone. There are whispers of it among a variety of peoples, but they are never more than contradicting claims built on foundations of sand. Just what is possible in this world of ours?

We've nearly conquered this small kingdom, and we are aiming for the capital shortly. It will be my first siege. The men are restless and . . . dangerous. I will keep an ear out for the rumors you've heard. Don't think about them too much. I know I'm a hypocrite for saying that! The moon shines a bit brighter.

> *Sincerely,*
> *Anthro*

Chapter VI

The Hope in History

Anthro leaned back upon the saddle of his nearly eighteen-hands-high warhorse of stygian fur and charcoal eye, observing the violent scene before him. Catapults launched, arrows soared, and men charged as another city felt the full force of the birth pangs of its own promised demise. An excited young soldier with a pudgy face and blond curls perturbing beyond his weathered helm raced toward the cluster of forward officers. "Sir, we've taken the outer wall!"

Anthro was now a decorated lieutenant colonel who had served the mighty cause of Tenebris for almost five years. His battalion, which was now under his direct command, had been a vital asset in conquering towns, seizing cities, and dismantling kingdoms over the last half-decade, victory after victory. Defeat was known, but rare.

In the foreground of his gaze a mass of military units moved upon the snow-covered slopes that lay before the icy city of Josias. In the background stood spires of jagged mountains that looked like a white, tooth-lined jaw upon the city's northern flank. To the south was an expansive river which, even at the height of northern winter, flowed unfrozen at its core. Between these two impressive natural barriers stood the entry point into the frosty but fertile lands of the Kingdom of Culpam. Josias was the necessary doorway into this country for any invading force approaching from the west, but now the city was experiencing the complete weight of a penetrating Tenebris siege. The battered structures and paths were overlaid with snow and sleet, much of which was now soaked red with death. What pristine snowbank remained untainted was quickly melting away along with the city's defenses.

Culpam was a peninsular country that bordered the northeastern lands of Tenebris. Starting with the lands of Psychosis, Tenebris had focused much of their expansionist efforts toward the multitude of minor kingdoms located to their direct south and east, all the while speaking continued promises of appeasement with their northern and western neighbors who were harboring more stalwart forces.

Had all the kingdoms initially united against Tenebris during their first assaults, it was unlikely that Tenebris would have gotten this far and amassed such a fearful and well-resourced army. However, whether it was due to isolationist policies, political maneuvering, fear, or a combination of the three, the other kingdoms had let Tenebris get a mighty foothold in the world. King Beelzebul was a cunning sovereign and he wisely refrained from overextending his resources, instead navigating his forces slowly and taking only a limited number of fronts at a time. He never pushed his armies too deeply into enemy lines before stabilizing what had already been conquered. With the southern front now well established, his steel blue eyes had turned north.

King Beelzebul fed upon the sluggishness of these other nations. Within his private assemblies he mocked their trade restrictions and economic sanctions. They were blind, having gorged out their own eyes to spare themselves from perceiving that he was coming for them next. But his vision was sharp.

He could see through the smoke and beyond the ash that must precede the rebirth of the world. Disorder. Dissent. Destitution. Waste. Want. Weakness. All would fade. All would be removed beyond even memory. But first, the release. But first, the severing of the shackles. Humanity was enslaved to itself, chained to a vision birthed within its past. A dream of what it could be—not wrong in itself, but flawed, unable, unwilling, afraid to recognize the necessary means required to achieve its ambition. To feast, it must first constrict. To swallow whole, first it must bite down. To live, life must first be taken. The ways of men and the ways of beasts are no different. Men have just forgotten the way. Beelzebul had begun to remind them. To awaken them. To unite them.

The populace—not just of Tenebris, but all those left standing in ruins—would follow, in due time. Once they sipped the sweet wine and tasted the richly buttered bread. Vision: this is what they needed now, until the material could fill the gap and then overtake it. So Beelzebul unleashed his poets into each newly captured realm. He let free his politicians and raised new ones up as he moved each budding piece of this universal enterprise. The soldiers were only for waging a battle in physical space. The other war was to win the imaginations of the brutes. He wanted them—all of them. One day they would see as clearly as he did. One day they would give thanks. One day, the mother of civilization would remember her pain no more as she held a child worth bearing in her arms.

Anthro had become far less concerned about—or aware of—the political agendas that went along with the War of Unification, a name King Beelzebul and his advisors had crafted for this campaign. He certainly thought about such things, but primarily his concerns were trifold, consisting of his military tactics, the lives of his men, and an unshakable desire not to annihilate the countries he was helping to conquer.

For certain, five years of blood-soaked warfare had nearly accomplished an even greater defeat: the sedating and subduing of his mind. He thought often, but more often than not, he thought about how much he did not want to think. Still, in spite of himself, Anthro tirelessly fought the hardening against humanity that warfare so easily produced; within him was an unceasing battle of mind and conscience that strained him far more than the confrontations before his eyes.

His letters to Keta were sounding boards and asylums that manifested his suppressed thoughts. He wrote to her often and visited her on the few rare occasions when he could, but he had noticed that she did not write as encouragingly as she had in the past. Her own fears had grown rapidly and her mind was elsewhere, focused on more urgent matters that surrounded her immediate setting.

Keta's replies never ceased to be soft and gentle, but they were laced with anxiety, with descriptions of what she believed might be the hidden work happening through and within Tenebris. She had come to suspect that the venomous fangs of their own kingdom were feasting upon more than just the blood of warriors and rulers. She spoke of the sinister idea that within the king's agenda lay a vast evil that attacked the very core of who she was. Murmurs from associates within Tenebris mingled with echoes from new contacts within the conquered kingdoms of the south, all speaking in nuanced whispers that delineated a cruelty beyond the grasp of her imagination: a living nightmare awake in the world to bring ruin to all that she had worked for, cared for, and loved.

Keta had been working with the mentally and physically handicapped for almost as long as Anthro had been in the business of making men both of those things. Her love for children had grown into a love for those who remained children. She loved them, protected them, and worried for them—now more than ever.

King Beelzebul's desires were in direct competition with her own deepest convictions. She could see beyond the serpent's stare and refused to be entranced by a vision that sought to eliminate concern for the means used to satisfy the dream. This reconstruction of humanity he was crafting would not view the handicapped as ends in and of themselves as she did, but as things best brought to an end. Severe limitations and prosperous utopia were incompatible realties. Quick, efficient, systematic, unsympathetic destruction was the obvious solution for those who would require more than they would provide. Unique puppets were far easier to dispose of than to work into Beelzebul's masterful act.

Keta was shrewdly circumspect in what she wrote to Anthro and in how she acted while she carried out what little resistance she could manage against such domineering oppression, for whenever one of her friends became overly vocal or revealed exceptional knowledge, that person disappeared with a story of being reassigned. Keta knew she would be no help whatsoever to those she loved if she was *reassigned*.

Anthro had stopped cautioning her that these fears were either unsubstantiated speculations or mere rumors. He had heard the occasional remark that spoke of a random soldier a comrade knew who had witnessed camps being set up. These rumors were neither specific nor first-hand accounts, but Anthro had gathered stories in too many places for him not to be convinced that there was at least some truth related to what Keta had heard from the start. The very dissimilarities of the rumors bore witness to their truth. Anthro had long since learned that nonuniformity in rumors typically meant a greater chance of an undergirding truth behind them. Discrepancies were not the same thing as contradictions, and they never stemmed from mere fable.

All the same, war was a distracting endeavor. It numbed the mind, bringing apathy to the conscience and forcing one's energies almost entirely on results in the present. Anthro watched as his companies stormed their objective. They swarmed over the fractured walls like angry ants, falling by the dozen as enemies within the remaining snow-capped turrets refused to yield or surrender.

Once the fighting begins they always keep struggling, even once defeat is assured. Is it because they are not aware of the eminence of their downfall? Perhaps. I've seen how feeble entire cities can be if they know that they are doomed. What will they not do to spare themselves? How many victories has Tenebris won by psychological warfare alone? It seems as though courage builds once men begin to act on it. You must get to the man, or to the army, before they can act on courage. Convince them of the futility of their bravery and you shall break them without so much as an arrow, but let them swing their sword in the name of country, the honor of spouse, the hope of victory, and they will be stopped by nothing but death. How quickly man can be swayed one way or the other. Always sitting on a precipice of advance, tottering on the edge of retreat, of honor or surrender, glory or shame. A single action, well timed, shapes their wills for the duration of the conflict.

His rear company moved in, advancing two mobile catapults along with it, as the other batteries provided the necessary amount of distraction. The wheeled mangonels were quickly positioned and took aim at the closest turret. Anthro watched his aggressive strategy unfold; with two well-placed shots, the weakened tower fell to pieces, turning bone to dust. Many of his own men lay scattered upon the slopes, disfigured, dismembered, dead.

After years of combat experience, Anthro knew that the

heavy losses taken by his first company had ensured the losses taken by the second were minimial. Despite his concern for their lives, he was willing to sacrifice a hundred men to save a thousand. Even if the balance tipped in the favor of one additional man, he would watch the slaughter of that slightly lesser mass with little-to-no direct effect on his conscience. The results were highly efficient and the justification sound. Who could unbiasedly argue against such tactics? It was the very concern for the lives of his men that motivated such seemingly cold and heartless decisions. Such was war.

When his mind refused to sedate, Anthro found himself wondering why he actually cared about his men so much. What caused that feeling? He was beginning to realize that it was not the men themselves that brought this concern about. He was fairly certain that he did not actually like many of them, if not most. On average, they were cruel, grumbled often, loved glory and spoil, and lacked true integrity. They were fond of grand and noble ideas, yet most revealed a lack of character that showed a great disconnect between the titans they imagined themselves to be and the actual men they were, in both action and deed. The songs they sang were filled with boasts of fame and honor, declarations of pride and virtue; yet whether it was their intent or not, this was only shallow lip service to those noble ideals hidden deep within the hearts of men but hopelessly restrained by the hearts of men. Their hands and feet spoke louder and more truly of their character than their lips and tongues professed. Were they willfully such hypocrites? Or were they just that lacking in self-awareness?

Nevertheless, Anthro had a deep concern for them. He would raise a mug with them all; he would give his life for many of them. The bond forged by war and blood was mysterious and strong.

* * * *

The people of Culpam turned out to be distinct from those of Tenebris, which was no surprise to Anthro anymore. Despite the desensitizing effects of war, the more he grew in his knowledge and association with other cultures and distant peoples, the less charmed he became with his own. The nationalism that had coursed through his young veins just a few short years ago had run dry. The enchantment had lifted. Little by little, his feelings of superiority had given way to thoughts of inferiority. Those whom he conquered were winning him, as a chorus of peoples from different tribes, nations, and tongues all singing a harmony that declared their value, praised their unity amongst diversity, and railed against the egocentric principles of his own army and nation.

These people of Culpam were not as easily distracted by the flashy pleasures and materialism that monopolized Tenebris. They were far more interested in pursuing the roots of beauty, digging into the depths of varied philosophies, and walking with the past in order to guide their future. These people, in stark contrast to the Tenebris standard, spoke with a careful nuance, crafted for the mere pleasure of creating, and lived with a communal mindset that did not neglect the individual. Anthro could not help but love them for it.

These thoughts made him wonder at times—alone and late in the night, always after victory, and with a bitter taste of rebellion and treachery left lingering in his mouth—as to who should be the rightful conqueror? What right did Tenebris have to extend its influence? It was more powerful than any other nation, but power did not equate to greatness. Strength did not guarantee goodness. More often than not, hegemony blinded and rarely, if ever, gave sight. Power and control made one feel as if they were in the right and yet, all the while, a hollow core of rot would grow unchecked and unnoticed as more focus was given to impressive outward matters and appearances. It was a recipe for ruin, a delicacy of disaster, faux walls of allure enveloping putrefaction. Anthro was coming to believe that this was true within both the hearts of nations and the hearts of men.

As Anthro explored the philosophies he found within the city Josias, as in most other kingdoms, he found that these people did not only deconstruct an idea or an object, as the Tenebris thinkers were so adept at doing. Rather, they sought also to fully reconstruct it, a concept foreign to the elite of Tenebris. Here, and in those many other lands, the breaking or dissecting of the thing was not designed to rip apart and gut out the object of its complex meanings. The goal was instead to see how the individual pieces fit together as they were taken apart, and to discern what that could teach the examiners about the network and meaning of the whole. This led to a greater appreciation of the entity and to a fuller understanding of the truth encompassing its entire reality.

The height of folly within Culpam were those pitied reductionists who were so consumed with the parts that they actually came to believe the parts were all there was. They had not eyes to see the richness of life and thought; they knew not beauty or truth. Such simplistic intellectuals were seen as those enamored with reason, yet devoid of knowledge, those obsessed with thought but unable to think. They were saturated wellsprings of fact residing in barren deserts of veracity. In his short time there, Anthro had developed a deep appreciation for the Culpam people, who were not kin of flesh and blood, but of thought and heart.

Following Tenebris's victory, Anthro had spent the last two

weeks here and would spend several more, as his battalion was always vital in setting up new governments and getting larger cities up and running again. His doubts about the supposed glories of Tenebris remained secret, but his interest in culture was well known, and his knowledge came in handy in many situations. Reconstructing a city was an art that required nuance, patience, and skill if it was to have any long-term success. Thankfully, Anthro's tactical finesse was not limited to the battlefield alone. Tenebris was not out to destroy all other nations—just to control them and to bring necessary changes that would allow for the Tenebris vision of complete global prosperity. Hence, the idea of unification.

Anthro was following his usual custom of talking to the city's leaders and thinkers after interviewing and disposing of the necessary higher up government officials. Tenebris had a strict policy that required a complete political restart or, more accurately, a complete cleansing of the upper government. As per his standard routine, Anthro had found an attractive female guide to help him navigate and study the new culture and to scout out potential candidates to be implemented into a functioning government. This method typically took some effort, but once the women saw that he had a genuine interest in their people and compared him to the rest of their guests, they warmed up rather quickly.

Anthro never settled for women who were anything short of fiercely intelligent, but acuity alone would not suffice. Beauty and brilliance were the consummation of his desires. He never gave thought to the potential shallowness of that behavior, the abeyant vanity that lay within physical beauty and the certain deceitfulness of charm. In fact, his sexuality was one of the few areas of his life to which he gave little thought. Anthro had been convinced from his youth that consensual pleasure was all that mattered in relation to the subject. He hated the idea of forcing women to do anything against their wills and saw rape or abuse as a sign of ultimate weakness in a man.

Without fail, he could spot the soldiers in his brigades who would seek to add rape to their spoils of victory, and they were always the weakest among them. Not physically, of course, but mentally. Holistically. To force oneself on a weaker vessel in an attempt to prove one's strength, right, or status, or to cause such trauma just to satisfy one's lust, only proved one's weakness, shame, and folly. Anthro had forbidden the act under penalty of death for those within his command, yet further than that he did not dwell on sexuality. In all reality, he simply used it as a thoughtless escape of rich physical sensation that acted as one of the few active remedies that could truly quiet his stubbornly restless mind. The more resplendent the body before him, the greater his mind was subdued; it was always a temporary rest, but powerful nonetheless.

"No. No. No! You don't eat it like that! You've got to break the shell first. You'll break your teeth doing it like that." The woman across from him had sleek black hair arranged in an elegant braid and wore a white dress of simple fabrics that brought out her own natural beauty more than any intricate fashion ever could. She had high cheekbones with soft ebony skin and was a prominent member of the city's historical society. Her heritage was from the desert lands in the southernmost regions of the continent, but like her parents before her she had spent her entire life in the north. Culpam was the only home she had ever known.

She laughed playfully for the third time that day, though each time Anthro watched her amber eyes dim when she realized what she was doing. Her city had, after all, just been defeated by Anthro's army. This time, however, the light did not completely vanish from her soulful eyes. She was in her early thirties, making her several years older than Anthro, but it did not show.

"Oh, that makes sense," Anthro said with a laugh. "Only . . . what part is the shell?"

"The hard red part, right there. Really, what else could be a shell?" Her voice carried a friendly tone and her face harbored a shy smile. She raised an elegant, mocking eyebrow at him. "In all the nations you've been to, is this the first one that eats animals from the ocean?"

"Diatris, I've eaten crustaceans plenty of times. I'm just not convinced that a crab, or even an animal, is what I'm about to eat right now." Anthro's eyes scrutinized the alleged crustacean before him, truly at a loss with its anatomy.

"This is a delicacy. You've no idea what it takes for them to catch it. As I'm sure you know, our northern border runs along the Glacial Sea and the waters are beyond treacherous." Diatris was a bit amused at the awkwardness of this modestly high-ranking military officer. It made him more human and less soldier, which was a difficult task as he wore a sword with him wherever they went and, until recently, had always been followed by a small posting of guards. She started to wonder about his past and his motivations. He was not at all what she expected when her supervisor had advised her that she would be escorting a military officer around for several weeks. Her heart had dropped then, but now—it fluttered.

After he laid another perilous siege against the beastly cuisine, Anthro finally claimed victory. "It is quite good, I'll give you that, but I'm pretty sure that there must be an easier way to eat this. It's so inefficient!"

Anthro enjoyed these moments of lighthearted conversation. On the rare occasion when they occurred in his life, he did his best to savor them. He and Diatris continued in an effervescent manner for some time. She seemed to have finally accepted that she liked Anthro despite his role in defeating her people.

Once their meal was complete, she leaned forward slightly, placing both elbows on the table and cradling her narrow chin with her confident hands. She stared into his rich green eyes, determined to know more about him. Anthro stared back and subconsciously rested a hand on the pommel of his sword, a thoughtless reflex whenever a mood changed. Her amber eyes reflected the sun, specks of brown shimmering within them as they cut deeply into his own. He was sure that his eyes had often done the same to others, but it was unnerving to find himself on the receiving end. There was something fascinating about this woman, intimidating even. He had enjoyed many meals like this with a variety of women, yet something was different this time—as if this woman could see something the others could not. It made him uncomfortable, which only increased his intrigue.

"Anthro, why a historian?" She spoke softly, her eyes unflinching.

"What do you mean?" Anthro leaned back, crossing his arms as his mind started to awaken. He began a conscious effort to keep himself from falling under the spell of her biting eyes.

"There are many beautiful artists, philosophers, poets, and researchers in this city. There are many women of different trades and talents who could be here with you this evening— whom you could analyze, whom you could sift through over the course of your stay." She radiated confidence, yet spoke like a dove. "Why me? Why choose a historian?"

What boldness! What conversational awareness! What a great question. Not once had he been asked something like it before. She could certainly think.

"I'll answer that, but first, why do *you* think I did? I'm sure you've thought of a few possible reasons." He leaned in once more, matching her posture.

Diatris gave him an amused grin. "My first thought was that you rotate your sources to get a well-rounded view of the world. In one city an artist, the next a historian, and so on."

"And that is no longer what you think?" *Who are you? That is what I used to do, but not now.*

"It's not."

"Well, what's your current theory?"

"I asked *why*, didn't I? Doesn't that show you that I don't know?" She laughed delicately, never ceasing her stare.

"For most people I'd assume it was that type of question. For you, I think it was already based on an idea."

"For me?" Once again she raised a thin eyebrow, sarcastic and sagacious. "What makes me so special?"

"I'll let you know that when I figure it out." *If I figure it out.*

"Ha, you let me know when that happens," she continued in her soft air. "I have a few ideas, but I asked the question first. It's only fair that I don't reveal all my cards from the start."

"Fair enough. I'll give you your answer." Anthro took a deep breath. He was not used to talking about himself or his thoughts in this way with anyone but Keta. Conversations had a way of working around all areas but himself.

"Just spare me the political part of it. I know that's one aspect, but I want to know why *you* chose *me*, a historian. I want to know why you have kept probing Culpam's history, myths, and legends. You're subtle, but not that subtle. I know you're searching for something greater than just a military or political advantage. You're searching for something for yourself. But what? And why with a historian?" She had read him like a child's book.

He gazed at her, deeply roaming her eyes, wondering at her ability to see through him. He delayed his answer for nearly a minute. The tone of the conversation allowed for it to move slowly. Anthro believed these types of conversations should give plenty of time for thoughts to process and words to be chosen carefully. Fear of an awkward silence should not drive hasty speech.

"I think about our world a lot. I've always thought about it. I've been taught so much about it, and I've experienced a great deal of it. But lately one thought weighs heavy upon me. One thought keeps me up at night." He paused, wondering if he should really tell this woman he barely knew the truth. He ran the fingers of one of his hands through his thick hair. With each promotion he had let it grow just a bit more, and by now it was just below his collar. "What... What if..." The words would not come. Anthro sighed deeply, leaning back and slowly writhing his hands as he gazed across the open balcony and out toward the looming mountains. Falling sunlight was reflecting off their ivory peaks. The crowds around the two of them seemed distant.

"What if?" Diatris suddenly took one of his hands, moving her fingertips across his coarse and callused palm. "What if . . .?"

"Diatris, what if we've missed something? What if there was an event in history that mattered, that explained something important about humanity, and we missed it?"

There it was. The whisper behind every misgiving thought, the shadow that seemed to surface every time he asked this world his favorite question: *Why?* Odd, he knew this, but contrary to many usual fears, this whisper grew louder the more he reflected on it. The dark dream seemed to grow in reality the more aware of it he became.

She surveyed the spiked mountain range herself for a few moments. Their bitter peaks seemed even colder as she took in his queer words. Tentatively, she returned to his eyes. "What causes you to think that we might have missed something? I've never had a thought like that myself, but it is interesting to me."

"I've watched this world. I've studied it and the people within it—especially the people—and if I can put it coarsely, I'm just not buying it."

"What does that mean? What are you not buying?" For the first time, her voice increased pitch.

"I'm not buying the story I've been told. The whole narrative. It's like we are missing something. It's like we're trapped in a cage of confusion and packed full of insufficient excuses for why that's the case. The answers I've been given seem too convenient and too inconsistent. I'm not satisfied with what I've been taught my entire life: that being skeptical is the height of wisdom, but somehow that skepticism is supposed to be restrained from turning in on itself. I loathe being told to embrace the darkness of this mystery while being promised that it is the way of light. That's what drives me. I'm skeptical of the skeptical answers that dominate Tenebris. They even pervade much of your kingdom's philosophies, though you are eons ahead of us." If an officer should say such a thing about his own kingdom, in this moment, he did not care.

"For skeptical people, we certainly make awfully bold claims about human beings and what we should or shouldn't think, how and why we should act, what we are or what we are not, what this world is or isn't, and what's possible or impossible." Anthro took a deep breath and continued. "Do you really think that this is it? Are you actually satisfied that humans are 'just here'?" He spread out his arms. "That *all* of this is 'just here' and that we should just live our lives accordingly?"

Diatris's thin eyebrows scrunched together and she softly bit her lower lip. "Anthro, what else could there be?" As she spoke her voice was sharper than it had yet been in Anthro's presence. "I mean, if we want to walk in our truth, we have to deal with the facts that we have, right? So whether we are satisfied or not, we can only deal with the facts at hand and make as much sense of them as we can."

"Exactly." He chuckled, smiling at her and softening the tone the conversation had taken.

"So, why are you so bothered?" Even with a guarded voice her speech was a melody.

"You said it yourself." He was not sure why he was starting to feel amused. There was something radically freeing about expressing suppressed thoughts.

"Did I?" This time both of her eyebrows rose sharply. "Please remind me."

"'We have to deal with the facts at hand.' That's what you said and I agree, but here is my dilemma: What if we missed one event, or even a set of them, that would actually explain this world—would explain *us*—in a far better way than our current worldview allows for? What if our base understanding of what is plausible and why that is so is in fact flawed? What if that error blinds us from what is not only possible, but what actually *is*? What actually has been?" A mysterious shiver shot down his spine—the kind of shiver that makes one feel very small in the world. "Imagine finding a fact that flipped this world on its head, that made the darkness tangible, the skepticism fathomable, the pain meaningful. A fact that actually reached the whole of humanity: mind, emotion, and being. Something—picture it as a key of light that penetrates this dark tomb—that actually gives a true and compelling explanation of reality far greater than the idle thoughts and dull speculations that prideful men have seen fit to offer it. You might not ever know that you had missed it, this fact, unless you searched for it. And where could such an overlooked fact possibly be found?" This time he raised an eyebrow at her.

"In history. That's a possibility for your line of reasoning, at the very least." She was not sure what to think. Who thought like this man before her? Was it insanity? Or was it brilliance? Maybe a lot of both? "But Anthro, do you seriously think that there could be a fact or an event that meaningful that was still overlooked by so many? As a historian myself, I say the very thought sounds outrageous."

"What if the event itself explained its own inscrutability? Or what if our methodological approach ruled out the event before we ever even examined the evidence? It's the problem of *what* we think is or isn't possible and *why* we think *that*. You see it in the sciences all the time. Before an event or material is studied, there is an entire philosophical system created a priori to the vast majority of the evidentiary research, many times without even recognizing this. Sure, certain patterns or histories of results can sway and mold that system, but ultimately, many results—if not most—are forced into a philosophical framework and plausibility structure that eliminates certain possible explanations prior to objective critical review. We don't always just believe based on results or findings, but we interpret results that are given based on a certain set of potentially limiting ideas that are often presupposed on our interpretive methods. At the end of the day, there is no getting around the fact that all knowledge is founded upon some base level of belief. Beliefs shape methods and methods shape results. Those results, in turn, shape beliefs and in the end it's circular, which means the whole foundation is legitimately questionable. Do you follow?"

Diatris calmly looked at him as she absorbed his ideas, treating them with both care and critical thought. "Yes, I understand. You're being reasonable, if nothing else. But I don't see how that applies to you choosing to search in history, of all places, for your missing puzzle piece. I get that something *could* be here, but why search here so strenuously?" There was no sarcasm. Anthro was too serious and full of candor for Diatris not to reciprocate that.

"Diatris, if there is one field that should be free of forced suppositions, it is the study of history. By sheer magnitude, volume, and fact, all history is truly unrepeatable. Certain variables—many, in fact—can never be reconfigured in exactly the same way, nor could all past variables ever be truly ascertained. Do you follow?" Anthro knew this was vital to his reasoning.

Diatris thought for a few moments, wanting to be sure. "Yes, by definition, that's correct. A truly objective study of history is essentially forced to work off of probability. Therefore, in principle, nothing should be ruled out, even though certain observations of uniformity should help to at least guide the ideas of what is more probable and what is less."

"Agreed." He felt relieved that she had been able to follow his thoughts. "This world is complex, dynamic, and mysterious, and so is humanity. I search in history because I'm convinced that we might have missed something, that we might have misunderstood who we are…or even *what* we are. We are historical beings, after all. I search in history because I'm skeptical that we are the wisest civilization that has ever lived. I search the past because I believe that there is a chance that an event of such magnitude need not be required to happen while I drew breath. Furthermore, I can't search the future—and keep this to yourself—but I'd say it's looking pretty grim. So why not rummage through the past at a time such as this? I haven't found anything yet—nothing more than patterns, anyway—but that doesn't mean my search will be in vain. I need just one event to give light."

"Do you really think there could be one event that strong? That powerful?" Diatris had so many new thoughts. Who was this man? Why had she been living with so many untested assumptions? Why so much confidence that she and her colleagues were on the right track? Just what was her epistemological understanding based on? What *beliefs* upheld it? Was her worldview really that compelling? That consistent and coherent? Was there any possibility that there was something they, or she, had overlooked?

"Maybe, maybe not. Perhaps it wouldn't even be a single event; maybe it's an event that would unlock an entire story, an entire history unseen, misunderstood, or misinterpreted. A cornerstone for a reconstruction of all that we know. What do I have to lose by searching? Where else should I go?" His final words were a queer tangle of nihilistic optimism.

Diatris stared at the bizarre man before her. She pitied his torment and the idea that he might be chasing after a false hope. She envied his lust for more, his dissatisfaction with a fleeting and chaotic world, and his willingness to enter any strange waters in search of a unique truth. "Anthro, I want to take you somewhere."

Chapter VII

The Parchment

Twilight had draped its way across Josias's polar atmosphere, the waxing quarter moon rising and the shimmering starlight appearing with the death of the sun. Daylight was falling in full, but new lights were emerging beyond those of the narrow crescent and glistening constellations. An eerie and mystical storm of excited particles wondrously emitted a staggering display of nature's marvels in the flowing form of electric jade and charged sage. The solar tempest tempted even the most glaciated of hearts to think afresh. This frozen, magnetic aurora produced a deep aroma of a longing for the extraordinary.

"This is it. I know that it was halfway across the city, but there is something here that I hope will make you even happier than our winter sky wonder." Diatris beamed at Anthro as the lights of her childhood fantasies emulated themselves within the enigma of his eyes. She wondered, with subtle fear, whether she was going to build on a false hope that would only later destroy.

Before them stood a building composed of thick hewn blocks of coarse sandstone. At the crest of the polished rising steps that led up to the Josias Museum of Historical Exploration stood a pair of intricate Corinthian columns supporting a soaring lancet arch. Carved walnut doors settled beneath this fine entryway.

"Welcome to my office!" Diatris had opened the oversized doors of the museum with a rusty bit key, revealing a dark, grand foyer. When her city was not recovering from war, she spent her days cataloging artifacts and sifting through new finds in the upper chamber rooms.

They walked through several crisp hallways as all light faded from the windows and skylights around them. Just inside the entrance, she had taken and lit an oil lantern for each of them, both for warmth and vision. Finally, they made it to a spiral stairwell and she led them down into bitter blackness. The fiery rays emanating from the lanterns cast a maze of unbalanced shadows all around them.

"I work on the top floor in the active research and field study section, but there is a room in the basement that's got your name on it." The flickering light of the captured blaze danced across Diatris's face, the flame and shadow creating a facial chiaroscuro of captivating complexity.

She stopped suddenly, causing Anthro to softly bump into her. She looked over her shoulder at him. Even in the dim light, her fear-laced eyes spoke. He put a hand on her left shoulder, beginning to gently move around her until she grabbed it and whispered in his ear. "No one else should be here. *We* shouldn't be here, but there is *no way* someone else should be here." She knew everyone who had access to the museum and was quite sure that they would have no reason to be in the closed museum tonight. She was certain they had not the slightest excuse to be in the frigid basement this evening, to be in the very room where she was taking Anthro.

The door, about fifty feet ahead of them on the left, was partially open and a lantern was clearly lit inside. Anthro expertly drew his sword, ensuring that it did not make a sound. "Stay behind me. Far enough back to let me swing, close enough to see into the room as I enter. Don't let me kill one of your co-workers. Got it?" He whispered the words, but still his deep voice seemed to carry more than desired.

"Got it." As they dimmed their lanterns, a soft fading light lingered in her eyes before being absorbed into the surrounding darkness.

Anthro moved slowly down the stony cylindrical corridor, working ever closer to the door. They could now hear movement from within the room. It sounded jerky and quick, like a scrambling animal hasty in its hunt. Anthro positioned himself at the door with his back against the ice-like stone while Diatris ensured that she was ready to get a line of sight on the person inside. A crash. Something had dropped to the ground. A silent pause.

"Could this be it? Yes, yes . . . the intel was good on this one."

The thickly accented voice came from a man. Even with the low volume, the sound was jolting as it echoed about in the quiet of the hallway. "My king . . . could this be another piece from Roma? An earlier one?" They waited to hear a response to the questions asked, but none came. "A small fragment this time, but the collection grows—no, it overflows. The grass may wither, the flowers may fall, but . . ." The man had to be speaking to himself and finished the sentence in a language that Anthro had never heard before. There was a greedy tone in his husky voice—like a miner with his gem, an athlete beholding his prize, a thief glorying in his plunder.

Anthro gave Diatris one last look, asking silently if she recognized the voice. She gave her head a gentle shake back and forth.

Anthro inhaled deeply, his lungs filling with the icy air

around them. Each pounding contraction of his heart fought the frostbite within. He paused at the threshold, releasing steam from his nostrils as an ox set to charge. With a fresh rush of breath, he spun into the room. A man of small stature was inside holding a piece of parchment to the light of his lantern. A hooded cloak was wrapped around his hunched form. A protruding short sword lay sheathed upon his hip. The man's head shot toward Anthro as he entered, two beads of light reflecting within the shadow of his face. The figure shifted backyards, drawing back his hood and drawing forth his blade in two swift motions. The small bit of paper he held remained clutched delicately in his free hand.

Anthro heard nothing from Diatris to slow him as his sword swung down upon this mysterious foe. Metal rebounded upon metal, sending a jarring vibration down both men's arms. Anthro's initial strikes were fierce but restrained. He did not want to kill, but was willing to kill. He desired to know who this man was, and he wanted information regarding the king of whom he spoke, but that would depend on the man's capabilities to parry a set of forceful attacks.

Piercing strikes of steel echoed about the chamber as the man was quickly pushed toward the rear of the room. A shift in his balance drew Anthro in, enticed by the potential opening. As Anthro's sword came down, the thief shifted again, bearing his weight low upon a sharply bent knee, defensively positioning his sword across his face. Anthro's blade slid across it, carrying on just inches over the man's scalp before slicing nothing but air. Anthro's momentum propelled his arm forward, pulling his body slightly along with it.

Time slowed. His eyes locked onto the man's. Anthro noticed nothing but the black depths of the man's pupils. He could feel himself falling into them, a victim of their bottomless pit.

Twisting, flailing, and desperate for control, he could see the tip of the blade drive forward, promising to cut him and feed upon his blood as it robbed him of breath. But at the very last moment, the thief spun the sword so that its pummel hit into Anthro's abdomen rather the tip. It was a powerful blow, but it was not one that would kill. Anthro fell to one knee, gasping for breath that would not come.

Diatris's screams pierced the night, beckoning time back to its normal flow. The man's head jerked toward this previously unseen woman. He took a step toward her, his blade reflecting the lantern's glow. Another gasp released Anthro's lungs as he staggered to his feet. Anthro could not understand why the thief had spared his life, but he was in no mood for such mercy.

Although the man made no advance, he was standing before Diatris with his blade drawn. In a daze Anthro roared toward them. The man leapt to the side, the parchment slipping from his hand for a moment, before he grasped it from the air. With a two-handed grip, Anthro swung his sword low, its tip scratching the ground below as it was then heaved in an uppercut motion. The thief blocked the edge, but was knocked back into a corner of the room. Tomes and scrolls crashed down upon him as he fell against the bookcase-lined walls. The little fragment of paper was still clutched within his grip.

Anthro ran forward, taking the man's throat within his left hand. Tightening his grip like a vice, he slammed the smaller man against the wall. The piece of parchment softly drifted to the floor. Anthro drew his blade back, ready to end this fight for good as he stared into those dark pupils. However, his blade hand hesitated, and his left grip loosened as well. The man took advantage of the brief doubt, pushing his feet off the wall and launching himself into Anthro, who tumbled forward as the man shot up and fled the room.

Upon entering the hallway he glanced at Diatris, stopped, then ran his dark eyes back toward the room where the parchment lay. Turning his head in resignation, he raised his hood and sprinted down the hall in the opposite direction from where Anthro and Diatris had first come. Blood dripped down Anthro's forehead as he recovered and was fast on the intruder's heels.

The thief outpaced him to a stairwell entryway, managing to slam the door shut long before Anthro could reach it. Whether he had locked or blocked it, Anthro did not know, but he was sure that the man had bought enough time to escape. He stood there breathing heavily, wanting to pursue, but not wanting to leave Diatris alone.

"Anthro!" Diatris ran up to him, wrapping her arms tightly around his torso. His unsheathed blade drew uncomfortably close to her, though she showed little concern. "Are you alright? How badly are you hurt? You could have been killed…"

"I'm fine," he said, placing a hand on her cheek. "He fought well, disciplined—but not professional. I made a very poor move that gave him a brief advantage, that's all." His touch was soft and gentle, his voice hard and distant. "What's in that room that would attract a thief like that, or even a servant of another king?" They slowly released their embrace and started walking back toward the chamber in question.

"Nothing. Not anything that should attract the attention of a thief or concern a king." Though she barely felt the surrounding cold, her body was shivering in uneven fits. "It's full of unclassified and untranslated literature that has been found but is not actively being researched. Not exactly a treasure trove, but I thought about what you were saying about history and was sure that you would be one of the few who would truly appreciate it." As they reached the door, she took in a long, deep breath of the frigid air, her muscles relaxing ever so slightly.

"There is a lot of material here." Anthro's eyes hungrily scanned the disheveled room. "Is *all* of this really not being studied?" Each scroll might be a key. Every tome a fresh path through uncharted territory.

"It's all been looked at to some degree or another, but we are very short on researchers and even more lacking in translators. It's organized, though. Rather, it was." She knelt down and looked at the parchment the thief had been trying to steal.

"Are you familiar with it?" Anthro bent down beside her and looked at the written script. It was a short message. The paper itself was torn and the writing had an odd format. It had a repetitive form to it that made it appear as if it were not written in straight prose.

"Partially. This is from a group of documents that were supposed to be sent out to other researchers who have more expertise in ancient languages." She brought the fragment closer to the light and placed it on a nearby table, treating it carefully. The value the thief had placed on it made it impossible not to handle the scrap with diligent respect. They both bent low and examined it closely, their eyes unblinking as if expecting it to reveal the reason for its worth.

"They were *supposed* to be sent out?"

"Yes. This one was going to be sent to a specific translator, the best there is, who just happens to be a prominent philologist in your capital. You'll forgive us if we felt inclined to hold onto it, considering the recent changes in the world." The bitterness in her voice was clear, but it was directed beyond Anthro and they both knew it.

"Romania? Romans? Romo?" Anthro murmured the words, trying to redirect the conversation a bit.

"Excuse me?" Diatris looked at him with her thin eyebrows scrunching together once more.

"The name. The name that the robber said. Did you hear?" He asked himself if this could be a piece from . . . "Romeny? What was it?" His eyes were fixed on the letters of the fragment before them. Each letter was a puzzle, every stroke a riddle.

"Oh . . . I think he said Roma. Yes, I'm pretty sure that was it." Diatris stood up straight and wrapped both arms around herself.

"Roma. Does it mean anything to you?" He stood up as well and subconsciously placed a hand on his bruised abdomen, his mind too active to recognize the growing pain.

"Yes, but only at a very basic level. The Romani were a people from a kingdom in antiquity. Much of their history is lost to us, but they held a good bit of influence in the world in days long past. Roma being the name of the nation, of course. My focus has always been on more recent study than that time period, so unfortunately that's about all I know." She ran her hands up and down her crossed arms. "Whether or not he was referring to them or the nation itself is hard to know. I can't think of any modern uses for the word. I've no idea what he could possibly believe about it that would make him risk his life for just a few lines."

Anthro looked at her, a wry smile spreading across his face. "We have to know. Diatris, we have to find out what it says."

For the first time since they encountered the man, she smiled at him. It was fascinating to think what those words could possibly contain, and his excitement was contagious. "Anthro—" She paused, her eyes now biting into his again as she took both of his hands into her own. "I hope I'm not wrong about you." She rose up on her toes and quickly kissed his scruffy cheek. "Take it. I'll explain the break in. I won't even have to lie." She winked playfully at him, attempting to vanquish the somber air.

Anthro stared at Diatris, still smiling, and wondered if she was right about him—pondered what exactly she might think about him. "I promise I'll let you know. I'm familiar with this philologist. We've had a few conversations during my visits to Babylonem. He'll be thrilled to have a new challenge."

Anthro quickly secured the parchment. As he did, Diatris, unable to restrain herself, went about the room and slowly began to replace fallen materials and reorganize the room. Anthro's eyes followed her as she moved about the dimly lit area. She leaned down to pick up a dusty, leather-wrapped book with an etched symbol upon its surface. She traced her fingers upon the markings, outlining an image of a crown that was split in two, half of it remaining as the rest crumbled away. She lifted the book up, arching her back to place it on a high shelf. He stared at her, a different kind of hunger in his eyes.

Anthro walked over to her, gently brushing back her hair from her shoulders. This enticed Diatris back to the reality of both the strange evening and his presence. She nuzzled up to him, feeling his warmth amidst the frost. Her amber eyes, lit with a soft flickering fire, looked up into his wild emeralds. Her hands rose to his chest and she gripped the clothing surrounding it. Rising onto both tiptoes and pulling him in, she kissed him slowly, hesitantly, freely.

Pulling away slightly and with a coy smile she whispered, "You'll get your answers one day, Anthro." Drawing back toward him, her lips up to his ears, she breathed out, "But no fun getting them all at once." Diatris, still in his arms, chuckled to herself as she pictured Anthro having—or trying to have—fun.

He smiled back at her but then winced as he took a deep breath.

"He hurt you?" She said the words as she delicately ran her fingers along his abdomen.

"Yes. But that's not what bothers me." He tangled the fingers of one of his hands together with hers.

"What do you mean?"

"Diatris," their eyes locked together when he said her name, "he was an amateur. He wasn't great with a sword, but he did have enough skill for the moment. I was holding back. Then, I made a mistake, a very bad one. A very costly one." He paused and in one move brushed back the scattered hair along her forehead and caressed his hand along her cheek. He drew her in and pressed their lips together once more. He then drew away just enough to rest their foreheads together. Locking amber and emerald together again, he whispered, "Why didn't he kill me?"

Chapter VIII

The Awakening

The great and mighty heart of Tenebris sat upon the nation's vast, rolling grasslands. Its impregnable walls soared upon the horizon, casting long shadows over fields of gold. At regular intervals cylindrical towers soared even higher, bringing humanity but steps from the heavens. From a distance the city was a mirage; within its shadow, it was a miracle. Reaching to the heights and extending to great lengths, the outer walls of Babylonem boasted with every brick. Their ghastly expanse teased of the endless stream of treasures held within her arms. Of her six gates, the eastern stood highest of them all. Its gatehouse towers were more like statues than structures. Carved on each side of the gatehouse was an identical woman dressed in purple and scarlet. Her eyes were haughty. Her form was envious. Upon her head sat a diadem with seven precious gems, each brilliantly cut into the shape of a decagon. Symmetrically, one arm rested upon each hip while the other shot high into the air. Together, they upheld a grand cup of pure gold. Beneath this grail the traveler would enter having read the words etched upon it: "My wine is costly, yet the one who drinks will never see mourning."

Anthro, flanked by his usual officer's guard, rode once more beneath the shadow of the women and their offer. Each time he went through was more difficult than the last. His disenchantment with Tenebris was just a bit stronger with every reentry into its capital, and now—after returning from his expedient conquest of more than a quarter of the kingdom of Culpam— his imagination would not be denied its craving. This time, with the bitterness deeply rooted and ready to bear fruit, he let the fantasies within his mind's eye roam freely as he envisioned what it would look like to sack this beast of flesh and stone, the great capital of his own kingdom. Would he be able to achieve it? How many men would it take? How zealously would it be defended? What would it take to reduce the head of the serpent Tenebris to mere smoke and ash? What great treachery filled his mind and played with his heart, and how little he cared.

Beyond the women, Anthro passed over the long, arched stone bridge that preceded the entrance into the core of the city. The eastern and southern edges of the capital were flanked by the largest river in the land, which had been integrated within the city's outermost boundaries. This was all to further the ceaseless flow of the plaque and clot of Tenebris trade. He then made his way through the next barbican and observed the numerous soldiers who were all standing proudly at attention as he passed. His eyes caught on those of the youngest-looking pikeman, who was roughly the same age as he had been when he first began serving Tenebris. The man, or boy (either term would suffice)—did he know the rotten core of what he was protecting? Did he understand the ideologies he would die for? Had he seen the ruin of war? Would he? Was he proud, as Anthro had been, to serve the mightiest nation in the world? What would he be willing to do for the name of country? Would there be any command he would refuse to obey? Anthro read his hungry eyes and they spoke to him of youthful inexperience, of a desire to prove oneself even if by reckless means, and of a blind patriotic loyalty.

Had his eyes looked the same just six short years ago?

Through the secondary gates his small troop went as the capital opened up before them with its large citadels looming high above them. Anthro breathed in the surrounding city air. The odor of infinite pride entered one nostril, the smell of limitless luxury filled the other. Their stench was nauseating. Within his heart the hour of judgment had come. A fire was burning within. It was beyond a fragile spark, having been rapidly fanned into a raging inferno.

Tenebris, your ascending colonel is here. My king, your honored servant has returned. Babylonem, you glutton, do you know the thoughts that I harbor against you? Your sentries salute me, your women pine after me, your men envy me, your children emulate my every move. How many could I turn against you? If I lit a match, how many would come to fan the flame? Or would all burn with your wretchedness? Are they already consumed? What could awaken them to your snare, your venom, your slavery, your rot? I know why I hate you, but why do I still serve you?

As he rode on, Anthro placed an unthinking hand on a small, leather scroll-case; this had been a subconscious action of his over the many months since he had come upon the parchment, looking for a chance to return to the capital and unwilling to trust any other to deliver it. At last, he had arrived. What had the thief been after? The little fragment's intrigue was fully dependent upon that man's behavior surrounding it. But the obsession had spread. There was something contained within its script that was worth dying for, but what?

* * * *

"This is certainly a unique document, Colonel. I must ask once more; where did you come by it?" The man before Anthro had a thick beard and an even thicker belly. His portly and blanched face assuredly saw far more light from candle than sun.

"As I've told you, Methero, I do not like to reveal my sources. Call it a paranoid officer's idiosyncrasy, if you will. However, I will tell you that there were many documents and books beside it, but it alone stood out to me." Anthro's voice was stern, though not threatening. Despite his appreciation for him, he preferred that the man believe that he had come upon this parchment himself. Anthro did not mention Diatris, the thief, or the fact that it had come from Josias and had even been destined for Methero's care if not for the war.

They stood together in a comfortable room overflowing with natural light and overlooking a garden of fern and flower. Anthro had spent the last three weeks becoming well acquainted with the landscape as he waited for the philologist to perform his work. Daily he checked on its status and always Methero would laugh at both his impatience and his faith in the philologist's abilities.

"Well, you certainly have a good eye. If you ever want to put your soldier days behind you, I can always use help here from a sharp mind like yours." Methero stood up from behind his desk, picking up an open notebook in the process. Beginning to pace, he continued, "The parchment itself is very old and its language took some time for me to decipher. However, it is undeniably linked with the era of Roma." His gaze was now upon his notes. The original piece of paper was in plain sight on an oversized desk of heavy timber.

Anthro took a step closer, his interest increasing even more with that statement. "Don't keep me in suspense! What does it say?" Anthro's excitement and enthusiasm had reached the end of a strenuous seven months of delay since coming upon the ancient fragment.

"It's rather fascinating . . . or, should I say, exotic." Methero turned away from Anthro and stared out at his modest botanical garden, clearly enjoying having someone so interested in his work and trying to prolong the moment.

"And by *exotic*, you mean . . . ?"

"I've studied many early documents, yet never have I come across one saying words exactly like this." Methero casually twisted around and began his lackadaisical pacing once more.

"Saying what, Methero?!" Anthro's tongue was nearly bleeding from his fight for restraint.

"Alright, alright. I can only keep you in suspense for so long." The translator now turned to face Anthro once more, and after a hearty laugh, a newfound seriousness came over his face. "To the best of my abilities—which, in my humble opinion, are rather trustworthy—I believe that it says, 'Their feet are swift to shed blood'—are you alright?"

Anthro's eyes were fixated upon his right hand, his mouth agape, and his skin tone suddenly drained of its vitality. In a fraction of a second he had felt a violent chill as if grasped by an unseen ghost. The haunting darkness of a moonless night came down upon him. The snapping sounds of crushing underbrush eliminated all surrounding noise. The smells of sweat and blood and steel offered no escape. But nothing compared to the burning upon his hand. Invisible, but unyielding. So distant, yet so unforgiving.

"Lad, are you alright? Anthro!" Methero shouted at him, attempting to awaken him from this sudden fit. He considered shaking him, but the sword attached to Anthro's hip made him go with another shout.

This yell awakened the dead man before him. "Yes . . . I'm fine." His voice carried with it a slight tremble. "Go on."

Never had Methero seen Anthro this way, or even imagined that his voice could sound so . . . weak? Timid? Afraid.

"From the top, then. 'Their feet are swift to shed blood'—" He paused, glancing up to see if there was another reaction, but Anthro was deadly focused this time. "'Destruction and misery are in their paths, and the path of peace they have not known. There is no fear of the King before their eyes.'"

Methero stopped speaking, the amiable atmosphere of the room standing in stark contrast to the seriousness and sobriety the tone had taken.

"Is that all?" Anthro asked, the lingering heaviness of the mood palpable.

The translator, still with a level of concern in his voice, replied, "That is all, Colonel. Does it mean something to you?"

"No. Well, I don't think so. You know of nothing like it?" Anthro asked, wrestling his usual demeanor back into his speech. He walked over to the parchment and stared down toward it, anxiously lacing his fingers over the back of his muscular neck. The color of his skin was still unnatural and sickly.

"I wish there was more of the document remaining so that I could do a better comparison, but from what I have, it is rather unique. Some similarities can certainly be drawn from a variety of sources, but the little message itself, with its order and apparent meaning, is on its own. One has to wonder what 'king' is being referred to. I will admit, that word itself has caused me the most difficulty in translation. The word may imply a divine status within that title, a holy sovereign of sorts, but I cannot say for certain."

Methero's mind now raced, thinking of any ancient king this might apply to. He had already done this before, of course, though to no avail. He cursed the gaps of the past that lay forever hidden, haunting those of the present whose only access was to that ever-restricting *remembered* past.

Furthermore, Anthro's reaction had added a new element of

oddity to this whole affair, multiplying Methero's intrigue. "Such interesting verbiage too, clearly referring to a violent people and apparently to—at least, the writer assumes—a benevolent king who demands more of them. But who? I daresay, I haven't the slightest inclination. Wherever you found this, I would urge you to either look in a similar place or go back and search for more of this document. The history! The mystery! It is marvelous to have come across such a thing. Would you like the fragment back?" The philologist inquired with a poorly disguised expression of pain upon his chubby face.

"Not yet. Hold onto it. In safe keeping, if you will." Anthro felt a lingering sensation of shock from what he had experienced. A part of him wanted nothing more than to burn the parchment into ash. Another part, a much smaller part, wanted to pursue. His mind briefly strayed toward Diatris, but more than anything, he wanted to talk to Keta.

"As you wish, sir. It will be held within my most secure vault to be seen only with your permission, Colonel." He said, with an almost childish glee, "And I daresay, if you do find anything relating to this in your travels, for you, my door is always open." He gave a genuine bow as he began to secure the parchment.

"Always a pleasure. You are a man of great skill and a good friend." Anthro returned the bow with all sincerity before turning toward the door, entering once again into the spiral of his mind.

*　　*　　*　　*

My stain awakens. In the condemnation of bloodshed, it has come back to life. Had it ever really left? It bites with all the same ferociousness of that first strike, of that wretched night. Though my body has been painted red one thousand times over, at mere words it burns afresh. Curse this mark upon this cursed man.

Who is this king? What is this path of peace? What of that thief who spared my life? A chasm of doubt is all that lies before me. A perpetual state of uncertainty, my only sure destiny. Shall I press into this unknown? Or shall I embrace it, surrendering to a life lived within the shadow of existence? A slave to its tyranny, oppressed by its sovereignty, overwhelmed by its mere possibility.

How difficult movement can be. How impossible even the simplest of life's actions can seem. An even darker shadow lies over me, one that I am not familiar with. It is suffocating as it seeks its prey. And yet, I cannot deny its temptation, its offer of escape. How it whispers of sweet silence. How it promises final rest of thought and fear. How preposterous such a solution seems until one is overtaken by the urge. But it is not the only voice. I hear you. Softly calling, gently persuading. Somehow I know that if I am to breathe again, then I must speak to you, Keta.

Chapter IX

The Reign of the Fittest

Twelve stallions approached the northern gates of Interitus, each beast carved with muscle and strength; any one of them was swifter than a leopard in chase, fiercer than a wolf at dusk. Though bridled they were far from tame, fearless and frenzied at the sound of a trumpet, snorting with pride at the beckon to charge. Quivers, spears, and swords rattled upon their sides. Though distant from it, they smelled of battle and war. Flowing manes clothed their necks as their hoofs clattered upon the cobblestone road. In groups of four they rode forward under the black and blue banner of Tenebris. Their speed was purposeful as they exited the maw of richly forested lands surrounding the city.

Anthro sat high upon his steed, trotting in the second row with two faithful lancemen positioned forward of their commander. The beast's fur was midnight black, a wild and hungry look filling its eyes. The green in the eyes of its rider was more subdued than its usual vibrance, as if death held the reins and had replaced the emerald with ashen. It had been two years since his last visit here—one month since receiving news of his redeployment to the southwestern edge of Tenebris. His army was already stationed at the newly erected border camp, the Kingdom of Vanus in its sight. Only more war and bloodshed on the horizon, the plague of Tenebris set to spread to yet another land.

However, a sizable remnant of Culpam had remained undefeated. This strategy was unlike King Beelzebul. Without fail he had conquered each kingdom in full before moving any forces on toward fresh prey. No reason was given, not even to high-ranking officers such as Anthro. Just orders. And Vanus was not the only target. Through the transition period, Anthro had learned of at least five separate fronts where Tenebris would now be on the offensive. Had the taste of blood and the thrills of victory only further agitated the beast within? Had the fresh wounds of the world only whetted the appetite of its predator? Now that the claws dripped with red, was it time for the teeth to bear down as well?

As the small cohort drew closer to the entrance, they noticed the first guard jump to attention, though their approach had been anything but covert. There was a shout heard beyond him. Several men with crossbows peered through the gatehouse window, only to disappear. The portcullis began to lower for a moment, then, just as suddenly it was raised again. Anthro ordered his leading knights to maintain their pace, all hands now rested over shafts and tangs.

Underneath the shadowed entryway of Interitus stood a lone officer of the guard, blocking their approach. While still a fair distance off, he raised his hand high and shouted, "Hail! Soldiers of Tenebris!" The greeting was atypical in its formality.

Anthro's two lancemen rode forward and returned the salute, "Hail! Guard of Interitus!" Their sharp lances were raised high in the air, slightly angled, ready to drop in an instant.

The officer stepped forward into the sunlight and offered an oversized bow. He was an older man, but still of fighting strength. His hands were fidgety as he bowed, his skin pale for a land this far south; though lightly armored on a temperate day, sweat dripped from his brow as he rose. "Interitus greets you fine men. Interitus welcomes you as comrades in arms. Interitus forever serves the King of Tenebris!"

Anthro clicked his tongue and drove his heels into his horse. His men knew to part to either side. He rode directly up to the man, towering over him. Anthro stared him down without saying a word, the grip of his long sword still clutched tightly as it sat restless in its sheath. He noticed blood. Dried smears of it, with signs of a rushed attempt to scrub it clean. However, there was no other hint of an injury.

"Have you seen recent battle?" Anthro's voice rumbled beneath the stone structure surrounding them.

The man's hands squirmed at an even greater speed and his voice noticeably stuttered when he replied. "N . . . no sir." His eyes darted around following Anthro's men who had created a defensive circle around them, their backs facing Anthro and the man, their weapons still held at bay.

Anthro drew his sword out an inch or two, just enough to show its steel. "You will not lie to me."

The guard raised his palms forward apologetically, a slight tremble carried down the length of his body. "Of course, sir. Of course. I dare not. I would not. I have not." The last phrase finally showed the first signs of stability. "Forgive me sir. I am only the newly appointed Captain of the Northern Guard."

Anthro let his sword drop to its original position. He drove his horse in a tight circle around the man, the man spinning round all the while to follow. Anthro pulled the reins back, the beast rising slightly upon its hind legs. "And what of your previous captain?"

"Err . . . executed sir." The man's eyes continued to dart about.

"For what reason?" A web of scattered doubts was rising to the surface of Anthro's mind. Slowly, he was linking together the whispers of the past with the worries of the present.

"Sir he, err . . . refused to follow orders, sir." The man inclined his head as if trying to diminish his own presence.

Anthro breathed in deeply before speaking. "Orders from whom?"

The man did not hesitate. "The King's Battalion sir."

* * * *

Hard heels kicked again and again into the ribs of Anthro's steed, the reins complementing the force on the animal's side, compelling it to give its all. Anthro had put enough of the pieces together. If only he had come sooner. His own heart pounded with a beastly zeal. Still, he did not know for sure. The lingering uncertainty offered the only ray of hope. Perhaps he had misread the signs, misinterpreted the signals. His travel escort was galloping down the compressed city streets behind him, the pounding hooves providing just enough warning for citizens to leap aside.

The group of men with him consisted of its typical party. One young squire, two men of lance, three bowmen, and five knights of the greatest skill. Anthro had hand-selected each of these men, balancing their talents with their personalities and convictions, and he was almost certain that each one of them was loyal to him before all others. He hoped it was a loyalty that extended beyond even the King of Tenebris if it ever came to it. He had spent years crafting each one of them, hours in long conversations over brewed bean and fermented hop. A few replacements had been due to his own choice and two the result of death, but this was his finest group to date. Their true loyalties and his own efforts were perhaps soon to be tested.

His intended destination, a white, three-story wood-framed building in the heart of the residential district, was now within sight, the well-manicured grass lawn and two sprawling maples adding a rare touch of nature in this overcrowded city. But an open door! Anthro understood that his fears were now all but confirmed. This door would never be left open and unattended unless something serious had happened. His emotions overtook him as he drew a preemptive sword. His subordinates unhesitatingly followed suit as the group passed the sign out front: "The House of Hope and Healing: A Place for All."

Arriving at the door, Anthro expertly dismounted his horse before the animal had even come to a halt. Prior to stepping foot in the building, he could hear her. Piercing his ears were broken sobs of anguish and despair. Sidesplitting cries of a heart turned asunder. Too late. He was too late.

Without a moment's hesitation, he entered the house of sorrow.

He started to scream her name as he passed the threshold but stopped the moment his eyes adjusted to the inner lighting. Before him lay a dead body. Prone. Pale. Lying in a puddle of its own crimson mess. And there, in the corner of the wood-paneled room, she sat as if still that frightened child he had seen all those many years ago; a husk of a human, an auburn veil casting shadows that could not hide the deluge of pain within. This time, emotion cascaded out of her as if all dreams of happiness and joy within had been brought forth and cleaved brutally in two. Anthro had never seen her lose control like this before. He could hardly take it, his anger starting to burn with the force of the sun while compassion flowed like a mighty river. Powerful emotions simultaneously occurring, yet highly conflicting.

He dropped his blade and ran up to her, passing the fresh

corpse. His men instinctively knew to vacate the building. There was no remaining threat.

The clanging of the metal caused her to stir and as she looked up Anthro stopped dead in his tracks, horrified. Feet from her. Miles apart. Dark purple like mulberry mixed with sangria red. Could those colors ever be seen as beautiful again? Around her left eye, and across her soft freckled cheek and temple, was a mangle of violent bruise and sharp laceration. As she realized who it was she stopped crying, though her body trembled fiercely.

"A . . . An . . . Anthro . . ." Her whole body seized as she said his name, fighting an assaulting wave of tears and howls.

"Keta . . ." If there were any adequate words of comfort for such a scene of despair, Anthro knew of none. He threw his body down beside her and she pressed into him with all of her being. Her wounded face buried itself hard into his chest as she continued writhing in misery. The touch of another human, especially this human, was the only thing keeping her sane. That thread of sanity was weaving within her and fastening itself ever so slightly to that steady heartbeat and soft breath of another. Finally, with the shock wearing off enough to think and to speak simply, she began telling him what had happened.

"I had received a secret message two days ago." Her body shook. He held her tightly. "Anthro . . . she said that I had a week. We were leaving tomorrow with all of them—at least, the three of us here were going to try. The others don't know what's happened. They are getting supplies in the city . . ."

He ran a hand across her scalp, brushing back what little hair had not already been matted by coagulated blood.

"Anthro, they were scared. They knew that those men were going to hurt them. Lazarus . . . Anthro, he knew! He had come so far!" Her eyes swept toward the body and she began to weep again. "Lazarus, he was a protector. He didn't know much, but he gave his life doing what little he could. A fork! He went against ten soldiers and their swords of steel with a fork, and I know it wasn't because he didn't understand his chances. Anthro, they could have so easily stopped him without even injuring him. He couldn't even use one of his arms." Another tremor, every muscle tensing. She felt so small in his grip.

"But . . . but I guess it wouldn't have mattered. I had been pleading with their leader." A look of motherly hatred that Anthro had never seen burned within her eyes. "I'll never forget his name. Captain Petros. He told me that all of them were being 'relocated' and coughed under his breath, 'exterminated'. That's when I lost control. He knocked me to the floor with the handle of his sword, and then Lazarus attacked him. Oh, Anthro . . . he laughed! The man *laughed* as he drove a sword through him! I was only half-conscious, but I heard him, loud and clear.

"And then his words . . . They're etched into my head. They'll never leave, even if I somehow wake from this nightmare. To have heard another human being say them, has taken something from me—I'll never sleep the same again. Anthro, as they were taking them away—the men, the women, the youth, the . . . the infant . . . she had just been brought here. The orphanage was just full . . ." Another shake, another tremor. "They were dragging several of them, and I was helpless on the floor . . . Anthro, that man said that it was about time to sing a new song in this world. He said that farm animals have more value than these useless cattle. He said that there is only one way for the world to be free from the burden of the crippled, and that I was a hindrance who was only lucky that I had some remaining usefulness left to offer society. With a cold smile, and that voice that will forever haunt me, he said that I should think twice about getting in the way of well-reasoned progress and human utopia."

The anger in her eyes had slowly faded and the pain was forever fixed, but now there was a sudden shift within her broken demeanor: a sharpening, a focusing, a pivoting of perspective. "Anthro, does Tenebris have nothing to say about the inherent value of humanity? Value rooted not in usefulness, self-awareness, or pragmatism, but in merely *being human*? Does it give no sufficient answers that can ground that reality? That can protect those who cannot protect themselves? What will we do to each other if humanity alone is left to determine our own worth? What won't we do? Anthro, are my beliefs—call them dreams if you will—are they so far-fetched when standing beside this kind of evil? Or . . . is this even evil to you?"

His grip loosened slightly—but for a moment. He would let her speak through her pain; his grip tightened once more. She was too overwhelmed to notice.

"Is there such a thing as evil in this world of yours, this world of nature and nothing? This world of humans and dirt? No lasting difference between the two of them, right? You've said it yourself. Oh, I remember; death is nothing to us. Life is nothing to us. Well, then, evil is nothing at all."

Keta's words stung, but her accusations were fairly reasoned. Anthro felt the full weight of her cries, hating their merit, unable to see an escape from the logic.

This ambiguous movement of matter . . . if all life ends in death, if life itself is determined to ultimately fade into frigid oblivion at the conclusion of our story, then no amount of chivalry, no extent of villainy, will be remembered. Good, evil, would be not only bound to endless chaotic interpretation, but, ultimately, it will be as if neither had ever been. No consequence from either of them would remain. Such an anticlimactic conclusion found at the completion of that loftiest struggle of the human experience, for in the end all that will be found is a cold stoic indifference to either course of history. This concluding apathy will be the end result of any evolution of events. *As memory in the mind binds the self to knowledge of its own existence, so oblivion of the final recollection of good and evil eliminates the ultimate meaning of either category. Such an impotent trajectory speaks heavily against any objective truth, for such terms are meaningless abstractions with many branches, but devoid of any roots of genuine reality in and of themselves.*

Anthro had no answers to give her, and at this moment, she wanted none. Nihilism cornered him, crushed him, called to him. That siren of vanity and futility would have him yet. He was sure that it would win the day, that it would claim victory over his convictions, but not yet. Not now. In this moment, he would hold her; he would do what he could for her, even while it destroyed him.

"Nothing! Tell me this is *nothing*! Tell me Lazarus was *nothing*! His murder *nothing*! Tell me the slaughter of them all is *nothing*!" Her crippled screams reverberated off of ceiling and wall, mind and heart, conscience and being. Weeping once more and with a cracking voice, she continued, "Tenebris, in its endless quest for reduction, has reduced human beings to nothing but predetermined parts. Oh, how have I heard you put it before: "We are just complex chemical cogs in a mindless machine of matter." But all this can only reduce evil to nothing of true significance. Anthro, tell me that such a belief is not worth greatly reconsidering and critically reexamining when humanity creates a world where anything goes, a world where humanity's victory over evil is wrought by us reasoning it into oblivion. No evil . . . no good . . . nothing."

At this moment, Anthro realized just how little he had told Keta about his growing disillusionment with Tenebris as a whole. He had mentioned his own nihilistic tendencies, which were the more convincing conclusions of Tenebris ideologies, but his mutinous thoughts were hard to convey in his position.

Now he hated himself for not discussing his rebellious doubts with Keta more openly.

"Anthro, I'm not asking for fairy tales, but at what point will we say that we are on the wrong track? On the wrong side of history? The wrong side of humanity? The wrong side of reality? Anthro, they're dead. Murdered. The most innocent of us all . . ."

Once again, she buried herself into his warm flesh that concealed his ever chilling heart.

*   *   *   *

It had been four days since all of the disabled in Keta's care were taken to their deaths. Anthro's men had discovered that there were none of the rumored camps. The handicapped had been taken far from the city and their bodies were left partially buried in pathetically shallow graves. When asked about the King's Battalion or the situation, surrounding villagers claimed ignorance. Citizens turned their heads, or, more often, suddenly found the ground beneath their feet of great interest. How easily humans could look the other way at the worst of crimes, wishing for a nonexistent ignorance, living indifferent to the darkness surrounding them.

His men had picked up a lead or two, and after digging proper graves, they were more than willing to ride with Anthro to conduct a slaughter of their own. His appreciation and faith in his men had grown steadily in these last few days. His hopes for them, and in them, were being realized. They knew what such actions could mean and they were calm, calculated, and unanimous in their desire for justice against this so-called King's Battalion. His men would have justice no matter the banner or title their enemy claimed. A justice of arrow and blade. A shedding of unrighteous blood. A cleansing accomplished by death. Eye for eye. Tooth for tooth. Life for life.

During this time, Anthro had stayed with Keta, ensuring that she was being taken care of. Her injuries were serious, but she was strong and was on her feet in just three days. Her two coworkers at the home were finding some meager solace and meaning in still having someone living to help. The visible effects of Keta's wounds were grotesque, even worse than they had been when he had first seen them. It was as if her body was unwilling to rid itself of the stain placed upon her soul that day. Her wounds were a living testament and memorial to those she had loved.

Each time Anthro looked at the bruising and the blood, his own blood boiled within. White-hot with rage, overflowing with a fiery anger. With every look he became more convinced of what he must do. As he watched her sleep, taking steady and shallow breaths, he stared at the wound, promising himself that he would destroy its creator. His mind would often stray to a vision of a field with fresh blood and successful ambush. One wretched enemy was left alive, one hated enemy left to slowly bring to death. Bit by bit. How crippled would Captain Petros become before he confessed that he was now less valuable than a cow? Would he at least have the honor to be consistent with his utilitarianism as he declared his own right to be eliminated? Anthro highly doubted it. He was conscientious to mention none of this to Keta. He hid it well. She knew him better.

Over the course of their friendship she had learned him, from minor gesture to grand articulation. She could see behind his ruse and penetrate his meanings in a way far deeper than Diatris was able to. It was precisely due to this knowledge of him that she knew she had to stop his inner fantasy of revenge from becoming reality. This grasp of him and his desires gave her strength. She thrived when helping and Anthro was a life to be saved.

She deeply regretted her verbal assault against him. Had she not already known that he wanted more out of life? Had she not been well acquainted with his struggle for meaning in a world that lived under the shadow of death? Why had she attacked the man who refused to get behind the beliefs that his fellow countrymen thrived in and lived out? She had tried to apologize, but he refused to let her even get that far. He did not blame her nor hold it against her. More than that, he would avenge her. For her, he would avenge those whom she had loved. And all of this would ruin him. That was now her greatest fear. Keta knew well that Anthro was on the edge of utter darkness; his letters had made that clear. This made her feel all the guiltier about her words to him, especially knowing he fought so hard against those ideas that swirled within his heart and arose from the very air they both breathed. He was a soldier refusing to yield, though hemmed in on every side.

She could tell that he was tired, feeling it more every time she saw him and read his next letter. How much longer could he fight against the contrast of life and the search for satisfying meaning that was so elusive to him? He thought so powerfully—perhaps too powerfully. He refused to live in the middle while remaining forever trapped there. At times he would talk with so much hope for an answer, with such eloquent beauty, that his description of life's goodness could bring tears to the stoic and charm the poets. Then, within the same thought pattern, the stark contrast, the broken paradox. The darkness and despondency sucked out the light of life.

She clung to belief in goodness and higher power, but he refused to accept their obscurity and lack of evidence when weighed against the overwhelming nightfall that was the human experience. Was it possible that a light could break through the darkness surrounding his soul? Shine bright enough for even him to believe? Could a true light enter this world and bring an enlightenment of clarity, satisfying both reason and longing? A light that, even if seen through a mirror dimly, could rescue his soul from death, his mind from callousness, and his heart from perpetual torment?

Now, at this moment, the blackness had a grip on him like never before and he had lost sight of how tightly it had wrapped around him. So little light remained behind the eclipsing sun of his soul, and yet the lustful moon hungered for total concealment. His anger clouded his usual self-awareness and his constant war against the night, and Keta feared he was at a line that, if crossed, he would never return from. Vengeance such as lay before him was a checkmate against his hope and conscience. He would not see this closing move until his target had stopped both breath and beat. Then it would awaken. Then it would fully consume. Then she would lose him. Finally, he would lose himself. The hardening he labored against so mightily would be set firm. His stone of heart would be forevermore.

She awoke from another cloudy slumber and watched Anthro as he stared at his hand.

He keeps doing that. Is it hurt? Why does seeing the action so clearly now make me think he has been doing it for quite some time? Should I ask him? I'm so afraid for him. What can I do? What does he need? Slowly . . . I need to work slowly with him. His hand . . .

"Anthro?" Her voice was dry and hoarse.

"Keta." His lost eyes lightened up, a dim ray of joy rising beneath a cloud of doubt and anger.

"I need to get out of this city for the day. And don't tell me I'm not up for it." Her eyes glared at him. Her mouth offered a weak smile. "I think it will be good for me." *And you.*

"Keta, I'm not sure—"

Throwing back a swooning hand and putting on the best "damsel in distress" voice she could muster, she said, "Would you really deny an injured girl her one request?"

Anthro could not help but laugh. Both of them laughed. Laughter, what an odd and wonderful medicine. It was too rare for the both of them.

"You're a horrible actress. You know that, right?" He stood up, stretching. He had barely slept through the night. Green irises were hedged in by crimson sclera.

"As long as it works," she jested in her most girlish voice as she rose from the bed, trying her best not to wince.

"Are you *sure*?"

She shot him a look containing the full measure of a woman's scorn.

"Alright! Alright. Do you have a place in mind?"

* * * *

Damp green moss covered the shadowy gorge of dark granite mountain slabs. The brisk air was inundated with a spray of water celebrating its newfound freedoms as it cascaded into the crystal pool below. The chilled basin had been carved wide over uncounted years of union between majestic liquid and silent sierra rock. The soothing roar of crashing cavern rain showered down from the restless waters above, endlessly echoing throughout the ravine. Branch of oak and wing of fir shielded the valley from the high noon sun in its position of pomp and nobility. Gentle rays of warmth were still penetrating through, a stubborn radiance of radiation dancing itself down between the canopies above. Specks of a wild blue atmosphere were scattered across the ceiling of broad leaf and wispy needle. Song of bird, sight of nature, touch of river harmonized with the senses and serenaded the heart, bringing a gentle caress of healing as if designed to guide toward the transcendent. As if manicured to free oneself from self.

This was Keta's refuge. When the toils at the home in which she labored were overwhelming, this was her place of rest. Not far from the city, but far enough. She came here regularly to meditate, and even to worship. She could not always define what she believed in (to the complete frustration of Anthro), but this was her temple. Nature was the place where she released her spirituality, where she directed it outward and was filled within. Did she believe in a god? A pantheon of gods? Or that everything was in fact a part of some greater and higher reality that could itself be called god? Natural matter infused with the divine and the divine a flowing circle of life, meaning, and spiritual energy. Did specifics really matter? She believed. For her, that was enough.

She was lying against the cool stone and watching Anthro as he stood with his hands behind his back, gazing up at the plunging water. He looked regal, reminding her that he was in fact an experienced military officer. How often she forgot that when they were together; he was no longer the conflicted boy of their childhood, but a far more confused adult of great accomplishment. As she watched, she let her mind wander into what he must have seen and experienced. Such imagination of the past drew in the fears of the present. What could she say to rescue him? What could she possibly do that could penetrate that stubborn heart of his?

After some time, with both of them lost deep in thought, he walked over to her and sat by her side. The damage to her gentle face kept him from any true sense of serenity. He began picking at some clovers and toying with their leaves.

"So, what do you think?" Keta asked, breaking the peaceful silence.

"It's beautiful, I'll give you that," Anthro said, slowly stacking the clovers's severed leaves into small piles with no apparent order. "Who would have thought there could be something this magnificent so close to the city?"

Keta stared at him, unsure of how she should approach this. "It's where I come when I need peace. It feels so untouched here, so right." She waited to see if he would respond. The clover leaf piles were quickly becoming mounds. She was watching his right hand. He was moving it with fine dexterity, so it could not be injured. Curiosity and concern were reaching their collective peak. Maybe it had just been her imagination? Only one way to know.

"Anthro."

The way she said his name made him look up.

"Did something happen to your hand?" At once she knew she had made a mistake. That expression. Was it anger? Fear? Both?

"What?" He stared at her with a quickly modified blank expression. He had heard her just fine.

"Did . . . did you hurt your hand or something? It's just that I've seen you staring at it quite frequently and it just made me think that you might have injured it," she said, while making every effort not to look at his hand.

"I . . . no, my hand is fine. I hurt it a long time ago, in an early battle, but it's better now. Maybe I look at it subconsciously because of the old pain. I hadn't noticed." He was talking in a breezy tone now and attending to his clovers once more as if the topic had merely caught him off guard. His ability to lie was about on par with Keta's ability to act.

"Oh. Well, that's good—Good that it's better, I mean." She

was willing herself not to push it. She knew there was a more important topic she must address, one in which she could not bend nor let him deflect.

They sat there in silence for a while longer. The last of the clovers within arm's reach had nearly been picked. Keta was just about to bring up his plans for revenge when he spoke first.

"I found something." He said this mindlessly, as if he was referring to an oddly shaped clover.

"What did you find?" She felt as if she were speaking to a child in her old orphanage, a child who had gotten into trouble and was carefully confessing his actions in an intentionally obscure and roundabout way.

"A relic from the past." He maintained his simple tone.

A relic? That's not what I was expecting. "An artifact? Where did you find it?"

"It's an old piece of parchment, actually. It was found in a city of wisdom." His tone was no different than if he had mentioned that the sky was blue.

Keta was used to this kind of patience-demanding communication (in fact, she specialized in it), but it was rather disconcerting coming from Anthro. He never spoke like this. *First lying about his hand and now bringing up this 'relic'. What's going on with him?*

"Okay, that sounds interesting. Care to tell me anything else about it?" She was doing her best not to sound patronizing. If it was, he gave no indication. She was slowly becoming irritated with his newfound fascination for all things clover.

"I've memorized what it said. It's short. Do you want to hear it?" Finally, he made eye contact with her again.

What was that look in his eyes? It matched his boyish tone, if nothing else. "Yes. Of course." She held his gaze.

He smiled ambiguously and looked down. Then he began speaking, slowly, line by line, in a disconnected voice,

> *"Their feet are swift to shed blood,*
> *destruction and misery are in their paths,*
> *and the path of peace they have not known.*
> *There is no fear of the King before their eyes."*

What on earth was that? He's looking at his hand again. "Anthro, what are those words supposed to mean? And what, may I ask, makes them worth memorizing?" Her flustered thoughts manifested in her shrill inflections.

Her change of tone snapped Anthro into a more appropriate level of seriousness. "They are from an ancient city called Roma. They're about some king who ruled long ago and, of course, his people. And yet . . ."

Now here was the Anthro that Keta knew, the hungry, serious, deep man coming back to the surface. The man of contradiction who permeated through with confusion, pain inundated with sorrow, hope misted and fogged over with grief. But why over this? "Yet?" *He doesn't even know he keeps glancing at his hand.*

"And yet . . . something makes me wonder about their meaning for the present." Anthro caught his glance this time and acted as if he had simply looked away in thought. "It might sound strange, Keta, but this is only a fragment from a larger document that I haven't found. I want to know more. I have to. I don't know exactly where to go or what to look for, but if nothing else, I want to learn more about this people of bloodshed and this buried king."

It was Keta's turn to look away, at a loss for what this was all about. He sounded crazy. What possible meaning could such words have for the present except to give a quick history lesson on the long-term violence of humans? Not much new material there.

But then, a thought. Maybe she could use this. When so little mattered to him, this parchment held his interest. Yes, she could use this for his own good, if nothing else.

"Anthro." She reached out, taking his hand and garnering his attention. "I'm going to make you a promise, but you have to promise me something in return. No debates, no questions, no objections. A promise for a promise." She had to take charge, make him less likely to object. "I'm going to help you with this parchment of yours. I can tell that it is of great interest to you and I'll do whatever I can to help you find out more about it. I'll work through anything you find out relating to it. Anything. No matter where it goes. No matter how long it takes." Now, for the catch. In normal circumstances, she would have done all she had just promised regardless of any commitments on his end, but she had to take advantage of this moment and the pull that the little piece of history currently had over him.

"Anthro, in return for this, you are going to promise me something." She squeezed his hand more tightly, knowing the importance of stopping him. "You and every one of your men are going to leave Interitus by tomorrow morning and go to the Kingdom of Vanus, where your current orders command you." He attempted to speak, but she refused to yield. "You are *not* going to look for the King's Battalion." Taking her free hand, she wrapped it around his cheek and bore her eyes into his, their faces inches apart. "Neither are you nor your men going to look for Captain Petros. You are not going to avenge anything that has happened here this week. Not now. Not ever." Her grip became a vice, her words were spoken as iron. "Promise me this, Anthro. If we are friends, promise me. If you are a man who cares about me, promise me this. If you are the man that I think you are, promise me."

Tears flowed freely now. She was at her limit. The new crystal drops drew his attention to her mangled eye and his grip tightened in her hand as she, following his gaze and knowing his thoughts, reached the point of desperation. "Anthro! Promise me! Promise me that you will not go after vengeance! Promise me, that *for me*, you will let this go! You will let him go. For me, Anthro, for me . . . if those flowers of the past meant anything, promise me." Her final plea—it was all she had.

She was shaking now and he was slow to respond. Why? Why was she so adamant about this? He almost asked. He almost argued. Had she not said those final words, he was sure he would have retorted. But that had stopped him. The memory within them had carried enough force to convince him that, whatever her reasons were, he must not avenge her. Somehow, against his desire, that was the more honorable thing to do. That was the right thing to do. That was the *only* thing to do.

Placing a hand delicately on her uninjured cheek and with a look of ferocious kindness, he said, "Keta, I promise." And she wept, for she knew that he meant it. A weight of anxiety and fear was lifting off her shoulders. She would not lose him. Not yet. Not like this. He had promised. The words were a mere compliment to the look of assurance and conviction he had given her. The rapturous scenery surrounding them finally reflected a bit of the peace she now felt. One was mighty and grand, the other feeble, but at last present.

Chapter X

The Moral Doubt

Six men with rough gunny sacks covering their heads were kneeling down before him. His personal guard was flanking him, positioned on either side of the raised wooden platform upon which they all stood. In the open square before him stood his entire regiment. Even many within the city had risked venturing out to witness the executions. Anthro would soon draw the edge of his sharpened blade across the hem of each one's neck. No trials. No delays. The use of his own arm of judgement would strengthen his message, solidify his statement. Crows were circling above them while buzzards perched like ominous gargoyles upon every roof line. These fowl of carrion cravings were well fed and soon they would gorge once more. All the while, additional foreign heads were drawing back their boarded-up windows, peaking out to watch this angry soldier who was, rather surprisingly, about to terminate men from his own country in this city of recent conquest.

"These men are not soldiers of Tenebris! They are not representatives of the treatment you will be given! They are cowards. They are vandals. And they will not be left to plague the people of this city."

One of the six began to tremble and moan; the others were

as still and silent as the death they would soon enter into. The crowds were hushed, but eager. His legion of men stood motionless and unsure. Never before had they seen their leader this enraged. They had witnessed him order many executions, but they all knew that he was about to perform this one himself—which was a first. The war in Vanus had been brutal, the most violent conflict any of them had yet to experience. Had the savagery of it all finally broken their most trusted brigadier general's resolve? Or was there some other fuel for this inferno of his fury?

"Tenebris shall not be known, as long as men under my command are walking among the nations, for this kind of brutality." Anthro shouted the words while still adorned in his full array of battle attire, its elegant onyx helmet and lofty blue crest setting him apart to all who observed as a high-ranking officer. "Have I not been clear? Have I not been consistent? Will anyone claim ignorance?" His voice was thunderous and stormy, his eyes of fire and flame. "Do any *object*?"

The moaning prisoner began to mutter rapidly, but was immediately silenced by a quick smash from the shield of one of Anthro's nearby guardsmen.

"No one, then?"

The quibbling man before Anthro was silenced for good. Justice.

"We are at war. No one denies this."

The next man fell forever breathless. Equity.

"Men will die on both sides. Civilians will be casualties."

Another sack turned red. Rectitude. Three remaining. The ominous shriek from a crow was the only other sound to be heard.

"If any of you citizens plan on revolting, know that my blade will be just as swift against you."

Two remained. Probity. Anthro's sword was now laden and

dripping with the blood of Tenebris.

"But my men, every soldier in this city, will not act like unreasoning lustful stallions neighing after every woman who walks these streets."

Another silenced. One more kill was needed to end this wretched week. Justice, not vengeance.

"Let marriage be held in honor. Let the single women be willing. *Let the young remain untouched.*"

The last man fell into a heap before his towering form.

Anthro had kept his word to Keta. He had not sought vengeance on the King's Battalion. These had been men under his own command and within his own ranks. Yet, this was the dark fuel for his righteous anger as his voice carried down alley and over rooftop.

"Let no one doubt that I am a man of my word. I have said this in every city with full and complete consistency: pain of death for unprovoked violence, unauthorized looting, and *rape* of any form." None could doubt the look in his deadly eyes. None could question the crimson on his steel.

Though he had not sought his true retribution, Anthro's passion for protecting the cities he was conquering had waxed full since the slaughter of Keta's loved ones. He would have his armies display the utmost honor and integrity. He knew many of his men would prefer to run wild and was sure that some believed he was robbing them of their rightful spoil. He was convinced that a relentless and unhesitating sword was the only way to maintain order. However, he also balanced this by giving his men plenty of freedom to enjoy more civilized debauchery.

"I will have absolute order in this metropolis from all sides." With full and final authority, he spoke, sheathing his saturated sword with eyes ablaze. "Captains, I will have you set up your districts from here." Then he turned toward his personal guard and, with a voice that would not carry, he commanded them. "Men, with me."

*   *   *   *

"Sir? Would you like us to force the door?"

Harpazo, one of Anthro's knights, was standing by a small, run-down home in a lower district. The rest of his men had formed a perimeter; the city had been conquered three days prior, but it was by no means secure. Anthro turned to Themata, the only other knight close by the door, and gave him a nod. The brawny, armored knight drew a steel war hammer that was clipped to his side.

Three hard swings above the lock did it. They drove forward into the house and were immediately met with screams. Inside, Anthro saw them: two women and a man surrounding a small group of people of all ages who were cowering in the corner of the dilapidated interior. The dark, candlelit room smelled of sweat, hardship, poverty, fear, and relentless love.

One of the women came forward with her arms spread out. She was trembling, but with a look of motherly determination, she began to speak. "Please, we have nothing here! Please just leave us be!" Her voice was strong despite her aged appearance. She stopped a few feet from Anthro, shivering with unmistakable adrenaline and angst.

Had this been Keta? Was this the type of scene the King's Battalion had walked in on—the courage of the weak boldly facing the cowardice of the strong? He was certain of it. "Are you in charge?" Fully armored, sword still drawn, war crest touching the low ceiling, Anthro towered over the older woman. He tried to speak softly, but his voice still carried strength and intimidation.

"I . . . I am," the woman was able to quiver out. "Please . . . nothing here." Though she stuttered, her brown eyes pierced into his own, declaring war upon anyone who would seek to harm those behind her.

Anthro placed his blade back into its sheath and his men followed his lead. The action caused the woman to raise her eyebrows in surprise. "I am not here to hurt you, any of you." He took off his helmet as well, trying to appear less intimidating and accomplishing little.

"Then why are you here? Sir, we truly have nothing here that your empire would desire." She spoke with her arms still extended as if they created a barrier between herself and those behind her.

"And there you are wrong." *Dead wrong.* "What is your name?"

"Sir? Truly, there is nothing here . . ."

Anthro stood in silence, waiting for her reply.

"Husterema, but everyone here calls me Ema. It's easier for those in our care."

"Ema, there is something here that the Kingdom of Tenebris will take." As he spoke every syllable, her eyebrows rose even more and her eyes widened. "I am here to try to prevent that."

He took a small step toward her, the candlelight revealing more of his shadowed face. His eyes. Ema had seen many things in her life, but never would she have thought she would see such a look from a conquering military officer. She could not fully describe it, but within the flickering emerald and ivory, she saw a mixture of pain and pity, sadness and sorrow, and something else, something deeper than them all. The look begged for trust. And, somehow, she was certain that she would give it.

"Tenebris will let me and a few other commanders reorganize this city and then they'll come. A certain battalion of men will come here. Not only to this city but to this house. They will come and . . ." He lowered his voice so only she could hear. "They will kill every single handicapped individual in your care."

Ema gasped and looked back toward the others. Why was this man, this officer, telling her this? Why would any kingdom do such a thing? Murdering the innocent; could men be so cold of heart to truly commit such a crime? What kind of darkness was this? How could such determined evil exist? And yet, she believed him. Why else would he be here, talking to her? They both knew he could cut through her if he so desired, and yet, with all this power in his grasp, the man before her was seeking to use such a thing for its true purpose—protecting the weak and the vulnerable.

"Sir . . . what must we do? What can we do?"

She believes me. Anthro sighed with relief. How often fear had clouded reason in those with whom he spoke, those whom he had given this same warning. How many lives were lost due to their unbelief?

With much greater ease, he began, "If you care for those here, you must leave. Soon. As soon as you can gather the necessary supplies and determine where you will go. I have nowhere to offer you, but I will tell you that you must stay away from the cities. Tenebris focuses its attention on highly populated areas. You must not let what you are doing be known to anyone whom you cannot trust with your life and the lives of everyone with you. You must leave quickly."

Now for the necessary protections on his end. "Should you choose to leave, you will spread a rumor of a contagious disease and will do your best to evacuate those here under the pretense of their deaths or required quarantine. If you can, pretend to burn their bodies. Take the bodies from a few graveyards. This will satisfy those who ask questions. My men will return and re-pair the damage done to your door. Create a false story of where you will be going and why. Leave one of you behind to provide answers. You must not fail. It goes without saying; you have nev-er spoken to me nor any of my personal guards."

Now the last protection, this one was a required threat. His tenderness vanished as if it had never been. "You will tell *no one* what I have told you. Even if you should stay and let all those whom you care for be slaughtered, you *will not* give the slightest indication that you have been warned. I travel from city to city. If you stay, I will be back here. So, be careful with your words, even if interrogated. You will not betray me nor sell me out. You will not deny me the opportunity to warn others as I have warned you. I assure you, should you speak of this to anyone in the King's Battalion, you will be punished personally by me. And, if you have not heard, my punishments for disobedience are swift and severe."

The woman trembled. This was no doubt a man to be afraid of. How thankful she was that he was on her side. She gave him a firm nod, understanding not only his orders, but why he gave them so severely. She knew what he was risking and she wanted so badly to thank him, but what words could convey her grati-tude?

She took one half-step forward, looking into his eyes and lowering her head slightly, and mouthed her thanks as a tear streaked down her face. Hers was such a small gesture, but with so much power within it. Anthro gave her a faint smile, inclining his head in respect, and left whatever was to be in her hands.

He could not fight this battle against the King's Battalion alone, but fight it he would. If he could not have vengeance, he would deny them their quarry. Anthro had now done this sev-eral times, finding every facility within his range and following this usual tactic. Always he was careful to be discreet. Always he gave different instructions to prevent repetitive stories. He knew what it could cost him, especially his men, and that only drove him harder.

Originally, his motivation had been exclusively his devotion to Keta and his hatred for the King's Battalion, but now—more and more—he found himself motivated by those whom he sought to save. The faces of the helpless now gave him his strength. On two separate occasions—one time an overweight middle-aged man and the other time a frail adolescent girl, both showing no trace of fear—had overhead his warning and boldly approached him, thanking him with a tight hug around his armor-clad body. This had startled both himself and his guards, but these actions gave new purpose to their efforts. Something about the simplicity of their love gave it a depth of meaning unreachable.

* * * *

Two days later, Anthro was slowly pacing in front of a stout, white-bearded man kneeling before him while two of Anthro's knights held bloodstained swords at the man's throat, towering over him like haunting statues. The conversation had nearly come to an end; the man had been more cooperative than most typically were. Anthro had now learned of a hidden armory within the conquered City of Consci, as well as different aspects of the Vanus culture and history.

Anthro continued to make this type of questioning his habit as he made his inquiries, groping for a hint of an ancient fragment or an unknown king, yet never directly speaking of either. This man was a wealth of knowledge, one of the top men on the Consci City Council, and a chatty one at that. He had dark eyes

113

that contrasted his white facial hair and pale skin. He was perhaps in his late fifties and seemed to be ready to face the death that was moments away.

Anthro about-faced, continuing his pacing while twirling his short sword between his hands in order to place it once again between himself and the man. "Well, Phusis, you have been very helpful. I wish that we had met under different circumstances, but I have my standing orders." Anthro's displeasure was palpable as he uttered that last clause. "As you know, we soldiers of Tenebris do not leave any high-ranking government officials alive." He dreaded this kind of killing. Executions for direct crimes, though necessary, were by no means pleasant; but these governmental cleanses that took no account of the individual's actions into consideration always left a hideous taste in his mouth for days on end.

"Indeed, our circumstances certainly are not the most hospitable for civil discourse," Phusis stated with dry genuineness. "But if this is my end, I suppose I am grateful that it will be *at the hand* of a man who shares my interest in society and culture." Hundreds of oil lamps, like distant stars, were burning along the outer walls, stationed above the rising, but noticeably empty, rows of bench seating encircling them. A roaring fireplace of refined ore stood in front of them, casting their long shadows across the council chamber and toward the unseen entrance of the dark, windowless cavern.

"Is that a request?" Anthro paused, then turned to look him in the eyes.

"Yes, it is," the man said, returning the stare as his voice lost its coarseness.

"It will be granted." The invisible stain that so often haunted Anthro began to throb once more. He was almost numb to its reaction, but never oblivious. "Any more?"

"You are too kind. Indeed, I have one more request for one such as yourself." He spoke with a very slight bow of his head, the swords at his throat preventing any more movement. If the gesture was laced with sarcasm, it was hard to tell. The man had a way of speaking with his inflection never quite matching his expressions. His communication style was proving to be rather bewildering to Anthro, but also slightly entertaining, if one could really use that word in such a situation. "I assume that this is just one of many such conversations a seasoned brigadier general like yourself has had. Am I correct?"

Anthro walked toward Phusis, his sword glimmering in the firelight. "Yes, you are." Curiosity was burgeoning within Anthro like a well-fed, oxygenated fire. Above them, the entire hemisphere that was the ceiling had a magnificent sun painted upon it. It was odd for a room so naturally dark. Hanging from the center point of the dome, held by a thick chain, was an intricate metallic globe. The light from the fireplace shone upon the suspended art piece, as if one singular lantern bid all to behold a marvelous spectacle. The shadows generated by the floating sphere gave the appearance that the chain that held the earth to the sun had been severed clean. Yet, amazingly, the world simply acted as if all was well, as if the time of its free fall was still not yet, despite the sheer madness of such a conviction.

"And you have had such conversations regarding culture, history, and philosophy with others in different kingdoms, have you?" There was a slight grin on the man's face. Still, Anthro could not read whether the forthcoming subject merely enthralled Phusis that much or if he might be planning something reckless.

"Again, you are correct. May I assume there is a request coming shortly?" Anthro was curious, but he was also ready to get this last kill over with for the day. He hoped that it was the last one needed in Consci, as the flow of bloodshed would usually cease with the successful establishment of a new government. In addition, attacks from guerrilla groups were at an all-time low for a recent takeover. Perhaps publicly executing his own men had carried that unforeseen benefit.

"Indeed, my request, in hopes that my loose tongue has been appreciated, is that you will indulge my own curiosity briefly. I am interested to know if you have found, or heard of, a satisfactory answer to a problem that has plagued me for decades." The man paused, but Anthro made no move to interject. "The core of my dilemma is found in the root of civilized human behavior. Morality."

Morality? Of all the things to talk about during your last minutes, he wants to discuss that? If you can even call morality a thing in this dying world of hopeless self-asserting valuers . . . well, let's at least see where this conversation goes. No need to close my mind recklessly to what this man may offer. How much I hope that he, and morality, have something to offer . . .

"Before I get to that, though, I must lay just a bit of groundwork. Are you familiar with the idea of a moral law? Or a natural law, as some might call it?" The fire before them, ignored since the start of this interrogation, was darkening. The softening of its light began to reveal a narrow entryway beyond their current gaze.

Anthro looked about the room as he thought about the man's query, to behold the hundreds of individual twinkling flames offering their own variants of light, opposing that more obvious blaze before him, but not one of them shining light upon the exit. "By this you mean a specific code of moral values for human beings, no matter the time, culture, or societal structure?"

"Yes and no." Phusis's slight, incongruous grin returned. "That definition is fine in part, but to be a natural law of *external* existence—and therefore unchangeable substance, similar to all

116

other natural laws—it must not *rely* on any of those factors for it to exist. The law is to produce the thing, not vice versa, so I would qualify your statement with that assertion. Now, Anthro, I have spent much thought on this natural law; across kingdoms, cultures, and certainly the histories I have seen, there is always a common thread of morality we humans display. Honor the aged, give to the needy, be just, speak truthfully, do not murder—these themes come up again and again."

Still the primary inferno waned, allowing the other flames to reveal more of their own visual sharpness within the doomed room. The only escape came from beneath a section of row seating, now only noticeable with the fading of the most captivating glow.

"I agree with some of that observation. I have also seen something similar. But I have also observed a vast number of discrepancies; have you not?"

The white-bearded man did not hesitate. "Discrepancies? Surely, though mostly around sexuality. Many times, the 'rules,' if you will, are actually quite different; however, the underlying values, normative assumptions, and reasons around which those rules are built are far too consistent to be mere coincidence. Is there a natural law of morality? To me, it seems almost certain."

"Alright, assuming that there is this moral or natural law," *and you've no idea the level of my doubts, old man, though you do make a fair point or two,* "what aspect of it could possibly cause you enough trouble to bring it up in your final conversation?"

The man looked away from him for once. His tone carried with it a taste of familiar and nagging doubt. "You see, I have found all this evidence for morality. And it is not just the mere external, I will add. There is also the *internal* force of the law within me that seems to be an aspect of my very being. And of course, not just mine, but all except those whom we deem insane

117

seem to share this force of law exerting itself upon us from within. Yet, despite all of this—and far more, mind you—one thing I have not found. I am not satisfied without having found this, so perhaps you have, and will be able to give me rest before my death. I . . ."

Anthro abruptly interrupted him. "Lower your swords, men."

"Sir?" His knights hesitated. It was an unusual and sudden order.

"Lower your swords. He is not a threat. I will be the one killing him, anyway." His stain reminded him of its presence with a ravenous bite.

"At your word, sir." The men dropped the tips of their long swords to the ground, each grasping the hilt with one hand and placing the other on the end of the pummel. It was a position of dignified attention while still allowing them to lop off the man's head at a second's notice.

"You are an intriguing officer and an even more fascinating man, Anthro." No sarcasm was to be found.

"You were saying?" Anthro was unsure why he had given his men the order. Was it that he could see the father figure he wished he had grown up with before his eyes? Or maybe even an older version of himself kneeling there? He was not sure, but those were his only thoughts.

"I was saying, despite becoming convinced of the reality of this moral law, I have not, with significant thought about it, found a way to fully ground this law on humanity. To justly bind this law upon an individual." Phusis shifted slightly, his knees sore. The guards flinched in response.

"Can you elaborate on that?" Anthro's mind had already begun to work, having laid aside his own doubts to follow the branches of this man's reasoning as they grew from the fresh

roots of his differing suppositions. Anthro took others' beliefs—those who appeared to have been even remotely thoughtful about such beliefs, at least—with the utmost seriousness.

Phusis continued, "I affirm that there is a moral law. I believe that morals are indeed a real entity working in this world
that are beyond a mere effect. That is, morality itself is the primary causal factor for moral behavior. Or, to put it another way,
morality is the original chicken that laid the first egg of moral behavior and continues to keep the egg basket full. I will elaborate
on the dilemma shortly. But first, this moral law is for humans,
right? Other animals do not seem to be burdened by it, correct?"

"We are in agreement there." It was an interesting thought
to Anthro, but it seemed obvious enough to agree on. He had
witnessed enough of nature to know that humans appeared as
freaks in a monstrous world of uncaring.

"So, we have a law for humans in regard to morality. How
that came about—how the *chicken* came to be—is of great interest as well, but not my main concern here."

"Before moving on, what do you mean by 'of great interest?' And why so much confidence in morality being the cause
of the existence of moral behavior? Why can't it be the other
way around?" With this present development of thoughts, Anthro was trying to see from all the fresh angles. Maybe there was
something worth dwelling on later in these areas of *interest*.

"Altruism? It's tricky. Perhaps not insurmountable, but in
a world such as ours, with nature out there looking anything
but self-sacrificing, are we *really* to believe that such a powerful
force arose by mere chance and necessity? Or through some rigid form of determined mechanistic action? That such a thing is
simply a twisted distortion of tribal survival instincts? It seems a
rather far stretch to me.

"And I assure you, dwelling on any of those as the cause of

morality certainly chills the desire to be moral. If morality is anything worthwhile, are we to believe that those who know its origins shall easily be drawn to kill the very thing created upon discovering its roots? What man wants to follow a force this strong knowing that it could have come out any number of ways? Or worse, that they themselves have no freedom in their own relation to it? Remember, I'm asserting an *external* law of morality. All of this is of certain interest when we start discussing how, and why—and even from whom—morality came about, though one's views need not even rely as heavily as mine do on the external to be reasonably skeptical."

"*From whom*?! Phusis, you've gone too far. Are you actually suggesting there may be some sort of *mind* behind morality?"

The man-made fire was becoming a mere smolder. A simple log would brighten the room once more, but such a rekindling would once again blind one from beholding the narrow pathway toward the outside sun in all its preeminent and real splendor. That sun was a far more extravagant sight to behold than even the human masterpiece adorning the ceiling above.

"Ah, yes. That whisper of a greater mind . . . well, it still nags my own mind from time to time. I do my best to avoid the thoughts. Honestly, I don't like the idea of such a . . . *moral being*. Who could? We've no time to get into what exactly the thing itself could be; however, as we approach my actual dilemma, we must focus on what the thing presents us with—whether that mere presentation is an end unto itself, or goes beyond itself, is not where my deepest problem resides. I have waded through morality; I am convinced that it is a part of human existence, and that it should not be, and cannot be, ignored. And yet, I am *not* satisfied with having a significant missing link. Perhaps your knowledge will be of some assistance. It may just be able to give me a little taste of rest before my death."

"Well, this conversation is yours; what exactly is it that you seek?" A pop from the fire attempted to draw Anthro's attention back toward the dying flames, but the noise was ignored.

"Anthro, what I cannot figure out is how to *bind* that moral law—or even just call it morality itself—that I so dearly believe in, to make it *require* something of a man. I can tell every citizen I have that there is this law, but I have no way, no richly compelling reason, to fully satisfy *why* they should adhere to it." As shadows danced across the man's face, he finally showed a clear expression of frustration at his predicament.

Anthro thought for a moment. He seemed to follow, but he failed to see a real problem—at least not one of such magnitude as to make it one's final conversation. "There seem to be many ways to bind a man. We are governmental, are we not? Surely as a member of this council you are in the work of binding men to laws."

"Ah, I've worked through this one at length and have found it to be woefully lacking. It is the age-old 'society binds the man' concept. It fails miserably—philosophically on one hand, and practically on the other." The man's discontented expression grew in length.

Phusis explained, "Beginning with the latter, on the practical hand, what society do you know of that has no need for prisons? What country is there where you can make a man act with a certain motivation in his will or without a hidden agenda behind his keeping of the law? You can punish a man for not keeping your moral requirements, or that of the people, but you cannot bind a certain code of ethics on a man. At death he is free; in life, more often than not, he is free.

"More troubling is the fact that we all have a similar strain of morality, but not one of us is in perfect agreement! How can we tell a man to act a certain way when no one can fully agree on which way is completely true to the moral law?" Phusis paused, ensuring Anthro had kept up. "On the more philosophical hand, what assumption free justification is there that is not comprised of self-imposed values but that would have a man believe he *should* care about what society tells him? Why *ought* an autonomous and sentient being obey the commands of anyone seeking to attack his own individual autonomy? Is his mind not free? Must his will be held captive to a certain number of others' views? If so, what is the number? And *why*? If that man cares nothing for society, nor its preservation, why *must* he do anything? He is free from this imposed moral vision." Phusis's voice was rising, evidence of the uneasiness within him.

"But even if society does not govern that man nor ground the ethic, we are saying there is indeed a moral law, are we not?" Anthro had followed the previous objections, but he believed he had the argument here.

Phusis looked hopeful, recognizing Anthro's confidence. "Yes, those are the grounds we are building on."

"Then that settles it, does it not? If there is a moral law that is truly acting on the will of humanity, is a man not bound to that law as a matter of simple fact? There is a law, it acts on man, therefore, he is bound." Anthro spoke confidently, suppressing his own deeper doubts, but still not thinking this was a problem of great magnitude.

That fleeting look of hope faded from Phusis's eyes. "Brigadier General, with my utmost respect, I do not think you fully understand the problem here. That conclusion is sufficient to say that there is a moral law and that it acts on all men, but it does not *bind* a man to that law. Does a man not have conflict against his own conscience? The conscience seems to present itself as the manifestation of the moral law within the individual man. However, a man may reason against his conscience.

He may ignore it. He may have emotions that conflict with it and choose to follow those more powerful feelings. Or he may simply trust his contrary natural inclinations and go after those.

"The conscience within may guide the man and the moral law outside may press on the man, but it does not *bind* the man. Even if it presents him with the appearance of a categorical imperative, it *fails* to give him an *absolute obligation*. The natural law may act on a man, but he may, while maintaining a sound mind and good reason—perhaps even *because* of that—chose not to act on it. Even if there is an objective good will within the universe, and it somehow presents itself within the rational human mind, why should a man bend his free and personal will to any but his own? Shall a man not fight the laws of gravity merely because they exist? What other forces of nature are we not free to resist?"

Though certainly intellectually stimulated, Anthro was not deterred. "But even gravity presents itself as external to man, whereas morality appears to be both outside *and* within him. If the law is in man, he would be resisting a part of himself in not obeying this law. And by shared human experience, we all admit that the vast majority of humans *can* and *do* follow this law to some degree."

The gentleman held his tongue, waiting until Anthro made eye contact with him to make his point manifestly clear. "Whether they do or do not follow the law is of *no concern to me*. The problem, once again, is not if a man *can* obey the moral law, but why a man *ought* to obey the moral law. Unless we wish to rest something as grand as morality on simplistic assumptions, we must establish the 'ought' beyond the mere presence of the thing. We choose to reject much within ourselves daily: cravings for things that are unhealthy, desires for things that are not ours. Why listen to a part of ourselves in spite of another opposing part?

"How can we convince a man who is determined to resist what we think is right that he *should* follow after the common thread of morality we share? The simple do this by instinct, but those who have wrestled through it . . . I've no compelling and consistent answer to give them, nor myself. In the end, all I can honestly proffer is a meager statement, though typically more eloquently put, that surmises to 'just be moral' . . . *but why be moral?* Because I tell you to? Because you have a conscience? Because you'll be happier? Bah! What thinking man could submit to such logic? But maybe . . . could it be that perhaps civilized society itself could not bear the darkness of the alternative? The haunting breadth of empty space . . . morality, within its mysterious nature, seems to demand much of a man, yet is this all the reason it offers for humanity's obedience? *It does not satisfy.*"

Anthro was starting to understand the man's frustration. "What are some factors that could help bind humanity to this law, whether or not they really exist?"

"Good. This is how I proceeded as well. I have thought of a couple: first, objective truth of this morality. This law *must* be universal and ultimate for it to hold enough weight to subdue the thoughtful. How to prove that as demonstrable fact, I haven't the slightest idea. But it can be proved to the level of being reasonable, if not probable, due to the very nature of this law we are discussing and the cross-cultural consistency that I've already mentioned. We need not fear cultural distinctions as long as there is undergirded unity and truth of the moral framework itself. Another factor is that it would need sufficient consequence that supersedes what we as a society are able to achieve. Death is always the escape for the stubborn." Here he stopped; he had never gotten much further. Death was the escape for any man content to ignore the moral law. In death—he was free, no matter how wretched he had been, no matter how opposed to society's laws or even the laws of his own conscience. Death was ultimate freedom. As long as that reality was there, humanity could not be bound.

"Consequence: it is influential, but in totality, it is an insufficient means. Can fear win a heart? It can guide or cause one to reconsider to some degree, but can fear truly bind all that is a man?" Anthro knew fear. He had seen it in hundreds of comrades and in thousands of enemies. Still, his most intimate knowledge of fear came from the fear within himself. It was a subtle feeling that spoke to him in the quietness of the deepest recesses of his being. He was afraid. Of what? He was afraid to know.

"Anthro, I am sure you know the power of fear. What will it not make a man do? A fearful man will sell his family, betray his closest friend, reject his country. Fear knows no bounds!" The man's animation caused the guards to tense once more.

"I do not deny fear's power," said Anthro. "However, I will deny that it is powerful enough for the question at hand. If a man is to truly follow the law from within and not just give it simple external lip service, Phusis, he must *want* to follow it. Ultimately, fear will never cause that kind of desire. One needs a more powerful motivation for that type of binding, and few exist." Anthro was speaking as fast as his thoughts, but he believed he was correct.

Phusis's face softened. "One such motivation exists . . ."

"Yes, one does. Cause a man to be motivated by love and that alone will give you the binding you seek. How you can cause a man, or all humanity, to obey the true moral law out of love is beyond me. Especially as we both concede that it is very likely that every man, to some degree, will require an adjustment to his moral code upon being faced with the true objective reality." Anthro felt the conversation nearing its end and resented the fact. He deeply wished that he could be friends with this man, to sit beside the embers of another dying fire with a heart made merry by just the right amount of quality beer and to dig zealously into the deep questions within every human heart, but openly discussed by far too few. He saw in this man a seriousness for life that he had rarely seen, and now Anthro would be the one to take that life from him. The thought filled him with hatred. Of himself? Of life? Or even of Phusis? He was unsure.

Phusis's eyes looked beyond this dungeon of his death. "Love. Not the feeble and wavering love of romanticism, but that love of action—love as a verb. The kind of love that humans so deeply crave and so seldom give. If you won a man by that to the moral law—or perhaps even through it—that could bind him. Not a perfect solution, since there are other factors we have not time for, but it is further than I've gotten before. Win the man with the law, the whole man, and you just might be able to do it. What would that look like? Anthro, can you imagine it: every heart set free from the law to be found in service of it?" His voice was almost childish as he stated those last few sentences. "What a thought. A good idea to hang on to at the end." Phusis lowered his head, that oblique smile of his returning one final time.

Anthro approached him, sword ready. He would be quick.

Suddenly, Phusis looked up.

"Anthro."

Anthro froze, his sharpened steel inches from the man's waiting neck.

"Thank you . . . but I am surprised. You didn't ask. So many questions around it, but not one directly about Roma."

The man knew. Had Anthro really doubted that? Phusis stared at Anthro, dark eyes seeing right through his own.

"I . . . I wasn't sure. I don't know . . ." Anthro stuttered, his voice like a fearful child and not a celebrated general in the grand Army of Tenebris. Thoughts of Diatris and Keta immediately filled his mind.

"You jumped around the topic several times. It was actually quite obvious. Don't give up. I can see that the secrets of that ancient city haunt you as morality has tormented me. There is more history hidden there than remains with us." The man's eyes briefly glazed over. "We don't have much here on it, but there is a museum in this city—the only one. In the upper room, you will find a glass display case. Within that case is a parchment we *obtained* from a kingdom called Culpam; you will find many here who will go to great lengths attempting to uncover the hidden secrets that surround us. I am not sure how much of it will help you, or if it will at all, but it could be a start. Who knows what you'll find? Or even what you have already found?" Phusis raised his eyebrows with a friendly and mocking grin.

So, there was indeed another one—another parchment from Roma.

"With that, I leave you," Phusis continued. "I wish you well, Brigadier General. You have my sincere thanks . . . a love so strong that it binds the man to the moral law. Perhaps unites him to it? Or shows him something about it that he never expected? That we never imagined? What lies behind the veil? Maybe this love even enlightens him to see through the confusion and to behold the true and complete law. What a wonderful thought."

Phusis bowed his head once more. In a flash, it was over.

*　*　*　*

Anthro sat on the railing of a balcony upon the Consci city keep. It functioned as his temporary lodging until his battalion moved out. Another perch. Another observation post. Another conquered city. Another parchment. It was protected in its case, which lay safely in his quarters. The retrieval the day before had been entirely uneventful; the only remaining museum attendee did not even say a word. He wondered why she was even there. Did she have no one left to go home to? For just a moment, he had thought he heard footsteps following him as he took the fragment back to his lodging. He had not been sure. The thought had faded.

War weighed excessively on his heart, heavier than it had in a long time. It was a millstone clinging to his soul and dragging him unrelentingly toward despair. Why did he offer any form of service to Tenebris? Does blood bring justice? Why did he have to kill Phusis? Why did men kill each other? If there was this inherent moral law inside of man, why was it so ineffective?

The streets were empty save the occasional passing night watches. The emptiness before him reflected the exact opposite of the activity that was occurring within his heart and mind. War. Death. The parchments. The mysterious king. What would this new fragment have to say? And what was he to do with these new thoughts on morality? Morals . . .

Why doesn't morality work for man? Despite the darkness of the future before us, by all other appearances, we are moral beings! But we—we rulers of this world, are so wretched! We spill the blood of the guilty. We spill the blood of the innocent. We spill the blood of our brethren. We spill the blood of strangers. We spill blood in the square. We spill blood in the night. No other being is like this. And yet we are the moral ones! What sort of freaks we are.

Wielders of morality, greatest of sinners! Curators of law, enemies of peace! Shining lights of reason, heralds of ruin! Beacons of glory, torchbearers of despair! Seekers of truth, purveyors of death! Coveters of knowledge, gluttons of corruption! Man, what are you?

Moral. Morals. Morality. What is this thing that courses through humanity? Could the world be bound to you through love? It's a dream: a nice thought for a dying man, a hope without foundation. Morality, are you a curse? Your very existence the ruin of man? Or is man the bane of morality? Are you weary of us yet? You who guide each man independently, yet universally run through us all—what are you?

A shiver raced down Anthro's spine. Sweat began to form on his brow, despite the cool breeze. His whole body fought a sudden tremor at this next thought. Was this finally proof that he was going insane? Or was it the most rational thought he had had in years?

Who are you?

Another shiver came, cold as ice and sharp as steel, electrifying his conscience, pulsating wonder, arousing fear. This thought, simple and unfathomable; elementary, boundless; the muse of a child, the ancient wisdom of the aged.

Who are you?

Is that so crazy a question? Is it insanity or clarity that brings one to consider this mind behind morality? Morality, you are a mystery to me; I don't believe you should exist. Where could you come from? You exist outside of man, yet you live within him. You crush his conscience but fail to restrain. You scream of objective standard, yet none prevails.

Who are you? Morality and humanity juxtaposed against one other—one seemingly good, the other an utter contradiction. Morality, we call you good, for a good man has you, follows you. Does he not? Yet, it is not just that—you exist in man. Man is a person. Of all the living things on earth, you have made your home in us, in those whom we call persons. Who are you? Not such an outrageous thought. You exist in persons alone. Outside of a person, you are a meaningless abstraction; perhaps there, but unrecognizable and pointless. Persons. Humans. Morality. You have tangled yourself in a web of human affairs, united yourself to our very nature. We know you are there, but what prevents your reign?

Were you not there, humanity would still be reasoning animals, yet with no ability to differentiate between right and wrong—no knowledge of discerning good and evil. That is your function, is it not? Without you, there is no good! Without you, there is no evil! They would be empty categories, even in the present! My greatest fear, restrained only by the hope of your existence.

But what of our function? Why are we here? Why can't we attain a truly moral society? Do you mock us, morality? Are you a jewel that is always kept out of our reach? Or have we misplaced you ourselves? Have we misunderstood you? Have we suppressed you? We treat you as philosophy, as a goal to be achieved, but are you more? You have to be more.

Another thought. Another chill. A shiver pulsating deep into the core of Anthro's being.

Could it be that you are from more? Is it 'who are you?' or is it 'who are you from?' Not only a law, but also a lawgiver? Do I sound like the archaic tribes I've come across, still thinking of a personal power like this? They call them deities and gods, but such beings have long since been disproven, right? Are they not only left to be believed in by the uneducated or by those of fideistic hope, like Keta? Or was that another act of our war against morality—casting aside its crafter?

Perhaps the moral law is yet even more of a reflection of personhood than it is the creation of that person? Are we waging war against the nature and being of that person from whom morality itself is defined? Morality is grounded in personality, whether within itself or from outside itself. What better explanation is there? Has humanity explained you? I've yet to be satisfied. Phusis wasn't satisfied. Who are you? Who are you from—or whom do you reflect?

Anthro maintained his eagle's perch well into the night. Only after long hours did he snap out of his trance of thought, the mystery of morality having distracted him from his heart's own anguish. Now he felt that sorrow creep back in, seizing upon his settling mind. Overlooking another city of his triumph, he knew there was no man as lost as he was, as utterly despondent. A man awakened to man. A man haunted by what he saw. A man baffled at the contrast.

The day had been long. His thoughts had been new, powerful, and overwhelming. Anthro lay down in his bed with the conundrum of man and morality still pulling on his mind despite his own mental protests. The weight of war, the struggle of life, the puzzlement of a consciousness plagued by a conscience, the images of death, and the subtle reminders of his stain—all pressed in on him, dragging him deeper into the darkness. All of this was fed further by the ever-present whisper of those haunting words: "Their feet are swift to shed blood."

What am I?

Anthro wept, bitterly.

Chapter XI

The Child's Dream

Not a cloud was to be seen across the clear blue sky in the crisp autumn afternoon. The sun gave its warmth, providing the perfect balance of comfort between chilly air and tepid ray. They were sitting on a hill overlooking the largest park Babylonem had to offer. Bright green grass still carpeted the ground, while vibrant orange, rich red, and soft yellow adorned every tree. Beauty in life, beauty in death. A gentle breeze was bringing in constant fresh air with each new breath.

Her head was resting upon his abdomen, their bodies perpendicular, as her eyes gazed into a canopy of color above them. He had his strong back buried into the thick, rough, half-living-wood of the single tree upon the park's most prominent hill. They had talked for hours, reunited after so long—but now they sat together in a peaceful silence only possible for those who are deeply comfortable with one another.

Anthro twirled his fingers through her sleek black hair, the physical movement a mindless reaction to his active thoughts within. He was watching a mother and her children play below the hill, their mirthful laughter carrying across the raised earth and filling both ear and heart. A boy and a girl, neither over ten, were enjoying themselves in the careless freedom found only in childhood.

What was it about children that could move the hearts of even the most calloused of men? Time and time again, Anthro had seen hardened men break like fragile glass at the word, touch, or sight of a certain child, many times not even their own. Children were little rays of light shining despite even the deepest darkness. The fruit of the womb was surely a reward and the crown of the aged. A man's children were his quiver; a woman's offspring, her joy. No child was the same, each was fearfully and wonderfully made, each a metaphor for something even the proudest of men ought to aspire to become.

Tenebris valued many things in this world and children were not lost among them. Despite Anthro's belief that placing significance on the young was good, he had seen parents who took this value of a child and had morphed it into something more. But what? What description would fit such behavior? What had these parents formed their children to become? Idols of worship. Like so many of those tribes, these parents too found something to bow before.

Fathers who were under the authority of their children were common in Tenebris. Yet the more Anthro observed, the more he saw that those who practiced this often destroyed their children in the process. Could such a small thing bear the weight of being a god? What a millstone of stumbling for one so young. Perhaps a society that no longer believed in a god was relegated to creating gods after their own images?

He had seen the effects of this in his own men. The ones who were the most morally healthy and emotionally stable were always those whose fathers had not spared the rod. Such fathers knew the difference between discipline and abuse, instruction and embitterment, patience and indifference—yet also held in delicate balance love against enchantment, encouragement without flattery, fatherhood and not idolatry.

And what of the mothers who placed children beyond the realm of mere human? What habit of their offspring could such women not excuse? How creative some of them could be with the defensives given for their children's vices. Never was this good for the child; never was it even done in love for the child themselves. It was a subtle and gross distortion of the parents' own self-love sought within that of others, over whom they held the most influence. Mothers too insecure in themselves would stop at nothing to have this child of theirs adore them. They adored in order to be adored, and in the process lost both themselves and their children. These mothers were ignorant to that reality, blind toward ultimate ruin.

What great balance was needed in parenting! What responsibility and power the position held. To instruct a child to walk in the way in which they should go was a task for the strong, for the committed, and for those able to see the crop of harvest among freshly plowed fields. Anthro did not think these things often, but now with Diatris resting upon him, he let his mind drift on to what could be.

The young girl below had dynamic blonde hair to match what was clearly a lively spirit. Her older brother seemed to be the timider of the two, but still held the playfulness of one in his youth. They were playing a game in which they leaped over one another without any apparent order or rhythm to it. With each leap, the girl let out a high-pitched yelp of levity and convulsed with rib-wrenching laughter. Such joy from such simplicity. Why did parents ever go to such marvelous lengths to entertain their children when children so often found the most pleasure in elementary activities?

For perhaps the first time in his war-torn life, Anthro continued to let his mind wander to what his children would look like if he and Diatris ever had them. They had placed no barriers against the possibility, yet it had not come to fruition. A womb not opened, seed not sprouted. They did not blame one other; they would not. At times Diatris blamed herself, but Anthro never let her maintain that opinion. Why was this their lot? He never had an answer to give. Futile words were of no comfort. Some things were beyond their control, and in this he comforted her. Although Tenebris offered many creative ways to potentially elude the barren womb, they had both agreed that they would not go to extremes to produce what was not freely given.

Secretly, Anthro felt some relief at not bringing a child into this world of war and death. Still, something greater drove his desire to be fruitful and to multiply. Was it instinct, or some deeper reality? If nothing else, he thought there must be some good in returning life to the world after so many years spent extinguishing it. Maybe his child would not defile the land with bloodshed as he had.

If that were ever to happen, what would their firstborn be, a boy or a girl? Would the child be healthy or unhealthy? Have green eyes or amber? He could only dream, but one thing Anthro knew: none of that mattered. The child would be life, would be human, would be loved.

He dreamed further. Surely, their offspring would have dark hair, but how would his own olive skin blend with Diatris's ebony complexion? Anthro was not sure of the imagined result, but whatever the color, he knew that it would be a wonderful mix: a unity of difference, a synthesis of skin, the reuniting of race.

Although Diatris still worked in Culpam, she had become an official citizen of Tenebris. This was typically no easy task, but being the lover of a well-respected general had its benefits. This citizenship allowed her to travel with significantly more freedom and enabled them to see one another with far more frequency. This was Anthro's first return to Tenebris with the second parchment in his possession. It was currently in the adept hands of Methero, the philologist and translator.

Despite their great differences, Diatris and Keta had shared similar initial reactions toward the revelation of the first parchment. Diatris, however, had made him no promises. In fact, she had become rather disinterested in the topic. Of course, the historian in her had found it intriguing, but she found the content of the message grotesque and had little desire to learn more, despite knowing about this second fragment. They both understood that this was Anthro's mission, not hers.

More than that, she had shown more interest in Babylonem than Anthro had anticipated. Certainly, she had her various critiques (though neither of them knew the full extent of the other's thoughts on this), but she found the level of achievement and innovation within the city sensational. She lamented that Tenebris had chosen such a method as war to spread its influence and often spoke of what could have occurred if the good within Tenebris and Culpam had been able to mingle and interweave: robust philosophy with endless resources; skillful creativity commingled with countless clientele; and charity guarding power. The match would be humanity combining its best to create even better.

Anthro kept the most heinous crimes of Tenebris from her, but he was drawn to her ability to find virtue and potential where he only saw spoil and deficiency. Would she still think the same if she knew the darkest of Tenebris's secrets? He did not know, for though they talked deeply with one another, he did not talk as widely or as openly with Diatris as he did with Keta. In Keta, he had friendship, vulnerability, and openness. In Diatris, he had passion, desire, and mystery. Both powerful, neither akin. The two women had never met, though both were well aware of the other.

"Anthro, do you think this war will ever end?" Her voice was dreamy and tired.

He did not speak immediately, but then queried, "Why do you ask?" The falling sun was just meeting the tops of the distant structures that stood beyond the trees.

"It's hard to imagine peace. But in this place, with you, it seems possible." She had shifted up next to him, cradling in his arms, watching the two children plead with their mother for more time to play. "Could you imagine a life together not separated by distance and uncertain return?" Apparently, her thoughts had not been far off from his own.

He pulled her in a bit closer. "I can. Not fully though. It always seems aloof. Like a dream just before you wake up. Close enough to touch, too far away to be real."

"I know what you mean. But what about you? Must this war end before we can start a life together? Will the king not release you from service?" She had never asked these questions before. What was causing them?

Anthro sighed deeply. He was nearing ten years of service, which meant one could petition for an honorable discharge from the Army of Tenebris, no matter their rank. King Beelzebul always knew how to keep a fantasy within reach, how to make one think they just might achieve the impossible. "Not me." A half-truth. "I'm in too deep. I am too valuable to his majesty's army." *Too valuable* against *his majesty's army.*

She laughed, playful and sarcastic. Talking to herself, she lamented, "Diatris, you placed your aim too high. You shot for the stars only to take hold of one *too valuable* to be forever yours. Shining brightly in the night, only to leave you with each new morning."

Anthro could hear her pain despite the playful delivery. He

felt it himself. "Diatris, how I wish ours was a story not birthed by war, but my love, such is our lot. What will the next few years bring? I can only speculate, but there are reasons to think things may be changing. The king has spread out our forces. We are on too many fronts. If we had not been so effective in establishing submissive governments, we would have long lost the strength to continue. But our advances are slowing. What will that bring? New boundaries? New attacks? I do not know."

She pressed into him. "Well, it sounds to me like there is at least some hope that I'll have you yet." She closed her eyes, her mind drifting into a half-conscious state of malleable dreams.

*　　*　　*　　*

Anthro meandered around the greenery that surrounded Methero's office as he waited for the translator to arrive. He had left Diatris early that morning. Now knowing that the parchment was translated, she was more interested in what the results were, but not enough to rise as early as Anthro had. Dawn was approaching and his heart was pounding. He had received a note from a courier the previous evening stating rather simply:

> *You'll want to hear this.*
> *Until tomorrow,*
> *Methero*

Where was he? Anthro had been hopeful that Methero would have risen early as well, but the old man always kept him in suspense.

To pass the time, Anthro walked among the flowering shrubs and savory herbs. The morning dew was still fresh upon each leaf and every petal. The soil was black and earthy, filled with life both visible and invisible.

He stooped down to observe a new seedling emerging from the dirt, its perishable husk of seed giving way to a resurrection of new life. What a wonder this tiny sprout was. Why did such a thing exist? Created from a drama between flower and insect, eaten by bird, buried in soil, given life by rain, and now hungry for sun. Its very breath gave life to Anthro, and his lungs returned the favor. What harmony! What a marvel! Such a grand mystery this was within even the simplest forms of life.

Finally, after Anthro had taken several laps through the garden, Methero opened his doors. "Major General, the rank still increases, but you're as impatient as ever!" He gave a jolly laugh.

"Forgive me, Methero," Anthro returned with some sincerity.

"Nothing to forgive, my friend. You simply entertain." Methero laughed cheerily as he gestured for Anthro to enter his office. He was in an even better mood than usual.

"First things first, then," Methero stated, walking up to his desk and, for once, seeming to cut to the chase. "The two fragments are indeed one."

Anthro, leaning over the desk, saw both pieces aligned perfectly. "Excellent, that is good news," Anthro whispered, running his fingers gently across the seams.

"Indeed, it is! In fact, I believe we have the entire piece. There surely may be more to the story, perhaps giving further context to the report, but I believe we can safely say that this is a full message. And what a message it is." Methero spoke as a taunting friend.

"I'm sure I'll agree in an hour or so when you finally get around to telling me what it says," Anthro said.

"Patience builds character!" Methero gleefully chirped, continuing his taunt as Anthro scowled at him. "In due time, in due time. Yet will you perhaps indulge my curiosity, if only a bit?"

"Perhaps." Anthro was indebted to Methero for his work, but still felt that he must maintain a certain level of secrecy. Maybe giving the old man a bit of information would speed things up.

"Always the careful tactician, aren't you?" Methero chuckled. "Well, I will not ask much, but I am hopeful that you will at least divulge if you found this new piece in the same location as the last?"

That was not asking too much. "I believe I can reveal that, but why do you ask? Would that make any difference?"

"No, no. Not with the translation, anyway. But are you not interested in what would cause the parchment to be torn in two in the first place?"

Surprisingly, that thought had not occurred to Anthro. He had been so preoccupied with what it might say that he had not wondered about either fragment's origins. What was their history? Were they an original autograph or a copy of an original? He could reveal what he knew about this to Methero. "It was not found in the same location. Quite far from it, actually."

Methero, stroking his beard, replied, "Curious. Curious indeed."

Fighting impatience, Anthro pressed on. "Yes, definitely something worth thinking about, but in 'due time,' perhaps? The words, what does it say?" That was still his main focus as sunlight began to give its life to the plants outside and its light to the office.

"Ah, yes, the message." Methero was becoming a bit more serious. "Do you recall the words of the last parchment?"

"Every. Last. Word." A wild energy and deep longing infused each word, only to be outdone by the hunger and fear that filled Anthro's eyes.

"Well, my friend, I will say this. The plot sickens."

Chapter XII

The Depth of the Darkness

With her head bowed low and tucked tightly between her knees, Keta sat on a cool stone floor amidst the darkness of her chamber. Eyes closed fast, her auburn hair draped around her pale face. A single candle was burning, a minute flame of life engulfed by obsidian. Her thoughts were unusually restless, but they were finally clearing. Or, if nothing else, they were becoming more organized.

While on his first reprieve from Vanus, Anthro spent a few days with Keta at the orphanage, then left Mori two weeks ago. After the destruction wrought by the King's Battalion, Keta had no reason to stay where she was, so she returned to her previous life of looking after those whom Tenebris had not yet decided to execute. Would orphans always be deemed worthy of life? Were any safe behind the never-settled line of value, where man was left to determine the worth of his fellow man? Yet for once, it was not these thoughts that assaulted Keta. For once, it was something unfamiliar. Foreign thoughts and powerful ideas circled within her mind and harassed her conscience.

True to her promise, she had taken it upon herself to try to understand or gain context around Anthro's parchments. She had not been shocked by the additional message of this new piece, having expected little else. Despite having only a faint interest in the writings herself, she had spent most of her free time in Mori's rather impressive library, searching for some kind of lead. All the while she kept a translated copy of both parchment's messages on her, reading them as a whole again and again, twisting the words every which way in her mind, hoping something would come to light. This endless study had been a welcome distraction from her lingering inner sadness.

Until three days ago, she had found nothing noteworthy. Then, all of a sudden, it had happened: a bizarre twist of events despite having obtained no novel information. In a sudden flash, as Keta read the parchment's words for the hundredth time, it was as if a light brighter than the midday sun surrounded her, hiding all else from sight except those few little rows of letters. And as she read those words within that light, this time, they started reading her.

In the twinkling of an eye the words had come to life. With a sudden spark the dormant text now stood before her in all the power and magnitude of the present tense. With just one stray thought, Keta had been brought to her knees, feeling naked and ashamed. *Imagine if they were speaking about me . . .* It had seemed such an innocent thing to do, a way to toy with the mysteries of the past and end another fruitless day of labor. But immediately, a voice had cried out within her, asking herself a startling question, something she had never given even the slightest consideration to. Her life's assumptions felt as if they had been built upon foundations of sand and were now in danger of crumbling into a heap of contemplation and doubt. This question—so much hinged upon it.

Am I good? Oh, that really is the question! Still, it really can't be separated from who is defining 'good'. Who could judge such a thing? Am I to be this judge? Is that not my contention with Tenebris, that we are the endless determiners of what is right and what is wrong? Shall I be the judge of the good in myself, using that same standard that I appall when used by others? Oh, this standard of goodness—it must rest in something more or on someone higher than myself. I've known that for quite some time. But where does that leave me now?

These words, they are like a spear to my soul. They haunt my conscience. They torment my heart and assail my mind. Now that they have awakened, can I ever have peace knowing that such a combination of words exists if I do not find a resolution? I cannot shake them.

Despite this, Keta felt a violent passion stirring within her, an urge to do anything to forget these words, to relegate them once more to their rightful position of a mere curiosity of days long past. She envied her previous indifference. She loathed that promise made to Anthro. She was about to curse even the flowers of their friendship, which then made her hesitate.

She took in a slow breath. Then another, and another. It did little to calm her. She shuddered as she imagined the ink of the words flowing through her veins, infecting her with the law held within the letters. How could so much power be contained in a few ancient sentences? She had read and studied her entire life, but never had she experienced anything like this before—this intrusion by text.

She felt as if the words wanted something from her. As if they had work to accomplish and would not relent until she had surrendered to their will. The thought repulsed her. The storm within her grew in its ferocity. If there was a question of goodness at hand, the words were in the dock, and she would be the judge.

Like a two-edged sword they pierced again, subverting the very thoughts within her soul and spirit, declaring that they would stand as judge of the intentions of her heart. The matter was not up for debate. Her heart would lie exposed, alone, unveiled; all whitewash removed as her heart was placed on trial and forced to give an account. Keta had always been careful with her heart—with all that made her who she was—never following after every stray feeling, desire, thought, or impulse. But now, a shadow of doubt had arisen. A sickening feeling hung over her, as her deeply hidden motivations stood ready to be revealed. Her heart, had she ever understood it? Had she ever questioned it or tested it against her conscience? Had she even once asked herself if there was any way that it might actually be sick? Had it ever wanted her to?

> *There is none righteous, not even one;*
> *There is none who understand.*
> *There is none who seeks after the King.*
> *All have turned aside,*
> *Together they have become useless.*
> *There is none who does good;*
> *There is not even one.*
> *Their throat is an open grave.*
> *With their tongues they keep deceiving.*
> *The poison of asps is under their lips.*
> *Whose mouth is full of cursing and bitterness;*
> *their feet are swift to shed blood.*
> *Destruction and misery are in their paths,*
> *and the path of peace they have not known.*
> *There is no fear of the King before their eyes.*

"There is none who does good." That phrase more than any other left her feeling bare and helpless. She repeated it over and over again, unable to deny its effect of making her feel seen. Nevertheless, only the charge had been leveled. The gavel had yet to strike.

I've done good. I know this cannot be about me. This king—whoever he is—and this message—whatever it is—they have nothing to say to the present! Nothing to say to me! I am good.

Not. Even. One.

Is there any way that I could be wrong? I've done good things—a lot of good things. I know it. But what about the bad? My self-centered desire for other's approval, my envy of those who receive such acclaim, my judgement on those who do not work as hard as I do at serving the marginalized, and my deep-seated coveting of those who actually feel loved. But it's even more overt. I've carried so much hate in my heart toward my mother. Her weakness, her folly, her greed—never will I be like her. And now I must ask . . . have I become her? Have I always been her? If I am judged by even my own standard . . .

Can my good outweigh the bad? Is the ratio one to one? Doesn't my good work count for something? Do these internal actions and dispositions count against me?

Not. Even. One.

Well, what about the good, then? I've helped the weak. I've served the least of the human race. I've given so much! I've practically given my entire life to serving the less fortunate! I have fulfilled whatever law there is upon humans to perform good. Oh, this can't be about me! Who are you to tell me that I'm not good! If there has not even been one, I guess I am the first!

Keta froze. She could feel herself falling into a void, endlessly flailing about, never able to grab hold of anything but air. Images flashed through her mind, telling her a story that she did not know. She was looking for a coin—frantically, desperately, infinitely searching about for what had been hers. She was pounding on a door, the sounds of joy and peace and acceptance just beyond the barrier. But it would not open, no matter how much she shouted and cried and begged. She was standing alone, in complete darkness. She was utterly alone, weeping and gnashing her teeth.

I am the first. Her own thoughts now joined the side of the prosecution. Her conscience seized upon them, calling them as a witness again and again. She had said them, but she could not believe them. She had said them, and now she could see them again and again.

Here is your firewood, old dear; now I deserve your praise and your love. This for that. Here is your toy, young child; you should want to be like me. The silent exaltation of self. Here is your soup, you poor soul; I'm glad I could serve you and prove that I'm not like all those other selfish people out there. The glory of humanity before your very own eyes. You over there! Guess what? I'm better than you. I am more kind, more thoughtful, and more giving, and you will never come near my level of caring. It is simple, really. I'm better than you. I. Am. Better. Than. You. All of you. There is not even one like me. Not. Even. One.

Keta knew that she had never had any of those thoughts so directly, but now, as she searched her heart deeply, her conscience sifting through her memories, she heard their ever-present whisper. Behind every charitable act was a lurking presence of some form of depravity. She saw, with new eyes, that even the very best parts of her were tainted with this lurking darkness. Her mightiest acts of charity were but filthy rags. What was she? She closed her eyes as tears rolled down her freckled cheeks in the night.

What am I? What lies within this heart of mine? What proceeds from this will within me? Look beyond what I want to see to what truly comes from within. Don't hold back, Keta; what is really in your heart? Conscience, show me! Someone, show me! Please, remove the veil!

Evil thoughts. Thefts. Murders. Adulteries. Deeds of coveting. Wickedness, deceit, sensuality, envy, slander. Pride and foolishness.

There it is. Is this my true nature? The real me? Has my never-ending quest for love and approval blinded me from knowing myself? Yet, was I ever that blind? Have I not warred with this endless charade of trying to be loved instead of being known? If someone knew all that was within me—my thoughts, my desires—could they ever possibly love me? If I knew all that was within me, could I even bear the thought of loving myself?

The best of me is tainted. The worst in me is evidence enough and testifies against me. The whole of me is corrupt. No part of me is untouched. Emotion, mind, will, body, spirit—all that is the person. My soul is unclean, and my will is bound to slavery and corruption. My whole life I have been free to choose, yet all the while my will has been shackled to yearn for nothing but self-exultation and death. I am dust and ashes. I repent!

But to whom? Who shall save a wretch like me? This king? I hear his law, but this only brings death. Where can life be found?

Keta remained there until morning, prostrate before the unknown source of this conviction. No longer did she push against this power, for through it she had seen in herself that which she had long ignored, that which she had relentlessly suppressed. It was as though scales had fallen from her eyes, as if the trance of self-deception had at last been lifted. She was weary. She was heavy ladened. She had wrestled with something of more strength than she could imagine, yet it had not left her truly broken. It only caused the necessary affliction in order to give her sight. As the first soft rays of sunlight landed upon her pale form and she lay in an unconscious state of rest, she heard a promise made to her, a gentle voice that whispered words saying: Come to me. Come, and be known. Come, and be loved.

Chapter XIII

The Thief in the Night

Diamonds of light twinkled within the midnight black heavens as if to say that empty space was not all that was. Myriads of messengers boldly declared a hidden glory. Each luminous herald shouted its own report, but the sky that bound them together spoke as if all were one great declaration. The magnificent expanse of cryptic emptiness told one to be patient when considering the story told between the stars. The glaring totality demanded that one at least consider its meaning.

An opaque smoke drifted over Anthro and his guard, veiling the heavens from clear sight. The light of a fading watch fire was being rekindled by his squire.

"Who are you?" Anthro had so many questions, but this seemed like the obvious place to start. Anthro was in a cotton night tunic with a short blade fastened to his side. The sudden shouts had given him little time to dress more appropriately.

"I am a servant of the king," the man before him said, showing no apparent fear at having been captured. Anthro knew that the word "captured" did not do true justice to the actions of the thief of Josias. Voluntary surrender more accurately portrayed what Anthro's men had described to him. Just as they had reentered Tenebris he had approached them, uninvited and unarmed. But why?

And this was not the only strange happening to occur recently. Anthro had been ordered back to Babylonem by none other than King Beelzebul. He spent just three months fighting in Vanus, only to be recalled so quickly. It was not a retreat either, for his army would remain in place. A slow edge of anxiety rose within Anthro with each step he took in the direction of Babylonem. Returning to the king's lair, on the king's orders, raised the hair on the back of Anthro's neck each time he considered the possible reasons. Had the forked tongue of Beelzebul finally caught onto his traitorous scent? He could only wonder, but in this moment even those thoughts would have to be suppressed as he focused his attention on the mysterious man before him.

"What king do you serve?" Anthro demanded. In their typical interrogation position, his men held two lengths of sharpened steel beneath their captive's throat. Despite the poor lighting, Anthro could tell that the man's appearance was not like those within any kingdom he was familiar with. He had not made this observation during their previous brief encounter. Most of the races within the lands surrounding Tenebris had been so intermingled through war and trade that few of them remained isolated or confined to the lands of their origin (especially within the major cities), but this man was like none he had ever seen. He had tan skin (brown with a yellowish hue), eclipsed sockets and dark brown irises. His weathered and foreign face was just beginning to show wrinkles. Perhaps the king of this distant race was whom both he and the parchments were referring to?

"The King of Kings," said the man as if that cleared up the matter. His thick, gravelly voice had a strange, gentle quality to it that only aggravated Anthro all the more.

"Of what nation? What land does your king rule over?" Anthro's voice was rising with the smoke, the light from the growing campfire casting deep shadows across the man's face. The spectacle of combustion before them reflected in his keen eyes.

"His kingdom is not of this world," was all the man said.

As they stared at one another, without thinking about it Anthro clenched his fists tightly; the answers he had long sought after were held captive by this thief's ambiguity.

After a long pause the man continued, "If it were of this world, his servants would be as you expect them to be. Yet as it is, his kingdom is not of this realm."

Not of this world? Not of this realm? What is he talking about? Why does he not just speak plainly? I want the truth! Why am I even pursuing answers here? The path of these parchments promises no peace. It offers only riddles and illusions. It inflicts only pain and incites only fear. Forever giving me just fragments of its story. Forever taunting me as a fool who seeks for truth. Truth. What is truth?

Rid of all patience and subconsciously afraid of false hope, Anthro drew back and struck the man hard across the face— bare knuckle against naked jowl—causing the thief's whole body to crumble.

I need answers. Now! Is this a dead end or not? Who is this king he speaks of? Who is the king of these parchments? Of course they are one and the same, but who is he? What is this other world that he speaks of? I shall get my answers even if I must hang him to a tree.

Before him was someone to blame, whether or not that was warranted. The deflection of his inward turmoil found an ally in directing blame outside himself. Anthro's temper raged as the man lay still on the hard ground. Without the slightest measure of guilt, Anthro began to wonder if he had knocked the thief unconscious. No.

Slowly and awkwardly, as he rose from the dirt with his hands still tightly bound behind his back, the man did the strangest thing Anthro had ever seen someone do. He had beaten many for intel in his military career; he had seen various reactions to the initiation of violence during an interrogation. But this? It did not fit with the circumstances. It did not fit with man. The thief did not spit nor curse; he did not beg nor weep; he did not struggle nor fight. Rising to his previous kneeling position, with the face of a lamb and the eyes of a lion, he shifted his head, simply turning the other cheek.

Silence hung in the air, shouting loudly into the night. Anthro's anger, thrown off by the man's behavior, was crushed into a heap of waning coal. He did not know what to do or even how he felt. He paced back and forth a time or two, nearly drawing his sword with each about-face. Then, stopping in front of the man, he looked down and spoke calmly. "Let's try this again. Who are you?"

The man stared at him for some time before saying, "I am not the king." The right side of his face was already beginning to swell.

Anthro sighed, half-amused but still partially infuriated. "I had figured that much out, but what do you say about yourself? Who are you in relation to this king? What kind of service is it that you render to him?"

"I am a voice. I am unworthy to serve yet called for that very purpose. You may think of me as an ambassador of sorts." He paused, his body trembling slightly. "It seems too much to say. It seems too high a privilege. How can one such as I represent one such as my king? I've no other task than to decrease so that he may increase."

Anthro took his hand off his sword and gestured for his guards to give the man a bit of breathing room. They were equally surprised at the man's benevolence. An ambassador: that was something a little more perceivable, at least. Anthro knelt down, his face close to the man's. Their eyes locked together.

"What is your name?" Anthro spoke without blinking, yet there was a discernible pleading in his tone that he failed to suppress.

"My name is not important, but because you ask, I will tell you. My name is Apostolos, and I am a servant of the King of Lux." The gentle tone Apostolos had been carrying was lost as he spoke the last three words. His inflection contained awe, wonder, fear, and love as he spoke them. Each syllable was spoken as a sonnet of subconscious devotion.

The King of Lux. I have it. Finally, I have this king's name. The King of Lux and his servant Apostolos. I've never heard of this kingdom, though. Yet earlier he said that it was not of this . . . what was it not of? This world? Realm? The Kingdom of Lux.

Anthro did not know whether he should laugh or cry. He could hardly open his mouth but felt as if he could scream with ecstasy and euphoria. He had a name. Finally, he had a name. He trembled at the very thought of it. Somehow this seemed to change everything. The very fact that there was now a name involved brought in the hope of more possibilities, and something about having it added a sense of reality where it was desperately needed.

Standing once more he continued his query. "Apostolos, what can you tell me about the Kingdom of Lux? You said that it was not of this . . . realm? I am not sure what that means, but you are an ambassador and you have sought the same parchments that reference a king. Surely, they refer to this king, but what can you tell me about his kingdom? Why do you serve him if he lived long ago and is not of this realm?"

"The Kingdom of Lux." Apostolos spoke the words with the same verbal fidelity. "General . . . that is your title, correct?" Anthro nodded; it was close enough. "Are you familiar with a mustard seed?"

Anthro could not hide the bewilderment upon his face at being asked about a garden plant in reference to this kingdom, but nonetheless, he replied while recalling Methero's garden. "Yes, it is the smallest seed used in our gardens, yet it grows up mightier than all the surrounding herbs. But what, may I ask, does that have to do with your kingdom?"

"Truly, you have spoken correctly. General, I will tell you of the Kingdom of Lux, but to understand it, you must listen to how it refers to itself. Otherwise, you will remain blind to the field of treasure right beneath your feet." Apostolos was speaking boldly, yet still his amiable spirit was present. "You see, this mustard seed has the smallest of beginnings, but it grows and spreads its branches out wide. If you were to have every seed in the garden before you, you would be hard-pressed to take notice of such a speck. Yet when all the seeds are fully grown, what had the smallest of origins is now the most noticeable plant that cannot be ignored."

"I follow the botany lesson, but I do not understand what this has to do with your kingdom."

"Does one such as yourself not understand? The Kingdom of Lux began as no other kingdom of this world has. One could say that it fully began with the death of the king. Who could see such a kingdom birthed by death? Yet it was born, and now it is alive, and still it will come."

"The death of your king initiated his kingdom? We'll get back to that. We'll definitely get back to that. But first, what do you mean by saying that the kingdom is already here but still to come?"

"The King of Lux came to inaugurate his kingdom. Despite any appearances, this kingdom will not be destroyed as it grows. The gates of the enemy will assail it, obscure it, and deny it. All the same, the enemy will not overpower it. The King of Lux will return to consummate his kingdom. Now he reigns, still he will come."

Anthro knew that he should wrap up this initial conversation and be patient with his questioning, but he had waited so long and was compelled to get just a bit more. "This night has been long enough. We have much to talk about in the coming days, but there is one more thing I'd like to discuss before retiring. Tell me of your king's death. Tell me about the death of this King of Lux."

"My king's death . . . it is my life." For the first time, Apostolos was not making eye contact with Anthro. His gaze carried beyond him—through him, even—like he was seeing something none of the others could behold. "By his death I live. It was for this very purpose that he came to this world."

Anthro stood there, willing himself not to be thrown off by the outlandish nature of the words being spoken. "Your king came to die?"

"He came to give life to the dead. He gave life, by giving his."

Anthro's men were all looking on with the same puzzlement. They had seen much following Anthro, but this was beyond their imaginations.

Anthro wondered for a moment. "Are you speaking in a metaphor? Is that what this is all about?"

"Concerning the kingdom, I spoke in metaphor. With his death, I dare not. My king was just, perfectly so, and he gave his life for those whom he loved, for those whom he would call, for those whom he had chosen. The just for the unjust." Apostolos again met Anthro's eyes. "Here I speak as plainly as I can. You will never understand the King of Lux if you do not understand his death. Nor will you ever see him if you believe that he is dead." The fire was once again dwindling; even Anthro's squire was distracted by the exchange.

Anthro took a deep breath, placing his hands behind his head. "An allegory?"

"No." His voice was forcefully resolute.

"How can your king have died and yet live? What do you mean?"

"Exactly what was said. My king came to die, and he always accomplishes his purposes. He was tortured to death and speared through the side for good measure. He was buried. He has risen. He has risen in the flesh. He has risen indeed." He spoke with no sarcasm nor poetry. If there was such a thing as a fact in this world, this is what Apostolos believed he was uttering.

Anthro felt a compulsion to label the man insane, restrained only by a more stubborn quest for truth. "But that's impossible. I've seen tens of thousands die. I've buried hundreds. The dead *do not* rise."

"Why does it seem incredible to you if the God of the universe raises the dead?" Apostolos spoke while shifting his uncomfortable knees. Blood from Anthro's earlier blow was dripping down his face.

Anthro placed two fingers on his forehead while closing his eyes and sighing. *A theist.* The two words combined in his thoughts as a curse. *Not just all this crazy talk about a death and another realm, but a theist. He believes in a god. That proves...*

Another thought interrupted his thinking. That shiver of old, that mystery of morality, that personality within morality returned to his mind again—though it had never been far. Maybe the idea was not so deranged?

"Apostolos, *it just doesn't happen*," Anthro said, his hand flaring to emphasize every syllable. "It's too much to believe when human experience is uniformly against it."

"Truly?" Anthro sensed the sarcasm in the word, but had not thought the man capable of it. "I do not claim that the normal course of events involving the dead results in them rising. It is an astonishing thing for a dead man to rise. But impossible? Surely it is *you*, General, who goes too far." The next words came with a stinging force that pierced into Anthro's lifelong doubts. But were they venom or elixir? "Do you have this universe all figured out then? No other possibilities than those that *you* think could or could not happen? I was unaware that your beliefs governed the order of this world." His tone was light but laced with a heavy sarcasm.

In that moment, Anthro stood before existence itself. The brute fact of its reality mocked his confidence and jeered at his self-assurance. Its baffling nature and chaotic course of events beckoned him toward perpetual agnosticism, its stifling beauty and haunting order pulled him in a similar fashion but opposite direction. He could not deny that there were other reasonable metaphysical possibilities besides the simple, deterministic material action and reaction that he boasted in. He could not admit this verbally.

Apostolos, continuing with his strange methods, began to tell a story. "There were two fishermen: one a man and the other a child. They went to a lake that was a moderate distance from the ocean. Both of them began fishing with small rods, but they were continually getting broken off. The child suggested they get larger poles. The man refused, stating that it was only possible for the lake to harbor a fish of a reasonable size that their current tackle could handle. There simply must be other reasons for their failures. The child felt no such restriction and left to retrieve gear worthy of the ocean.

"The man continued his fruitless task, making countless excuses for why he would not upgrade his tackle, and ultimately ended in frustration, returning home without a catch. The boy returned to the lake, ready to test just what was possible—humble enough to admit the possibility of his own ignorance as to what *could be*. The boy cast his line into the water and got another heavy bite that did not break his line. He landed a massive salmon that is exclusively found in the ocean or in wide rivers, never in lakes. He returned home with food for the entire village. Now I ask you, General, was what this boy did unreasonable?"

"No, I suppose it wasn't." Anthro thought for a moment before continuing, "But are we *really* comparing fishing to rising from the dead? They're categorically different."

"From a certain perspective, yes. But the parable is not as unrelated as you think. You have focused on the face-value situation, not on the overall meaning and wisdom contained within. Such is the path of narrow thinking. We are discussing approaching a situation without making sweeping and restricting assumptions. We are cautioning against those who only bring their own past experiences to the table of possibility. The child's humble recognition of his ignorance resulted in a different outcome when put to the test."

Anthro saw that he had missed this, and that fact greatly surprised him. It fed his conflicting emotions, aggravating and humbling him.

"In the story, a nearby river had flooded in the past during a migration of salmon that allowed for a small population to take root in the lake. This was unusual. It went against the normal order of things. But it was not impossible. It is certainly not a perfect analogy, of course, as I am proclaiming an event which has no *natural* explanation, but the proverbial truth within it bears weight to this conversation.

"The best course of action to see if an unusual event has occurred is not to say that the event cannot happen simply because one hasn't experienced it. This is especially true when all parties admit that the event would be a stunning and amazing reality! The best course is to investigate the claim at hand, and to then—and only then—determine if it occurred. The resulting conclusion may open your eyes to a new understanding of what is possible and challenge the uniformity of your experience. If uniform expectations rule over objective observation, one will never have eyes to see anything but regularity."

It was late and Anthro was feeling the effects. Furthermore, for an ambassador, Anthro could not understand why the man spoke indirectly in both riddles and parables. It was almost as if his manner of speech was selected so that one would not understand. A dying king ushering in a kingdom? A kingdom not of this realm? A mustard seed? This King of Lux rising and returning? It all seemed so incredible and unlikely.

Anthro had a sudden and powerful urge to stop the conversation—to just claim that Apostolos was a madman and to try to forget he had ever come across the parchments. Why, though? Why stop here? He walked into the shadowy perimeter of the firelight, standing on the edge of what was seen and unseen, gazing into a darkness above and beyond. Why did this conversation seem so unbelievable?

Is it because Apostolos is speaking against reason? Is that why I feel this way? No. No; nothing said yet defies reason, it just defies what I expect and assume. I expect to find nothing outside this world. I hope for it, I even search for it, yet I assume that hope is merely a dream that will ultimately die along with me. Is that reasonable? No. To rule out possibilities without listening to the reason for that possibility is what does not make sense. I know that—I've told Diatris just as much—but still, this doubt. Why?

This universe. Who am I to determine if it is a closed system or not? Who could truthfully argue that reason prohibits this universe from being open to the influence of, or even originating from, another realm? It is merely a philosophical presupposition based on some level of uniformity in my experiences, and on a certain interpretation of my observations, that makes me assume that this world is functionally closed.

It is actually reason that makes me object to holding dogmatically to my belief in a closed universe. Certainly, the very existence of a universe of matter, time, and space should make one open to the possibility of an outside influence when studying this planet. We are a universe of observable causal dependence. What about the first cause? What about the millionth cause?

Logic itself demands an explanation and knowledge, a foundation. If all events ultimately flow from a causal chain not bound to follow any rational path—a chain from which these events cannot escape—then all ideas and thoughts are merely events based off those irrational causes. Thus, knowledge in such a system is nothing sustainable, nothing substantial. It bleeds to death after cutting its own throat.

We are in a universe that is bound to a state of cooling corruption. Just how reasonable could it be for a dependent universe held together by laws of decay to bring itself to life through its own independence? Life: a complex web of vast information and required reproduction. Yet, I see life in count-less forms and can even contemplate its very existence. Life interpreting life. Thought proceeding from life and reflecting on its being, on all being. I've only scratched the surface. Why be so closed to possibilities in a world such as ours?

To follow a methodological system of thought that only adheres to my experience is narrow-minded. To adhere to a thought pattern that rules out possibilities that cannot be disproven is misguided. Tenebris has hardwired me for that kind of closed-minded, circular thought pattern. But if the cir-cle of possible explanations of reality is beyond my system of determining reality, it is my system of belief that is faulty and prefabricated to mislead. Such thinking could quite possibly, if not probably, cause me to misinterpret the very nature of the universe—the very nature of nature.

I know all of this! This is exactly why I started this search for the parchments in the first place. Why then the struggle to even listen to this man? Could it be that somewhere deep in my heart I really want a closed universe? That I think the darkness has already won? That it should win?

Do I truly want an explanation that could give hope to a world of death such as ours? Is my experience working against my reason? Are my inner feelings clouding my reason? I've no reason to close myself off to what Apostolos is saying. Reason demands I press on. Truth, whatever it may be, requires it.

Anthro ambled back to Apostolos, positioning himself before him once more. He continued, his voice a bit kinder than before. "Alright, I see your point." Anthro knew the man was right; his own methods were not the truly objective ones. Nevertheless, the words were hard to verbalize before even this small crowd. Like never before, he felt that powerful pull—that almost irresistible urge—to stay safely nestled within the comfortable perimeters and explanatory confines of his own assumed frame of reality. And yet, he managed to press slightly forward. "But what you're saying—this king, his death, and his . . . *rising*—how could someone even investigate such a thing?"

Apostolos stared at him, this time with nothing but lion in his eyes. "One could read the reports."

Anthro's eyes widened. "There are reports?"

"Yes. In fact, there are four testimonies from either direct eyewitnesses or their interviewers and disciples."

"Do . . . do you have them?" Anthro stuttered. He felt as if he was losing his mind asking for such a thing.

Apostolos was looking at him in an obscure fashion. "Not on my person, but I believe I could get them for you with time."

Anthro's heart dropped just a bit. More waiting. Still, maybe this was not the dead end he had feared it would be.

Apostolos must have noticed his crestfallen expression. "However, General, I do believe that I have something that will intrigue you. You have read my king's report in the two parchments you collected. Is that right?"

Another parchment! Anthro's mind was jolted awake. "Yes. I have had it translated."

"Good. In a hidden pocket of my cloak, there is a copy of another document that I am certain will be of interest to you. You will find that it is in your own language, as years ago I had used it to practice your land's native tongue. I now read more complex books from your own society to continue my studies of your language and culture, but this passage is so dear to me that I have not been able to part from it. This document, if properly understood, may shed some light on the reason for the report you have read. We call it the *Manifesto Regnum*. It is a proclamation of the Kingdom of Lux—the morality given from the Most High."

The remnant of the campfire was dwindling into fading embers as Anthro's heart was kindled afresh. This was a feeling far too rare in his life, a sentiment far too fleeting for him to ever trust.

Chapter XIV

The Two Brothers

Once more, the haughty gates of Babylonem opened wide to invite Anthro and his personal escort inside the city of his heart's animosity. As Anthro made his way down the illustrious streets, he noticed that his men were carrying themselves just a bit differently than they had in the past. Although always having been proud men, they now toted a certain boastfulness—almost an arrogance—along with them. The core of this haughty disposition was fed by a thriving spirit of defiance—that brazen feeling of satisfaction at knowing your opponent's ignorance of their own betrayal. It was a sword through the back, with the friend's face never seen. Having spent the last few years smuggling the mentally crippled from beneath the grasp of their would-be murderers had granted his men (and himself, for that matter) a bold confidence against that unseeing malevolence.

As they had traveled through Tenebris toward Babylonem, Anthro and his men had met up with several other Tenebris officers, all returning on the king's orders. This had alleviated the fear that Anthro was leading his men to their deaths. Before this knowledge had come, he dreaded the possibility that the king had called him back after discovering his treachery. Still, not one officer disclosed what had caused this homecoming of commanding military leaders, whether in ignorance or sworn secrecy. In three days, they would know. All the officers had their orders to meet at a military complex in the industrial center of Babylonem. The time frame allowed for the stragglers to be present. But for what reason they would gather, and despite the growing pit in his stomach, he did not know. He would simply have to wait.

Upon entering the city outskirts where Anthro's men had now set up their camp, all the requested officers received an additional message that contained a rare order demanding that they come to the meeting without weapons nor guard. For some of the army's leaders, this was the capstone of insult. However, Anthro thought it a wise move if King Beelzebul was going to be present, which was the assumed norm for a distinguished gathering such as this.

During their return, Anthro had heavily considered the idea of an assassination attempt. Would the snake wither with its decapitation? Or would the wriggling corpse regenerate a head of malice, wielding an even more vicious viper? Even without this new order, he had come to believe that the work he and his men were currently doing was ultimately creating more good than any assassination would do.

During their short stay, Anthro had decided to leave Apostolos with two members of his guard whenever he and the rest of his men ventured into the capital for the day. He thought it best not to disclose that he was traveling with a captured spy from another kingdom. Though Anthro still kept him bound and under guard at all times, the man gave no appearance of trying to escape, holding his bonds with stunning contentment. Apostolos was a freak of a man who could sing in chains.

Anthro now carried the *Manifesto Regnum* on his person at all times and had been severely grieved to find out that Methero had died recently in his sleep. Anthro had been intending to share this new document with him, regardless of it not needing to be interpreted. The words contained in this script were fascinating, yet humbling. They were captivating, but frightening. They were convicting, and yet still alluring. For someone who had been contemplating morality with the utmost attention, this other king's ethic was certainly a jolt to the conscience. There was much to consider within it and Anthro would use his free time these next several days to do just that.

* * * *

Anthro left the officer's meeting with new information—novel material that needed to be analyzed. Maybe an assassination attempt would have been worth it if he had only known about this prior. Had he really expected anything less?

Anthro was walking the crowded streets of Babylonem's financial district as he hastily made his way out of the city and back to his camp. Although he had not thought it possible, for the first time in weeks, the parchments, the King of Lux, and the newly acquired king's manifesto were far from his whirlwind of a mind. King Beelzebul's *revelation* was now his singular cognitive occupation.

Anthro's strides were lengthy as he sifted through the conflux of travelers and citizens alike. He was eager for the quiet of the grasslands beyond the high walls of this city of his captivity. After all these years, Tenebris would not release him from its greedy claws. Whenever he began to hope and believe in something more, the monster would return to remind him why he should relinquish such a forlorn quest. There was one more district between him and his escape; how desperately he needed to be beyond the barricades of the city's defenses. The physical nature of the capital itself was a testament to its wretched hold on him. Anthro wondered if . . . then he saw him.

Despite the crowds and his own restless mind, there was no mistaking who it was. Towering height, tightly shaven black scalp, muscles of an ox bulging within a soldier's uniform. Aradis. It had been far too long since they had seen each other or even written to one another, but perhaps that was all meant to be so that Anthro could feel joy in this moment, when he once more so desperately needed it.

Like brothers in their late youth and comrades in arms as they both became men, Aradis and Anthro had a bond that could survive the separation that came from their progression through the Army of Tenebris. Some friendships needed no words or affirmations to remain as strong as the union of forged steel. The mere clasping of forearms was enough to fashion the friendship back to its former glory. There is a jewel of a friend that is closer than a brother. There is an extraordinary type of love in such a friendship that can even surpass the pleasures of any passions shared among lovers. Such friendship is hard to find. Such friendship is worth finding. Such friendship is worth preserving.

"Aradis!" Anthro shouted the name as if he were in a former life back in Mori, calling after his friend to chase down another adventure and caring not about the many glances given by those sharing the street.

Aradis turned. He knew that voice; time could not keep him from remembering it. "Anthro!" Aradis pushed his way easily through the throng of people between them.

The brothers—the word was more fitting for the two of them—grasped forearms while beaming widely at each other. Both had aged much, and both had somehow survived nearly ten years of savage war. What were the chances of such a thing? What were the odds of meeting here? Aradis had not been at the king's meeting, so why was he here?

"I figured you'd be here, Anthro."

Did he? And what was that look in his eye? Had it been fear? It was gone in a moment; too quickly it fled for Anthro to be sure if it had been there at all.

Aradis continued, "I had hoped to see you, but I wasn't sure . . . I . . . I wasn't sure I'd find you. You're not the only general in town, are you?" He then gave Anthro a friendly wink and a shove.

"No, there are far too many of us here for my comfort." Anthro laughed, though now with mild reservation. He had been sure that there was an odd look in Aradis's eyes and a stumble just now in his voice. "But what brings you here?" Anthro's eyes glanced over the patches on the shoulders of Aradis's uniform and he then asked, "You haven't caught my rank yet, have you?"

"Ha!" Aradis's voice boomed in reply. "I would've thought there would never be a chance of that, but word is that you've stalled out at major general despite other opportunities that many men dare not even dream of achieving. You just can't get off the front, can you? In case you didn't know it, there are other ways to serve Tenebris than risking your neck in every battle."

The two men had subconsciously made their way off the busy street and onto a far less crowded side road, pivoting into a high-walled alley. The sun was fading beyond the peaks of the citadels above them as the surrounding streets began to glow—literally—with Tenebris's latest public technological advancement.

Anthro continued the conversation, "You know me. I've got to be where the most action is and where my tactics can thrive as they are tested. But what about you? You've been keeping better tabs on me than I have on you, apparently." Anthro's eyes were drifting down to the golden crest on Aradis's coat.

"I guess you could say that I've been serving the *king's* business."

Without even needing the emphasis, it had registered. Anthro knew *that* crest. Four gold, crossed swords formed a star with a small crown in each gap. This symbol was outlined over the blue uniform with a larger crown of etched gold encompassing the emblem. There was only one group of the king's servants who bore that crest.

"But why talk about all this here?" Aradis said. "I know all the best spots around this city. What do you say? Let's you and me hit the town, just like old times. Anthro and Aradis reunited once more! The ladies won't know what hit them!" Aradis slapped him on the shoulder and tried to tug him along back toward the main avenue. Anthro was frozen in place, unmovable as he fell headlong into thought.

Not this. No, anything but this—anyone but him. No. He couldn't. How long? How long!

"Anthro, you alright? Don't start spacing out on me like you used to!" Aradis smiled, but that look of fear returned. This time, it lingered.

Anthro went to rest his right hand on the hilt of his sword, only then remembering that the king had required that he not bring any weapon. He felt naked without it now. "How long have you been a captain, Aradis?" His voice was quietly fierce.

"What?" Aradis took a step back.

Anthro's mind was now crystal clear, his eyes ablaze, his slumbering stain awakening along with his anger. "I spoke clearly. How long have you been a captain?" He paused as he shifted his own body between Aradis and the open street. He would need no sword. "I'll make it even easier for you. Aradis, how long have you been a captain in the *King's Battalion*?" Anthro said those last words with the fullest amount of hatred he could muster—hatred against everything that name stood for, disgust for the crest adorning his friend's chest, enmity for everything his friend must be, and, ultimately, a horror beyond words for what his question could imply.

The larger man took several more steps back, not unarmed, yet neutralized, nonetheless. He did not want this. Not this. He had not wanted what had happened, but she *had* gotten in the way of Tenebris. What else could you expect?

"Anthro, I . . . it's not what you . . . it's more complicated than it . . ." No words for it. The defenses in Aradis's heart crumbled on his tongue. The weakness of his justification was not even worthy of verbalizing before his friend. He stepped back as Anthro pressed forward until he finally hit the cold stone wall of the alley. That stare—who could forget the sight of recognized betrayal revealed in a brother's eyes? No other words from Aradis; none but three.

"Is she okay?"

With the speed and skill of all his experience behind him, Anthro bolted forward, hammering his left boot into the side of Aradis's knee and dropping the beast of a man to his knees in an instant. With both hands, Anthro grabbed Aradis's throat with unyielding force, driving the back of his skull into the solid wall behind them. Just like that, Anthro had him at his mercy. In seconds, he would have his revenge—not on Captain Petros, but on his accomplice. On his replacement? On his disciple?

But then he heard them penetrating through his anger and convicting him despite his deepest inner protests. Shouting from within, he heard those recently memorized words, phrase after phrase. Words from the *Manifesto Regnum* cried out from conscience and mind as Aradis struggled and gasped for breath.

I say to you that everyone who is angry with his brother shall be liable before the court.

This is righteous anger.

Anthro's grip loosened just an iota.

Again:

I say to you, do not resist an evil person; but whoever slaps you on your right cheek, turn the other to him also.

This is justice and retribution. Who could follow such a ridiculous ethic?

He had seen it lived out in Apostolos.

One of his hands went slack, the other still clung to windpipe.

And again:

I say to you, love your enemies and pray for those who persecute you.

Where does such love come from? It is beyond what is in me to muster.

Total release.

Aradis collapsed onto all fours as he drew in fresh breath, wheezing at first, then slowing down to deep inhalations. Anthro stood back from him. He had been so close to killing him, to murdering him, and to murdering again. The King of Lux had saved him from dealing yet more death, whether deserved or not. Vengeance, in this case, in this manner, would have been murder. Anthro knew that much. Vengeance, retribution, and justice were needed, but not like this. How, then?

Aradis looked up, his ordinarily black face slowly recovering from its oddly pale complexion. "Anthro, I'm sorry. I didn't know Keta would be there. How could I have known? What could I have done? You, of all people, should understand that sometimes there is nothing we can do as subordinates. She just *wouldn't* stand aside."

In his eyes Anthro saw genuine sorrow, but not the kind of sorrow that leads one toward repentance, only the kind that produces death. Aradis was ashamed of what he had been a part of, not ashamed of what he *was* a part of. He did not regret the destruction of the weak, only that a former friend had stepped in the way and that he now found himself paying for it. His name and character were tarnished with his best friend. It was a betrayal of trust of such a kind that no amount of worldly gain—be it silver in pocket or golden rank on shoulder—could ever make it worth the cost. It was the type of regret that only leads to self-preservation instead of reconciliation, even if preservation is only found in self-elimination. The power of a man's broken but firmly abiding pride can manifest in the most obscure and radical fashions. Few paths lead to true humility and penance.

Anthro beheld his friend, and though it felt odd, he pitied what was before him. The same man who could plead with him for understanding could run his spear mercilessly through a damaged mind beseeching him for life. What a wretched thing to be. It was horrifying. It was sad. It was pitiable to be a human of such blindness, such heartless indifference, such abject hypocrisy. Even in Anthro's many sins there was always complex existential torment. In Aradis, the only lasting anguish was the harm done to his own reputation and standing.

"Some orders are worth disobeying. You of all people should know I believe that." Anthro stood tall over Aradis. "Some captains aren't worth replacing, aren't worth following." Should he risk saying it? "And some ideas, no matter whose they are—no matter how much power supports them—are worth fighting against. Are worth *dying* against." With that, Anthro disappeared into the blur of people as night fell over Babylonem.

*   *   *   *

In the twilight, in the evening, in the middle of the night and in the darkness, she came to meet him. After three days of unforeseen delays from returning to her love, she seized him and kissed him. While beholding those brazen eyes of ember glow, while delighting in her soft skin of dark velvet touch, upon a bed of myrrh, cinnamon, and aloe, he drank his fill of her love. From within the hold of blended arms, the language of love flowed forth from his beloved's flattering lips. She whispered the praises of pure siren into his longing ears. Ivory, gold, sapphire, emerald, and ruby, all pale in comparison. Most beautiful of women, who shines like the dawn of winter solstice, as seducing as the full harvest moon, pure as the sun of high noon. His left hand was under her head, his right hand embracing her flawless form . . .

And then he heard them, those other new words which festered in his mind . . .

I say to you . . .

No. You can't have this.

He presses her tighter to him.

172

Again:

Everyone who . . .

Not this. This is my beloved. Many waters cannot quench this love. It is stronger than death.

His body and mind chase further his distraction, his devotion.

And again:

If your . . .

Not her. I am my beloved's and my beloved is mine.

Complete embrace.

Chapter XV

The Great Divide

Despite his quest for distraction, the King of Lux could not be silenced. In the form of silent whispers late in the night or as ghostly echoes with every waking hour, his words would surface within Anthro's mind. Life could often keep them at bay, but not always. Whenever Anthro would succumb to entertaining their existence, he found most of his focus was drawn toward the ethical system of the king. What was its purpose? Was it just another moralistic construct—perhaps even the true one—but nothing more? What did it all mean?

These thoughts battled for his attention as they fought against those competing spirals that would ensue whenever King Beelzebul's unveiling and Aradis's betrayal came to the forefront of Anthro's mind. The King of Lux was proving stubborn; even with the vast amount of mental draining the other two subjects caused, the King of Lux still found a way to occupy some space within Anthro's restless mind.

Anthro knew of many ethical systems in the world (even well beyond those found in Tenebris) from enlightened gurus, ascetic monks, boastful philosophers, and everything in between. Yet, had he ever found teachings equivalent to what was contained within this *Manifesto*? What kind of moral structure was so radically against violence that Anthro was not even sure what its teachings were in regard to the validity of self-defense, and yet still taught of a final judgement to come? What system of belief instructed not only to do no harm to one's neighbor, but to also love them *as* oneself—with the same tenacity and care? That positive imperative of maximal requirement . . . who could do such a thing? Anthro doubted even Apostolos was capable. This king took a common teaching of silver and had morphed it into a golden rule that was a real moral advance, at least for anyone already committed to a silver system of neighborly benevolence. Yet the entire ethic was . . . exhausting? Needed? Persuasive? Fanatical? Beautiful? Impossible? Compelling?

More than that, this king's ethos was of such lofty height that it went well beyond external actions and demanded rigorous performance of the heart as well. A lustful look was adultery within the will. A hateful thought was murder in a reality of judgment. An envious demeanor was sinfulness in the core of man. Anthro could see probity in this moral law, but with the recent events with Aradis he could not stop wondering about the purpose of such a strict code and severe law. He pondered and greatly doubted its ability to ever be fulfilled in perfection, but this was its requirement. Would this law not eventually burden the conscience until the follower broke at the seams after repeated failure? To seek excellence at this level would crush the man or woman who remotely knew themselves. No one could follow this law wholeheartedly and expect success. Not even Keta? Well, maybe Keta. If anyone, Keta. But she was the anomaly. Anthro had learned long ago that to seek truth in matters of law and behavior, one first must shift through the general circumstances and *then* understand how the extenuating affairs fit together. Let the transparent give sight to the opaque.

So then, what was the purpose of this law that could not be

followed? What lesson lay hidden from Anthro's sight? Was it a gift or a curse? The King of Lux seemed too dynamic to merely seek to crush his followers, yet was he not the same king who declared, "There is none righteous. Not even one"? If all have been shut up under sin, who is left to follow? If there was a personal god, as Apostolos believed there was, and such a being required this law of humanity, would it not create an insurmountable gulf that separated humanity from god? Would not the barricade of moral failure have to be removed for a relationship with such a being to be made possible? So why the law? Was there merit to the idea of it being a reflection of the very character of the god whom Apostles believed in? Was following the law an act of following after the character of god himself?

Anthro was well aware of his fluctuating thoughts on there being a god or not. How long could he remain neutral on such a monumental question? This belief in *this* god of morality was one with too many implications for life—and for death—for one to remain forever fixed upon a fence of skepticism. His gradual development from societal atheist to reasoned agnostic could only be dragged out for so long before he either just became a theist, or he once more and forever embraced atheism, this time having chosen it for himself.

What a fearful thought: man being the final determiner of such a conclusion within his own conscience and mind. How could one live in peace with such a conclusion when, by his own epistemological standards, he not only failed to disprove god's existence, but could not even establish the reality of his own being with absolute certainty? The gentle brush from an unseen leaf would be enough to frighten one to reconsider. There would always be that insuppressible fear of the scythe of death coming down to reap and to put one's godless hypothesis to final test.

Once thoughtfully and openly studied, could a human conscience ever be so hardened against the idea of god? Would not denying such a universe of personal accountability need to be unceasingly and restlessly sustained for the rest of one's fleeting existence? Always the arguments would have to grow in complexity to further convince oneself. One would always need more convincing to sustain his professed loyalty toward a certain set of atheistic beliefs against an opposing, cross-pressure exerting, cumulative package of alternate theistic beliefs. One would forever have to live with the perennial knowledge and abiding temptation to follow theism's conflicting take.

The devout atheist would always be left hoping that the most nagging and stubborn of humanity's thoughts are indeed man's greatest delusions. He would always endure that terrible worry whispering in the moments of doubt that "the fool has said in his heart that there is no god," and that god's existence was evident not only from the formation of the human mind and the natural flow of man's thoughts, but from the human heart as well. Man would be forever doubting in mind until resting upon the presumption that god was true, forever restless in heart until finding his rest in god.

Even for Anthro, there were times where it could seem as if humans were wholly designed to love this personal creator god with heart, mind, soul, and strength. But then, why the confusion? More and more, Anthro found himself never clearly on one side or the other. In one line of thought, he would reason as if the most fundamental need for humanity was to set one's mind on the fact that god *is*. In the very next thread of logic, that suppression of deity would flow forth as if such a denial was the height of human wisdom. How terrible the idea that humanity could consider both possibilities.

* * * *

All of these questions were actually a welcome distraction from Anthro's other concerns, but he was about to seek his answers to some of them and he had called in help.

In a small Tenebris town, Doceo, in the upper story of a musty antique bookstore, Anthro and Apostolos waited for her. Mori was too far a detour for Anthro's current orders, but he had sent a rider to request and escort Keta to meet him in this town. She had made him a promise; he had upheld his end. And he was now calling on her to uphold her end of the deal as well.

He had left her with the second parchment months ago with no communication from either side since. Had this second fragment finally had the same effect that the first had on Diatris? What would Keta think of Apostolos? Of the *Manifesto Regnum*? She had always been the more morally adept of the two of them, so hopefully her insights would be constructive here.

The loft in which they sat was no larger than a pair of carriages and had one narrow window near its ceiling. Soft rays of light made their way through the thin pane of glass, reflecting the otherwise unseen dust that filled the sultry shop. Anthro sat with his back against a carved wooden column on the far side of the stairwell as Apostolos made his way through bookshelves, flipping pages of the various volumes seemingly at random. Anthro had recently decided to let Apostolos walk without restraints during the day. The man acted no different whether slave or free.

"Anthro!"

Keta ran toward him from the upper creaky steps, barely giving him time to stand before giving him an energetic hug. "I didn't think I would see you this soon. Is everything okay? I was actually in the process of finishing a letter for you when your rider showed up. Is this man with you?" Keta had just noticed the older man who, with a slightly comical tilt to his head, was observing the two of them.

"Keta, it's really good to see you too. Yes, this is Apostolos. Apostolos, this is the friend I was telling you about, Keta."

The two of them shook hands, exchanging the customary pleasantries. However, Keta's face was unusually difficult to read. Anthro rarely talked deeply with her when another person was around, but from the little she had gathered from the rider, she was under the impression that her friend wanted to have a meaningful conversation. The trio took seats on the warped hardwood floor, as the otherwise vacant ground was without seating.

Anthro jumped right to it. "Keta, do you remember that promise we made to each other? Well, I've upheld my end of the deal." Anthro had firmly resolved not to mention his new knowledge of Aradis's involvement. For some reason, Keta had not told him this and, as it was her tragedy and not his, Anthro would respect that secrecy despite his longing for a fuller picture of what had transpired. "But now, if you are willing, I've asked you here to uphold your end of the deal."

Keta's face remained indecipherable. Her wound had healed much, but still there was significant disfigurement around her eye and Anthro was sure that the damage that remained would be permanent. Perhaps that was what added to the inscrutability of her gaze?

"A promise for a promise." Her inflection was atypical as well. "No matter where it goes." Doubts started to surface within Anthro's mind. When Keta had received the second parchment, she had only seemed mildly interested in it. The nervous knot in his stomach made him wonder if he had missed something back then as well. She glanced over toward Apostolos as if seeing him for the first time. "And this man . . . he has something to do with the parchments? With . . . with the king?"

The visible dust in the room faded back into spectral particles as dense, raven clouds moved in over Doceo. The storm on the horizon had arrived; the decision for an indoor meeting location appeared to have been wise. "Yes, he does."

"You do?" She looked at Apostolos eagerly as if needing him to affirm.

"Anthro has spoken truly. I am a servant of the King of Lux, a herald of his kingdom." He spoke with his genial tone and thick voice. For some reason, he had been far more direct with his identity to Keta than he had been with Anthro. They had posed similar questions, yet how different their query. Homogeneous words from heterogeneous hearts.

"The King of Lux." Keta repeated the name slowly, but was bursting for more. "What can you tell me about him? Was he good? Who were his people? Were they really that bad? What of his kingdom remains?"

"Keta, slow down, slow down. We'll catch you up on what I know and then go from there." Anthro said, alarmed and amused. Keta was far more interested than he would have imagined. He was utterly grateful for that, but unsure as to why she held such a strong interest.

For well over an hour they spoke of the king, his other-worldly kingdom, and his *Manifesto*. All the while, Keta sat by Apostolos's feet and listened with rapturous attentiveness. She was beyond distraction—impervious to worry, immune to bother. Keta had but one necessity—to learn more about the King of Lux.

* * * *

"So, if I understand correctly, all I have to do is repent and believe in the King of Lux and that reconciles me to God?" Keta asked as the conversation turned to a place that never failed to bring Anthro discomfort. The floodgates of the heavens had opened during the course of their conservation, the rain echoing ethereally off of the hollow wooden shingles above them.

"In a simplified manner, yes, but there is a lot in that statement you made. So much depends on it. Let's break it down and fill in those terms a bit." Apostolos and Keta were like pedagogue and pupil, his whole demeanor less charismatic and more directly didactic with her. Two traits, however, remained steadfast: his gentleness and patience.

Anthro had already come to know that Apostolos would go without sleep or food and spend days in ceaseless two-sided conversation with anyone asking about his king, with perhaps a little hearty proclamation thrown in from time to time. It was as if from within the deepest recesses of his heart he wished that whether in a short time, or in a long time, all who heard him would become such as he, a servant of the King of Lux.

There was much Anthro still did not understand about the man or his beliefs, but one thing was clear: if the King of Lux was who Apostolos thought he was, then the rest of humankind was in serious trouble—of such a degree that it was difficult to fathom. If Apostolos cared for his fellow humans, then that love for them would compel an almost relentless effort to seek the conversion of men and women of every kind, class, and kingdom. Apostolos might be many things, but Anthro found his outspoken evangelistic demeanor to be perhaps his most consistent quality. The man was stubborn and outspoken, but Anthro had yet to see anything he would describe as coercive—only simple words spoken of what the man believed was the sober truth.

"Let's start with belief. What do you think it means to believe in the King of Lux?" Apostolos had leaned forward as he asked the question, looking Keta directly in the eyes, and then, upon asking it, had leaned back as if to signal that the floor was hers.

"Well, I think it's obvious that at a minimum it means 'cognitive ascent' regarding what the king came to do. Agreeing with his death you spoke of and with this rising that you mentioned as well." Apostolos listened carefully without distraction and did not speak during the silence as Keta thought more. "And you mentioned that the king was the Son of God too, but also that he was the only God? I'm not sure how that works, but I think something like that would have to be of the highest importance, right? Believing correctly about *who* he was? To confess that he is lord over all *is* to confess him as God, so the confession of the one implies the other. They're symbiotic. I mean, if we're talking about being reconciled to God, how important it must be to *understand* God!" Keta was linking distinctions and recognizing logical conclusions with ease. All the while, the knot in Anthro's stomach had only wound itself tighter.

Apostolos smiled. "Do you think that is all?"

"Well . . . well, no that can't be all." Keta was thinking fiercely. As iron sharpens iron, so Keta and Anthro's friendship had put an edge on both of their minds.

"Why is that?" The question was crafted to hone, but not to lead.

"This king, the King of Lux—I still don't know much about him, but a mere acceptance of a certain set of principles in relation to him cannot be what it means to truly *know* him, to *believe* in him. Belief in this king goes beyond the list of propositions and into the will and the heart. The full human is involved in belief. Belief . . . it means to follow. It means to submit to, to be transformed by, to walk in the footsteps of . . . but—and here is where the distinction really matters—is it by not trusting in yourself? Oh yes, that's it, belief is a commitment to trust in this king which will result in obedience and transformation based on a confession of this core set of facts revolving around the king and his work. So, basically, belief is a giving over of oneself in confidence to the king's promises and work, and *then* following after him."

Keta let out a breath. A part of her wondered if she was making this more complicated than it ought to be. Or was she treating this king seriously by examining what it meant to follow him with scrutinizing detail? She was collecting facts and counting costs so as not to begin construction of a house only to fail to complete it. Why lay a foundation if only to give up on the labor due to poor initial consideration? Why set out to battle without weighing the requirements for victory? This king's claims were far too grand to handle lightly.

Apostolos smiled once more as thunder roared from above. "'Giving oneself over in confidence to the king's promises and work.' Yes, that will do. The facts are essential: the king's nature, his death, and—most importantly, his rising. Without them, there can be no belief. We are a religion that rests upon a set of historic facts, but if it is *only* sheer consent to them, there is no belief. For true belief—genuine giving of oneself toward such a king—will certainly manifest outwardly in actions that are reflective of a heart that *wants* to run after his commands. You have answered well." He paused before continuing to let the ideas absorb. "What of repentance?"

Keta thought for several moments. "Well, I think it means confessing that I'm not good and that I need to turn from my own moral efforts in order to trust in this king. It's accepting the king's report that I'm not righteous in and of myself, and it is a turning from self to God through the reconciliatory work of the King of Lux."

"Are you sure that you do not have more of our books in your possession?" Apostolos asked with a happy chuckle.

"Wait. This is where you're wrong."

Keta and Apostolos both looked at Anthro with interest, as he had been quiet for so long.

"Keta doesn't need to repent."

"Excuse me?" Keta's voice was filled with surprised affront.

"You heard me. You don't need to repent. I'll buy that someone who has lived the kind of life that I have needs to do something to get right with god, if there is a god. But this entire repentance idea, if it's anything at all, is for people like me. Not you." Anthro was determined not to cede ground here. He had thought for sure that Keta would be on his side in regard to her own righteousness and was shocked to hear her even entertaining the idea of her complete iniquity. It was nothing short of outrageous.

Apostolos held his tongue. Keta took a deep breath before speaking, holding back certain words with restraint. "Anthro, I know you've seen me do a lot that looks good from your perspective. I'm not sure if Apostolos would agree, but I believe that at some level, it is good. Let's call it a horizontal level, an angle that is seen and done from humanity's perspective. But what about the vertical level with God? At this final judgement to come, when I stand before this king of absolute holy perfection and penetrating light, what shall I do with those horizontal good works in contrast with my bad deeds? Shall I offer them to this God? Shall I really believe that even they are free from blemish? Shall I bargain with them? Would I not then be using such deeds as a means of coercion against this God? Just how good could such works be? Anthro, what about my sins?"

"You don't have any." Did he believe that or was he afraid to yield even this turf? He could already follow some of the logic. Where would the line of sin meet the scales of meritorious works? Would the scales of justice held by this . . . holy God be one for one? Anthro very much doubted that.

"Oh, take the blinders off, Anthro. Even in my best light, I am far from this king's law. If you don't see that, then you don't know me." Keta was matching Anthro's defiant stance. She had accepted this conviction of wretchedness well before reading the *Manifesto*, and having heard a good part of it now, she was convinced beyond doubt.

Anthro's forcefulness was abated by her words. *Did* he know her? Yes, of course he knew her. This was Keta: provider for the widow, hero to the orphan, defender of the weak, protector until death. He did not only disagree with this idea of the evil nature of her deeds, he hated it. Still, he possessed the interpersonal awareness to know when not to push an issue.

"Alright, let's just keep going. I'll move forward, only for the sake of the argument. That's the best I can do." There was an ache in his voice this time that calmed Keta down as well.

"Alright, Anthro." She spoke his name tenderly. She could sense his agitation; it permeated the stale atmosphere. To some degree it was flattering, even if surely faulty. "Well, what's next?"

"This whole idea of morality still has me at a loss." Anthro broke the silence, willing the aggression out of his words. "The King of Lux has this entire *Manifesto* with a complex moral code and clear commands to follow, but then he has this report saying no one can follow, so which is it? Are humans supposed to follow or are we to know that we can't? And, if that's the case, why even bother?"

Apostolos eyed Keta to see if she would take the question. She did not, so he spoke. "Anthro, you are not far from the kingdom of heaven."

Anthro laughed aloud with tepid sarcasm. "I am farther than you can imagine."

"I speak seriously. Few men realize the weight of this law.

Fewer still *feel* the weight of it. Keta is wise to recognize the importance of distinctions with these beliefs. They are needed here as well. God is holy, which literally means separate in perfection. In fact, that declaration is one of the most stressed aspects of his nature within our beliefs. Humans go beyond mere contrast with such a being. We are not just unholy; we, by nature through inheritance, are anti-holy. If God is such, and humans are such, do you see the chasm this morality creates before humanity and God?" The rainfall above slowly began to subside its strength.

"Of course, but then why follow if doomed to failure?" Anthro asked, his emotions oddly gaining placidity alongside the rain.

"Anthro, why did the King of Lux come to this world?" Apostolos returned.

Anthro reflected for a few moments before speaking. He had talked to Apostolos on this subject several times now. "To die."

"Why?"

More thought. Then, "To reconcile humanity to God."

"How?"

How? How did this supposedly work? "Through magic," Anthro said half-heartedly.

Keta would not let that go. "Anthro, you're intelligent enough to know that anyone willing to mock a prudent question is not sincerely after the truth." She spoke with a confident, rebukeful warmth.

"Fine . . . sorry," Anthro said without looking at either of them. "How?" He mouthed the word to himself as he weighed the thought in his mind, sifting through all that he had heard, and considering the potential solutions.

The problem . . . sin—human nature set against divine nature. The solution? This king . . . dying. This king . . . rising? Why would God have to come in this way? Why would he have to die? His death must be the key. But how was his life . . . his human life? How was that related? Why would this Son of God, this God-man, need to be killed in order to save humanity? How would that reconcile man to God?

Then a word materialized in his mind, a word that carried strength and burden when considering a holy God. A word that seemed universal throughout human experience so that its hope could resonate with all. Yet, if it was to ever be found in full—if it was more than some abstract concept of man's musings and desires—did it not stake a claim on every single human being?

Justice.

Anthro once more looked at Apostolos. "Justice. The king came to justify sinful humanity before God." Gentle tones of peach and coral were infiltrating the room as the sun overpowered the remnant of clouds one final time before its daily demise.

Apostolos eyed Anthro for some time before speaking, "What would be needed for such justice to be accomplished?"

Anthro gave it more consideration, new thoughts forming and connections growing. "Well, I think a couple of concepts would need satisfaction. Sin, if it is what you say it is, requires payment. All true justice does, right? A faithful judge cannot dismiss a criminal without consequence. To neglect the requirements of the law would be corruption, not justice." Apostolos inclined his head slightly. This next idea was the most consequential in Anthro's mind. "So, there's a penalty for sin . . . that penalty . . . Apostolos, what are the wages of sin?"

"Death." Apostolos said the word with somber finality. Keta simply observed the two of them with her eyes and mind riveted.

"So, there can be no justice without death. This God, he is just?" Anthro was calm, his calculating and tactical mind recognizing the enemy and determining the necessary course for victory.

"Indeed, infinitely so."

"Then the king died, as a . . . a substitute?" A network of scattered perceptions were weaving into a coherent web of understanding. "But he couldn't just be any kind of substitute. He would have to be holy, innocent, undefiled, separate from the sinners, as he was seeking to save others by offering himself. But then . . . then how could one man satisfy this need for justice? Wouldn't he only be able to save one man—a life for a life—assuming he was even all that was necessary for such an atonement?"

Apostolos looked once more to Keta. She was slow to speak, wanting to be sure, but she was positive. "And that's why he has to be more than *just* a man. He has to be God. Only God can save with such efficiency while still satisfying justice. Besides God himself, there is no savior. I wonder though, Apostolos. I'm sure there is an answer, but for the king to die such a death, wouldn't it be unjust for God to allow him to die? If he was truly sinless, for him to die, he would have to have . . ." She could not bear to say it. Her perceptions of the greatness and nobility of this king of divine royalty already made this seem like a task of extravagant humility beyond the heights of human imagination.

Apostolos completed her sentence. "Become sin on our behalf so that we might become the righteousness of God in him." That gaze of foreign sight once more returned within the deep brown eyes of the king's servant as he spoke a prose of wonder. "The King of Lux, he was pierced for our transgressions, he was crushed for our iniquities. The chastisement of the Almighty fell upon him, satisfyingly crushing whom he loved for what he had taken upon himself. By his wounds, we are healed. All of us, like sheep, were lost and had gone astray, each one turning to their own way, but God caused the iniquity of us all to fall on him. In anguish, in sorrows, in grief—in his blood he justified the many,

pouring himself out unto death, bearing the sins of his sheep."
The tapestry of color was dulled as the sun fell deep beneath
the earth.

The group was speechless for a moment, two lost in glory, one lost in speculation. It was Anthro who spoke next. "We
probably have overstayed our welcome here, but let's track back
to morality quickly."

The deaf shopkeeper was lighting a few scattered lanterns
on the lower floor, either oblivious to or unconcerned with her
three guests.

"The relationship of the moral law and this king . . . we can
say that he, in fact, fulfilled the whole law, then? And that was
one of the requirements for him to be an acceptable sacrifice?"

"Yes, yes, but more . . ." Apostolos said while not fully in
the room.

"Could . . . could it be?"

Both men looked toward Keta.

"'Become the righteousness *of* God *in* him'. That's what you
said. But could that mean that, in addition to the king having
taken on our sins, his fulfillment of the law is somehow transferred to us?" Keta knew the radical nature of these thoughts;
this would change everything.

"That, my soon to be surpassing student, is the heart of
being justified before God. Humans do not only need a removal
of sin; we also need an alien righteousness to clothe us in the fulfillment of the requirements of the law. It is a cosmic exchange
of imputation: sin absorbed by the sinless and obedience robing
the disobedient." Apostolos paused to let the words soak. "It
is by no mistake that a prophet of old declared that the king
would be called 'God *Our* Righteousness.' It is by this garment
of perfection that we are adopted as children *of* God and are no
longer his enemies. There is no hallway between the courtroom

of God and the family room of God. They are traversed only by instant adoption through propitiation. That is the extravagance of grace. That is the scandal of the king's death. That is the good news we proclaim. That is the salvation *of* God."

Keta bowed her head as Anthro opened his mouth. "So, morality is pointless, then? No need to be moral if you've been justified like that. You can do whatever you want."

That lion look of Apostolos arose with the velocity of that beast in chase. "Anthro, no one who has experienced such grace could ever say that. Only those outside the gift can see that as an actual possibility. Grace such as this is antithetical to willful sin. Grace has freed us from the law. Love has won us to it."

Anthro was silenced verbally while cerebral chatter occupied him once more, an old conversation returning to his mind.

"Apostolos, I have one more question. Forgive me if it is dishonoring, but I already feel the doubt." Keta spoke with a rare fearful tone. "How . . . how do we know—how do *I* know—that the payment was enough? That there is no longer any condemnation for those who believe?"

"There is no dishonor in such a question, only sight. Death could no longer hold the King of Lux. The sacrifice was sufficient, and it became impossible for death to hold him. The penalty was paid in full and his rising was the announcement of that satisfaction of sacrifice. He bore our sins, paid for them, and *then* he rose. The King of Lux was vindicated by God and our debts were forever left behind us as if buried in the tomb he walked out of."

Apostolos took on an even more serious tenor as he continued. "If that one fact were not true—his bodily resurrection, his vindication—then everything we are would crumble into dust. Our entire faith would be worthless. We would still be in our sins and we, more than all of humanity, would be most of all to be pitied. But in this we rejoice: the tomb is empty, our redeemer lives, and at the last he will stand upon the earth. In his flesh he rose, appearing to individuals, small gatherings, and a group as large as 500. The doubtful were given his wounds and flesh to touch and see.

"The earliest witnesses to see him were women. This was a shocking claim for one who knows that society's patriarchal history. The risen king showed himself with enough proof to convert previously unbelieving brothers. Anyone with siblings will know for certain the difficulty of this. But not only kin did he win, for even the most violent enemy of his followers eventually joined their ranks. It is not simply by a subjective burning in our hearts that we believe with confidence, but on the proclamation of an objective fact in history with much corroboration from even hostile outside witnesses in regard to many of the details. By all this we believe that, in the flesh, the King of Lux rose and that, in the flesh, with our own eyes, we shall behold him in glory."

"Worthless? The whole faith would be worthless?" Anthro questioned the word. More than anything, it caught his attention as he was surprised by such a confession. He had not believed that Apostolos was the type of man to even consider such a possibility, let alone admit it.

"Without the slightest shred of value," Apostolos replied simply. "More than that, if the king has not been raised, my preaching is in vain. All who follow him are fools chasing vanity and bearing false witness to whatever there is in this universe."

This one admission added a credibility to Apostolos's testimony that Anthro had previously been unable to give. The man believed the resurrection of his king to be true while knowing that it could be objectively false, which would render his beliefs meaningless. What other surprises were to be found in this man?

Chapter XVI

The God of Suffering

Ash filled the air as if it were a dense fog. It fell from the sky like dirty snow. It rose from the earth like polluted pollen. It came from the east. It came from the west. It could not be outrun to the north. There was no escaping it to the south. Like a volcanic plume it rose into the heavens as it blacked out the sun. It coated the skin and filled the nostrils. It made breath short and burned the eyes. It consumed all that it surrounded, but it would never conceal what had given it life.

Anthro rode through the thick of it. His guard surrounded him. Those closest to him appeared grainy and unclear, those furthest, invisible. Besides this ashen covering, they were all free of any physical injury. A battle had been waged. One side left unscathed; the other was annihilated. What had Anthro and his men just witnessed? What had they just done? They had crossed some unforeseen line that not even war would forgive. This was not battle. This was not even war. This was slaughter. This was massacre.

Syntri, the capital city of Vanus, had not just fallen; it had been decimated. The men of this country—so strong and valiant and brutal—had been left to cower in the ruins of their last stronghold, begging for mercy as their mighty fortress crumbled upon them. Beelzebul's revelation had come to fulfillment in this extinguishment of the living. These cold metal contraptions with their explosive shells and energy were merely the final contractions that preceded the rebirth of civilization—the last birth pangs before the singing of that new song. There was indeed to be sorrow for the night, but joy would come in the morning.

For peace to last there must be an unquestionable power undergirding such progress. The fruit of this technological advancement was unpleasant, even in Beelzebul's eyes, but it was necessary. As a woman no longer remembers the pain of giving birth while holding her infant, so too the world would forget this fiery trial of pain and death. Though the tears would fade, the memory of uncompromising power would remain. A child knows its place once afflicted with the rod; civilization is no different. That child goes so quickly from the beating to begging once more for love and affection; civilization is no different.

This type of onslaught had been King Beelzebul's plan ever since dividing his armies (a tactical move Anthro had long scrutinized). It was masterful. It was dreadful. It was for this purpose that so many officers had been called to Babylonem to announce these new weapons of destruction, and right now, Anthro was confident that this horror was unfolding throughout the continent on various fronts. Modern military strength of a disproportionate power was reshaping the world at this very moment. Anthro was just one of many harbingers of death.

He had known that these weapons were coming. Yet it had all seemed so distant, so unreal—until the first cannon had erupted in the quiet morning air, until the first shell carried beyond the heights of the outer wall, blasting fire and stone into the sky. An endless blaze of unearthly hail then proceeded to rain down upon soldiers and civilians: the young and the old, the strong and the weak, the small and the great. What had humanity just invented? In the ceaseless race of war, how had such advancement in killing potential ever taken so long to develop within the rapidly industrializing nation of Tenebris? Perhaps the old ways were already so capable of laying waste to countless numbers that few gave adequate thought to the possibility of a developmental shift of this kind of weapons technology. That had been Anthro's only thought as he watched the city burn in unholy fire.

He and his guard, still encircled in the haze, were nearing the command area miles beyond the desolation. As they were riding, something happened within Anthro's patrol that had never occurred before. A man broke rank. Not to the left, nor to the right, and certainly not in retreat. It was Themata who raced ahead of them all at a full gallop toward the unseen pitch of canvassed tents with their flying black and blue banners. Two of Anthro's other knights had called after the sounds of fleeing hoofs with no reply. They shouted to Anthro for a command, and he had them maintain their formation.

Themata had spent seven years under Anthro's command and four years within his personal guard with no deviations in his service. He was quiet, reserved, strong, and faithful. His reserved nature was Anthro's greatest reservation in recruiting him into his trusted service. It was difficult to get to know the man, but Anthro had been drawn to him after overhearing a statement Themata made that had been most unpatriotic. Themata had feared that he would die a traitor's death; instead, he was brought into Anthro's intimate circle.

The runaway's horse raced into the camp and toward Anthro's command tent. As Anthro and the guard neared the encampment, Themata reappeared in a blur, but he was no longer alone on his mount. Apostolos was awkwardly seated behind him, his bound hands wrapped over Themata as they galloped right through the escort of knights.

The entire guard reared and gave chase, this time maintaining a closer proximity. As they entered through the scorched gates of shattered marble, Themata came to a stop near a solitary horse and had Apostolos mount the orphaned steed. The transfer gave his pursuers the necessary time to close all distance.

Before the affronted superior could say a word, Anthro's knight and Themata's dearest friend, Harpazo, positioned his heavy clad stallion in front of his erratic companion. Drawing his blade, he shouted, "Themata, how dare you desert your company! How dare you abandon your commander! Explain yourself!"

Themata stared his brother down, his eyes blood red from the ash, his square face expressionless, and his thick beard hiding sealed lips. His dangerous eyes dared Harpazo's burning black ones to attack as if the sword before him was but the harmless complement of an aging spinster's thimble, but Themata made no move for his own war hammer. He drove his horse forward, shoving Harpazo forcefully out of the way.

Harpazo, with a look of the betrayed on his young charcoal face, cried out, "Prepare yourself!" Commanding his horse around, he raised his long sword high in the air. Sunlight glittered off the reflective steel despite the hazy smoke surrounding them. Themata took no notice and carried on with a rope attached to Apostolos's horse, pulling him along as well.

"Harpazo, stand down!" Anthro roared, finally intervening. He would see what had overcome his underling's senses—without killing him, if possible. Harpazo aggressively sheathed his blade, falling in line without comment as anger swirled around him. The youngest of all of Anthro's knights, he was certainly the most pugnacious, both vocally and physically, but he was also the most compassionate and determined toward the heart of their rebellious cause. The man was an odd mix of violent tenderness.

The group traveled through the many ruins of white-marbled battlements and turrets. Syntri had been a city of beauty that rivaled even Babylonem, but instead of collecting a mix of materials and creating a tapestry of construction and art using many mediums, the builders had primarily used just one: pure white marble. Houses, roads, walls, and keeps, were covered in it, whether thin sheets or thick as mountains. The marble was everywhere, with splendid silver acting as the outline and covering the grout in most areas. Anthro could only imagine the capital as it had been. Even with no structure left undamaged, there was still a beauty left lingering in the ruins, like the haunting, melancholy song of a bluebird amidst a flock of shrieking ravens.

Along the outskirts of the city, Tenebris soldiers were executing the severely wounded enemy combatants. Upon Anthro's orders, the walking wounded were always to be spared. Under the threat of death, it was amazing how little a human needed to be ambulatory.

The deeper they traveled into the core of the city's remains, the uglier the scene before them grew. The projectiles had carried further than expected and had been difficult to restrain. The farther they had flown, the more they had met civilian rather than soldier. As they neared what had been a cleared field, the smell before them—although never pleasant—grew almost unbearable. All the while, Themata never spoke. In fact, no one spoke on this tour of human destruction and woe.

Piles of bodies were being burned in the field before them, and the odor of human flesh was enough to nauseate. Normally, this would have been done outside the city, but this place was too far gone to be re-inhabited. Its desolation and ruins would forever be a fixed monument to the dead.

Being thrown into the fire were men, women, and children.

Sex, class, age, health, intelligence—none of that mattered. Here, there was no discrimination in death. Anthro desperately wanted to ride away, hating the raw reality before him and knowing that he had overseen its accomplishment. He loathed himself now more than ever, but he looked on, gazing, feeling, hurting. Anthro would stare human suffering in the face; he always had. He refused to look away from humanity's most rotten spectacle and forbade himself to deny its brutal existence.

If ever he found an answer in his quest for truth, it would have to account for this wretched reality. It would have to make some sense of the hollowness found within this hell. He did not need every explanation, but he needed something tangible. Currently, his working resolution—his only account for it all—was a meaningless and indifferent world of hopeless vanity. How could there be anything else? That answer alone satisfied both the intellect and emotion surrounding human suffering. What else could?

Still, there was doubt. Anthro could not help but find this apparent emptiness and complete vision of darkness wanting in light of all that his eyes saw, of all his mind thought, and of all that his heart longed for. It was this doubt that would delay his embrace of the ever-calling mistress that was a universe devoid of ultimate meaning, purpose, and design—at least, for now. In a world with suffering of this magnitude, a person who refused to embrace the mind-numbing distractions and worldly pleasures that so many others turned to could only remain agnostic for so long. And still, a thought lingered. What did the King of Lux have to say about this?

The company, led by Themata, worked its way out of the city, passing the crying, the weeping, and the broken. Sight, sound, and smell—a trio of senses took in the misery of humanity before them. There was no escaping the lament of life and loss wherever one looked, the dirge of dreams destroyed drumming loudly from the dying, or the stench of society degrading into seared sinew and sizzling skin.

Finally, after two hours spent within the city, they came to a stop on a bluff that overlooked the burning ruins of Syntri. Themata dismounted and helped Apostolos do the same before sitting down on the rocky plateau, where even at this distance, smoke clouded the air. The company, not sure what else to do, followed suit. Then, with a misted gaze toward the vestiges of civilization, Themata began speaking into the air, and as the words came, he spoke Anthro's heart.

"Another city has fallen—this one astonishingly so. This ruin is as vast as the sea. Beyond healing. It has been thrown down without sparing. On grounds of beauty lie virgin daughters and young men of vitality stripped naked by death. People of aged wisdom and humans of great stupidity. They have fallen by a weapon greater than the sword. Slain. Slaughtered. Terror on every side. No one could escape or survive this annihilation. I have seen affliction since my eyes were opened to the evil of our race. All the while, the natural world hangs as a curse over us and is sure to finish off whatever little remains of this race of men. I have walked in this darkness and not seen light.

"Rotting flesh. Wasting skin. Broken bones. Bitterness and hardship. Humanity hemmed in on every side, held by a heavy chain with no one to hear our prayers. Like beasts, we tear each other apart. We are desolate, alone, filled with bitterness and drunk with wormwood. Peace has been rejected. Happiness is forgotten. Destruction and misery are always before us. Strife abounds and contention rages. Justice is never upheld, and if any comes, it is perverted. If our race had strength, it has perished. We have watched for a nation to save. We have even believed that we were that nation—but no nation can save. Our end draws near. Our days are finished. Our end has come. The crown has fallen from our race. Woe to us. We have no hope in life nor death."

There was silence for some time as the entire company felt those words on their skin, tasting the bile of lament and smelling despair as they gazed at the burning wasteland before them. Anthro knew that if he closed his eyes this night, with these as his final and unrefuted thoughts, he would let the darkness have him in full.

Harpazo was seated on a fragmented piece of granite, leaning forward with his sword tip deep into loose earth and doubting that he would be needing it much longer. His hands were crossed over the pommel, his stubbled chin resting upon scarred black knuckles. It was he who broke the dead air. "Themata." He spoke his name as only a beloved friend can. "I've no answer, but I can only wonder; why? What purpose lies behind your actions? Who shall deny that it is a wretched reality that is before us?"

"I believe all shall admit the horror before us." His eyes cleared as they shot toward Apostolos. "But I wonder . . . shall one not admit that it is horror above us as well?"

Apostolos met his glare, but only with compassion in his eyes.

"You . . . you ambassador!" Themata's voice began to rise, reverberating off the surrounding stone. "I've heard you speak! Night after night, telling us of this 'good' God, of this 'good' king who is worthy of all honor and worship." He paused, collecting his thoughts, eyes filling with limpid liquid. "How dare you! How dare you look at the state of this world and tell us that someone who has power actually cares! I've no problem with believing in *a* god if that's what you want. But a *good* god in this world of suffering is ridiculous!" The short man was puffed full of emotion, standing over the unwavering eyes of Apostolos.

"How dare you even believe such a thing yourself! You are either blind, idiotic, or, if you do have eyes and a mind—demented! You . . . you 'servant of the king,' explain yourself! Either deny your king or give light to your twisted belief in him! With such destruction as our witness, I demand it!"

Apostolos knew many defenses for these charges, even beyond those of his immediate tradition. His conviction to love God with all of his mind had led to a lifetime of endless study. His belief in the unity of the king's people had driven him to understand those of differing perspectives that still faithfully flew the banner of Lux. From the mere intellectual level he could retort from various angles, not to provide a complete understanding, but at the very least offering a reasonable defense.

But none of these he offered, despite their rational merits. Over the years, Apostolos's mind had sifted through and wrestled with such explanations. But in his heart, he had learned to rest in the inscrutability of a creator God who is light and in whom there is no darkness at all—a God who forms light and creates darkness, who brings prosperity and creates disaster, who both gives and takes away. A God who is simply, just God. But Apostolos would not present even these precious truths to Themata. Not at this moment. They had all been learned over a lifetime, and even they did not hold him on his darkest nights. Furthermore, he could see that beyond the angry accuser stood a broken man. Therefore, he would offer himself.

"My little girl was beautiful. She had fair skin like the soft clouds of long winter evenings. Smooth black hair of onyx that glistened as the reflection of sunlit rainfall in spring. Her eyes . . . her eyes were pools of swirling fallen hickory leaves. Her laugh was summer."

Apostolos's voice cracked and his whole body shook as he bit his lower lip, eyes closing for several moments. The memories he so rarely spoke of inundated him with fresh pain drawn from a well of his own deep-seated suffering. He would drink this cup of sorrow for his fellow man.

No one spoke; they hardly moved. There is great power in the raw tears of a man.

"My love for her was beyond the grasp of metaphor. Skies above simile. She was my life, my gem, my joy—and she was ten." Apostolos was progressing past tears, though the pain of voice was palpable to all.

"My wife . . . I shall not let you hear me describe her beauty." Apostolos managed a choked laugh. The mood was impossible to lighten, but the joke managed to add a touch of his gentleness, even within his innermost sorrow. "She was all a man could ask for in a partner. The proverbial woman of wisdom. A value surpassing all worldly wealth. An early riser of perpetual labor, her hands only worked in delight. Girded with strength and a lamp that would not go out at night. A hand extended to the poor, arms stretched out to the needy. Never did we fear the snow, for she clothed us in scarlet. Strength and dignity were her clothing and she smiled at the future. The teaching of kindness was on her tongue toward strangers, friends, and family. And, with a holy love, she feared the God who took her and my daughter from me." Apostolos regained composure by taking several deep breaths and wiping his eyes.

"My daughter and I watched the life slowly drain from her eyes. Is there a worse experience in this world than to watch the flesh of your flesh and the bone of your bone fade away? I know of none, but one. For two years the sickness ate her body away. The worst part? She so rarely complained. At times she even rejoiced. She would tell me, 'Apostolos, I consider any suffering this world has to offer not worthy of comparison to the joy and glory that will be revealed to us because of the King of

Lux.' I lost myself in anger when she went so far as to say that this suffering had been 'granted to her.' My heated response was nearly my last words to her; how selfishly I spoke." He delayed, still feeling the guilt.

"You see, we had both been raised as believers in the King of Lux, but I came to find out that only one of us believed. The belief I thought I had about the king and this good God wasted away with her. She hoped and trusted beyond last breath. For her, to live was to know the king and to die was gain." The surrounding leaves were still, nor was a sound of bird to be heard in the air.

"My daughter—what did she know of this world? I heard her prayers continue in the night as darkness eclipsed my soul. As she prayed with childish trust, I wrapped her tighter around my heart, all the while shutting my mouth to God. War came through our small town and arrows flew. Why would they hit her and not me? Could providence exist with such torture done to a man? I was beyond belief. I was not indifferent to what remained of the community of believers in our town after that. I wanted to destroy them."

There was a hollowness in his voice, a weakness, an anger, a conflicted cry still buried within as if a deep wound lay festering just beneath healed skin. Even in Anthro's wildest imaginations, he would never have believed this would have been Apostolos's story. Why had he assumed that Apostolos had not faced such sufferings and such pain? Anthro regretted that he had never cared to ask.

"I knew the people; I had grown up in their community. Several were experts at giving me pompous, dirty looks for my rebellion and I was all too happy to encourage their behavior. Far more of them had sought to serve my wife as she was dying, and even more had tried to give comfort when my daughter was taken. I hated them for their kindness and ripped their charity from my memory. It was easy to look down on them when I forced myself to only focus on the few bad apples among the bunch.

"My feeble efforts to destroy them were futile. They were stubborn in their belief as I turned to strong drink. I had long since reopened my mouth to God. Daily, I cursed him and begged him for one pitiful act of mercy: my death. Even this he would not give. Daily, I shook my fist in the air as I put God on trial for this world of torment. Daily, I found him guilty. I was no longer the town's enemy; I was simply the belligerent drunk. Men stood between their wives and children as I passed in the streets, and even the best of the believing community eventually abandoned their efforts to help me. I do not blame them. I was a nasty man. My grief was an endless supply for my anger. But not all gave up." A minute glimmer of light returned within his dark-brown cavern eyes.

"There were two who remained. An old man, very old. I think he may have been deaf; it would explain his toleration of me. He would supply me with small amounts of his rations. I'll never forget his mutterings, 'As he is now, so I was.' It was all he said and I cursed him for it. Again, I do not know if he could hear me, though he did mutter faster whenever I began cursing, so perhaps he could.

"The other was a very young man, not fully right in the head. He would clean my room once a month, even my sheets. Bless that man. I was slower to curse him, but to my shame, I still did." The remorse was written upon his face as he spoke. He seemed to have aged years in just these few minutes. "The man—or boy, really—never spoke for the first several months. After a while, though, he would stop at the threshold of the door as he was leaving and look me straight in the eyes. He was the only one in town who could do that." Another long pause. "Then he said it.

The first time only once, the second time twice, and so on. His memory for such things was astounding. He would simply say 'Read. Read. Read.' An interesting word for an illiterate man with numerous handicaps. I didn't remember his name, so I started calling him that. I thought it was a fun way to mock him. He did not relent.

"Finally, after a little more than a year, I found out what he was talking about. I believe I knew the entire time. On a cold winter morning, as I wallowed in my drunken filth, he showed up with them . . . all four of them. 'Mine.' He said it over and over again. That stare . . . how could he hold my gaze? Then he combined his two words as he said, 'Mine. Read. Mine. Read. Mine. Read.' The books were precious to him; even I could tell that. Something about him making eye contact with me stopped the impulse I had to destroy them. He put them next to me, on the only clean spot. 'Mine. Read.' Still he would not relent. I cursed him as I picked up the first one. Maybe if I started reading, he would shut up. I hadn't held a book since I had read nighttime stories to my daughter."

That hollowness of voice had resurfaced, and with it had come fresh tears and clenched fists. Yet this time, the light never left his eyes. Now, a spark of hope could not be hidden beneath the pain.

"He had stacked the deck with his favorite on top. Sneaky kid. 'In the beginning was the Word, and the Word was with God, and the Word was God.' That's how it starts, with the divinity of the King of Lux. Somehow through my groggy hangover, I felt the weight of such a claim, even a hint of the wonder. I stopped for several minutes. 'Read. Read.' There was only one way to mute the kid, so I read on. I didn't get far. 'And the Word became flesh and dwelt among us and we saw his glory, glory as the only begotten from the Father, full of grace and truth.' What possible glory could be found in the flesh of this world? I had forgotten. Had I ever really seen?

"I read on . . . I no longer needed the boy's prompting. He smiled as I picked up the next book. He laughed when I started the third and fourth. I hated him, and I loved him. He sat there for hours listening—for the entire day—as I read of a Father and of a Son in whom he was well pleased: his beloved and only Son. I read of a God of eternal relationship and perfect triune fellowship both sending and being sent to purchase a people with his own blood. His Son had not counted equality with God a thing to be held onto. This King of Lux had humbled himself by taking the form of a servant, by taking on the flesh of humanity and dwelling among us. He came as a servant, not of kings, but of rebels.

"I read of a divine rescue mission, with all persons agreed and willing despite tears and bloody anguish. I saw humans doing what humans would do if there was ever a truly just man in their presence: torturing him slowly, ensuring he would die a gruesome and definite death, and mocking all the while. Not just what man would do to a perfectly just brother, but what man would do to *God* if they could get their hands on the real being. What . . . what man did to God *when* they got their hands on him. As I read of the King of Lux, of God incarnate being crucified, I must confess that I did not at first identify with those who mourned and wept, nor even with those who fled. I am convinced that I would have joined in on his murder. I'm no different than they who nailed him to that tree." Apostolos paused once again, yet an even brighter light rose in his eyes.

"I read as if all reality bore witness to the Word, with my silent partner beside me. Again and again, I read of a God who knows what it's like to lose an only child." He bit his lip hard. "Who knows what it's like to *give* his only Son for a world of hostile enemies. This is the cosmic act of love God showed the world: sending his only Son to die for it. Anyone who has loved a child as I have knows *that gift* is truly the greatest act of sacrifice. I would have given my child for no one, certainly not for myself, nor my best friend, nor even my treasured wife. Yet God, to satisfy justice in the greatest act of love imaginable, gave his Son for those who loathed them both.

"I read, time and time again, of a God who *knows* what it is like to suffer and weep and bleed. Not in some far-off, abstract kind of way, but *in* raw, naked, human flesh and experience. I read of a king in rags and of a suffering savior well acquainted with grief. Of a messiah who was forsaken by God in ways I will never be able to fathom, as, for the first time in human history, innocent human blood was spilt in a sacrifice of God and man. And it is that blood of the Son of God that has purchased, cleansed, and redeemed human beings in both body and soul.

"In these four precious books, I read of a king who dies *for* his enemies, a husband who dies *for* his adulterous bride, and of a God who pours out the terrors of his wrath in the loftiest drama of his unfathomable love . . . And I read of an empty tomb, the vindication of the Son. I read of the dead man who lives." Apostolos again had that gaze from his first conversation with Anthro. He was seeing something beyond them all.

"In those four fragments of history, I saw the good God of this universe in the person of his Son stripped naked, mocked, scorned, beaten, and then nailed to a tree. He hung on the most tortuous instrument of death humans could create. Literally becoming a curse for his wayward flock, his arms spread out wide as he declared what the love, power, and glory of God looks like. The Son explained the love of the Father in himself. He who has seen the Son has seen the Father, has seen all the fullness of deity in bodily form—the radiance of his glory, and the exact representation of his nature. At the foot of this cross, and only there, does a good God in this world of ours make sense to me. Without that cross, I daresay, I fear that I would be far too weak to believe. With it? Well, there is a power enough in that cross for me . . . there is a glory enough to be found at the foot of that tree . . . for me to cry out, 'Lord, I believe; help my unbelief!'"

Quiet hung over them as if sound itself had been silenced.

Chapter XVII

The Call to the Sick

Strokes of rose, sweeps of titian, sun of daybreak—all illustrated a canvas of new birth. Damp dew was misting off rock and leaf as it met the breath of the sun. Scent of sap, perfume of petrichor, whiff of the wilds—all permeated the air of the dawn. Sonnets of songbirds, hymns of awakening branches, callings of various creatures—all united as one chorus. The anthem of the early morning thicket.

Several battalions, the entirety of them now subject to Anthro's command, were camped along a rocky upcropping that stood tall above the surrounding forest that marked the border of Ultimus. For several days these peaceful sounds and this beautiful scenery had surrounded them, but Anthro knew it was a lie. Nevertheless, it was a lie he willfully clutched onto within his imagination. He let himself dream of the nation before him laying down their arms, surrendering without a fight. He conjured up images of himself standing upon the western edge of the continent with Ultimus resting securely behind him, intact and unharmed.

Maybe the annihilation of Syntri would provide the necessary deterrent to engage this all-consuming invader. Maybe the conquering of every surrounding nation would influence a military abdication. Maybe this time blood would not reach to the bridles before he reached the coastline. He could only hope; he could only dream. But even now he heard the sharpening of spears. Even now he heard the shaping of shields. Even now he heard the people say, "We will fight before we fall." Peace, even in his imagination, was a lie. Even once Ultimus fell, he wondered if Beelzebul would turn his army into a fleet and send ships to conquer the western world across the sea which were Apostolos's homelands. There was always the possibility of more bloodshed. Peace was a lie.

A thin tendril of smoke was still rising from the coals of a smoldering fire as the full light of dawn approached. Ever since Apostolos had been freed to move within an established camp as he pleased, he was always awake before Anthro and his men, whether well rested or not. Anthro knew that he spent the daily quiet time of the new mornings reflecting on memorized scriptures and praying to his God. Anthro had been shocked by the informality of it all, especially with the knowledge of just how holy this God was. Could a man pray to such a being with his eyes opened as he stared into the ashes of a dying fire? No charades, no rituals, no required posturing—none of that. Was the King of Lux's mediation so efficient?

Apostolos prayed with the frequency and tenacity of a beloved child, with the rich mosaic of generous praise that flows forth from an adoring spouse, and with the constant recognition of being a sinful, yet justified, creature approaching his hidden creator God. Fear and trembling, love and faith, humility and confidence—with all of these, Apostolos approached the throne of his God of mercy and grace.

But not only this Father God being prayed to in the name of his Son—there was also this mysterious Spirit by whom Apostolos said that he prayed. Even this Spirit was involved and fervently interceded for the prayers of Apostolos. This mystery—or as Anthro saw it, this contradiction—of Father, Son, and Holy Spirit apparently all being God, and yet there still being only one God, was on Anthro's mental agenda to confront Apostolos with as well. But since learning about the man's past, Anthro had been far more patient with his questioning. He was more careful to enquire about Apostolos himself, knowing that in time, his questions would at least be given a thoughtful response. Even with that knowledge, Anthro knew what must come next.

"You know that you're free to go, right?" Anthro said as he took a seat of fallen timber opposite Apostolos. Besides the usual sentries in the main camp below them, they were the only ones awake to greet the freshness of the morning.

"Free?" Apostolos was just becoming aware of his company.

"It's been over five months since that first night. Don't you want to be free?" Anthro was staring at him through the thin haze, but Apostolos kept his gaze fixed upon the pile of ash. He took a stick and swirled the remnants of flame once more to draw out final life.

"Freedom? I believe that freedom is overvalued." A slight smile came over his face.

"You don't think humans should be free?" The morning grogginess was quickly wearing off.

"From tyranny? From oppression? Of course. But freedom? In the complete and usual sense of the word, I believe there is no such thing." Apostolos looked up to meet Anthro's curious gaze.

"How can that be? Surely, those who do not serve a king are, in some sense, free? Or those citizens of other nations that have democratic reign must be free? A man with no master, no country, no children, no spouse, no responsibility—even if he is a scoundrel, he is free, is he not?" The morning artistry had reached its peak of proclamation.

"Is such a man free? Perhaps he is, in fact, a slave to his thievery. Man always has a master he serves, whether that tyrant be another man, a driving ideology, or an unquenchable vice." They both turned from each other in order to appreciate the display of light and color on the glowing horizon, but their conversation continued.

"But still, if the man is serving himself and no other—and his will is to do as he wills, and he is able—is that not freedom?" Anthro asserted.

"Ah, is there no greater slave master than that of the self? It is not of wisdom that one thinks a will free to do as the self demands is in fact free. There is a deep and frightful bondage in such a reality. True freedom is only found in surrender, is only found in denial." Apostolos paused before he came to his point. "I have freedom enough in the truth that the King of Lux has given me. In him I have freedom from many things, but perhaps what I hold most dearly is the freedom that he has given me *from self*. Having lost my life, it has been saved. The king has rid me of that most demanding of task masters; he has delivered me from that most frightful of tyrants who cannot find satisfaction no matter how full. He has cast down that unending, idolatrous nature of autonomous, individualistic self-expression. I am free, for it is no longer I who live—but oh, how I have life." His last sentence remained in the air as dew does in shade.

Being free from the self . . . that's not an entirely new thought. It certainly strikes at the very heart of Tenebris's understanding of the sovereign self, but I've come across something similar before. Those monks followed a similar way, talking of freedom from desire and the illusion of the self. They claimed enlightenment and peace are found in losing oneself—in becoming one with all. In being nothing and yet being in all things. But did they confess to have this kind of life that Apostolos declares to have? And surely

Apostolos's views deeply contradict the many so-called illusions of this life. But still this overlap of freedom from self. Why?

And not just here, but over and over again. This man's beliefs converge with so many other views. It's never exact, but there are always connections. It's as if blind men all had their hands on a great beast with varying parts, each touching something but failing to recognize the whole thing. It would be the height of arrogance to merely assume to be an enlightened man with distant sight. For even if just to say that all the others were blind, one would have to assume that he, in fact, had sight enough to see that. Such a claim would be one of superior knowledge, and in essence, would not be of a different kind than all the others. Just a bit cockier. Perhaps even more blind. To say that all other beliefs are talking about different parts of the same whole is a statement of belief similar to all other claims, nothing more.

But what if the beast spoke? The men are blind, not deaf. What if it could describe the variances and yet interpret how they came together as one? When it comes to knowing the nature of reality, one has to wonder, in light of the King of Lux: What if the creator spoke? What if the creator, whom many were still groping for in darkness, came here to give light? Came here as the light?

Apostolos isn't saying that every belief system is entirely wrong—quite the contrary. When I think of the beliefs found in our own history and in the nations less affected by Tenebris, it is actually Tenebris stating that all of those past peoples were woefully ignorant and completely off base. Apostolos is asserting that the majority of them were actually close—certainly closer than Tenebris—but they were still grasping in the darkness of sin, at times connecting with various truths, but just missing the Truth.

Apostolos coughed, drawing Anthro's presence back out of the realm of thought and reminding him of what still needed to be said. It was more necessary than ever. "Apostolos, I've told you that you're free—in the sense of no longer being my captive, anyway—and still you remain here. Why?"

"Simply stating my freedom to go shall have no effect on

my circumstances. As long as you are still a searching man, and do not turn me nor my king away in finality, I shall be joyfully shackled to your quest." His ovoid brown eyes reflected the bright light of the rising sun as they met each other's stares once more. Could such radically different men ever come to a mutual confession of ultimate truth?

Nearly a minute of silence persisted. Anthro knew the time had come; he must speak. He must say it now. He did not trust himself to voice it at another time.

"Apostolos . . . I want you to go."

Apostolos did not flinch.

"No, I need you to go." Anthro hesitated. He knew what he was asking.

There was no hasty response from Apostolos, but after a protracted pause he began, "I will do as you wish." Slowly his agile body rose, his muscles taxed by time, but still nimble. His joints ached with age, but still spry. His voice was even heavier than usual. "Anthro, it has been my—"

"Apostolos," Anthro interrupted. "I need you to go. I'm asking you to go . . . but I *beg you* to return." He quickly stood up. "If you are truly bound to my pursuit of truth, then I plead with you; leave here and go wherever you must for you . . ." Anthro, for reasons even deeper than he knew, was afraid to ask, but he had to make this request. Conviction overcame anxiety. ". . . for you to bring me back those reports of your God in flesh."

It was out. He wanted to face them; he wanted to face *him*. Anthro desired to read the full testimony of the King of Lux, not without doubt, but neither with forced conclusions. What could this king say to him? Would his words cut through him, or would they fly overhead? What actually happened to this man? Who was he? *What* was he? How did he die? *Why* did he die? Was it *possible* that he had risen? Anthro was ripe to see for himself.

* * * *

Preparations were being made to have Apostolos travel to the southwestern border of Vanus, where he said that a small group of the King of Lux's followers were secretly established. He referred to the place as an Ekklesia and spoke of the people there with a particular fondness in his voice. That is where the additional parchments were being collected and sent back to Apostolos's homeland. Apparently, a great number had been found and were now being analyzed with what his people had retained to ensure the most accurate transmissions of the texts were being performed.

Anthro had discovered that this people's understanding of their scriptures was far from simplistic. He had probed Apostolos at length about these religious texts as soon as he came to realize this had been the man's goal in Culpam: finding older versions of his religion's scriptures to ensure the highest levels of accuracy. This people did not believe the divine inspiration of their texts meant that the books fell from the heavens, nor that the original writers had entered into a trancelike state as they composed them. By the text's own admission, it was even possible for uninspired words to be added and for inspired words to be taken away from their copies.

In fact, the work of Apostolos and others commissioned by the Ekklesia had resulted in a passage or two being removed from the current copies of their scriptures, including what had once been a beloved story about a forgiven adulterous woman. No matter the sentimental value, his people had no tolerance for any post-apostolic additions to their texts (that is, the work of any besides those messengers who were commissioned by the King of Lux directly when he walked this world to establish the foundation of his universal Ekklesia). Some of this had bothered Anthro greatly and he questioned how a belief system could be under the authority of such scriptures.

Apostolos had recognized Anthro's concerns but had pressed the point that ontologically the words within the scriptures—including their relationship to their meanings—were inherently different from standard human texts. By the nature of what God had ordained and the means by which he had chosen to use his Word, despite the need for interpretation, translation, and other various nuances, it was—by its very nature—infallible and authoritative.

The status of the written texts themselves was not the primary concern. Even though Apostolos had much to say about the positive validity of its current state, the Word itself could never be truly lost, no matter the condition of the manuscripts on hand. The Word was ultimately *immaterial* in its nature and had merely been given through a physical means. Thus, the original documents were of great importance, but not required for sure faith and true governance.

Anthro still had several reservations about such holy texts, but Apostolos had advised him—as one not within the covenant family of the king's people—to simply read them as he would any other document of antiquity, without ignoring the knowledge that these had superior testimony and more reliability than any other ancient documents known to humanity. Furthermore, he pointed out that the very fact that Apostolos's people had removed small sections of manuscripts actually increased the reliability of the far greater majority of the remaining texts. In all fairness, the fact that a part could be shown to be inauthentic within a faithfully derived, textually critical method added to the authenticity of the parts that survived such criticism.

This Ekklesia was also where a large number of completed

books were being sent in preparation for the retaking of a fallen land. The attack would be driven not by weapons of warfare such as swords and arrows, hatred and violence—weapons of the flesh—but through a divine power set to besiege the height of wayward speculations and determined to destroy the fortresses of philosophical captivity. The fight would move forward through armaments of the Spirit, weapons of love and truth, and soldiers of self-sacrificing service brandishing the weapons of the Word.

Apostolos had said that Tenebris—and several of the surrounding kingdoms—had once served the King of Lux in a past not rightly remembered, a past filled with dubious reconstructions. His own nation (and many of the lands across the wide sea) had been brought the message, the gospel of the King of Lux, from Tenebris itself. The message had spread with fragmented growth like seed scattered widely across a field of various soils, yet water for the sprouted crop had eventually stopped coming as persecution in these lands had intensified. Ancient Tenebris believers displayed so much urgency in the beginning to promote the message of the king, only to neglect what had been initiated.

Spiritual confusion had set in across Apostolos's own lands; cults, heretical sects, and false teachings had arisen with force. The early Tenebris believers had been so eager to make converts that they had failed to properly train those who had believed. Failure to faithfully and patiently disciple had led to the gross malnourishment of the fields of faith now littered with many weeds. But not all was lost; steps had been taken to preserve what remained. Plans were being made to not only strengthen his own lands, but also to recover those of Tenebris and the surrounding nations.

Following the great outreach and then the initial decades of silence, envoys had been sent to learn what had caused the shift. Apostolos's great ancestors were shocked to observe what had transpired. A great darkening had fallen over the land. Toxin had seeped into philosophy, ego had cut out the backbone of science, and the very beliefs that had been the bedrock for human equity and reform had been discarded frivolously, as if all those who had fought to win such freedoms were mindless and ignorant fools.

Arrogance abounded. Chronological snobbery spread like gangrene. Exaltation of man birthed his demise. Yet ironically, Tenebris still retained some semblance of the very values wrought from the coming of the King of Lux, from the work of his servants, and from the arguments of his people. The people of Tenebris had thanked him for his radical, self-giving love and then told him to return to his tomb. They had taken his gentle hand toward slaves, children, and women, and acted as if their own free-roaming reasoning was sufficient to protect the poor from the power of the rich and the weak from the rule and dominion of the strong. They deluded themselves into thinking they did not need God to uphold human worth; they gnawed through the blessed restraints of moral objectivity, tore down the pillars of veracity, and demolished the foundations of inherent human equality. Confessing themselves enlightened, they walked blindly into the heights of human folly as they ripped apart reason, dismantled dignity, and trampled upon truth. Beelzebul was simply awakening them to their own contradictions.

Such was Apostolos's view of history, though Anthro had searched the past enough to contest various interpretations of those views. Still, the foreigner had offered a fresh and detailed perspective that shed light on the many fractured pillars that were still invisibly upholding Tenebris's ideals.

Apostolos was not strictly one-sided in his condemnation,

for he was swift to point out the many failures of the King of Lux's followers along the way. Some he confessed were beyond egregious. However, Apostolos was just as quick to remind Anthro (who was all too ready to jump upon these criticisms) that he was continually critiquing those of the past for not living up to the king's own code of conduct. Remove the king and there was great difficulty in maintaining the rebuke, aside from asserting values that found a much surer foundation within the king himself. With the king, the critiques were valid; the condemnation of all atrocity, no matter the allegiance of the condemner, was well founded.

Furthermore, Apostolos had little concern in a return of political power in the name of the King of Lux. His desire was for the truth to spread, the poor to be served, and the king's servants to live in humble subjection to the government, regardless of its confession. As critical as Apostolos was of the history of Tenebris, he was every bit as trenchant against the desire for power expressed by many who had claimed to serve the King of Lux. If political power came, God be praised; if it did not, God be praised. The abuses of and unbecoming struggles for worldly power had no place within this mysterious Kingdom of Lux.

* * * *

After yet another discussion on the history of Tenebris and the King of Lux, Anthro lay restlessly in his tent, unable to sleep because one aspect of all of this talk was not adding up. There was something cloaked within the histories told by Apostolos that lacked a proper connection. Anthro had focused his search for truth within history, and he simply could not believe that the initial revolution of the King of Lux—with all its magnitude and implications—could lie completely buried out of sight without even the slightest trace of its confessors.

However, Anthro had made a few minor connections; increasingly, things that had seemed to be simple trinkets of the past were linked with the king. He could determine that much. But there was still this tremendous expanse of disconnect. Historical revisionism just could not be as powerful as Apostolos declared it had been, no matter how determined its fabricators were. But how? How could such a gap exist?

Late in the night, after hours of consideration, a wave of insight arose within him. A dawn of understanding emanated from the ashes of this hidden history.

Yes. This is it. But even this seems almost too much . . . could they really have let it happen? Could they actually have been the ones to proffer such a monumental distortion prior to the modern touch of Tenebris? But it fits. It even links with much of Apostolos's account. Ever since I came across the first words of this king's parchment, I've failed to look here . . . for they were that far from his Word.

From within his scattered puzzle of historical recollections, Anthro recalled a group of spiritual people who had so hated the term religion, and so neglected their own holy sacraments, that they must have driven a fatal stake into the chests of their precious inner relationships. This group was so determined to convert all that they themselves had been indoctrinated by the world whom they had sought to save. They were an entire people who were ignorant of the depths of the law while overflowing with empty and endless moralism. They hid teachings of truth so far behind therapeutic practices that all true meaning of grace had vanished from sight. As the darkening onslaught pressed in against the sacred walls surrounding what must have been the fading house of those supposed Trinitarians, all that could be found within was a den of doctrine-less deism.

The first fruits of the darkness came forth from within the ranks of those confessing followers of light. But this king . . . even I know that he did not come to bring peace, but the sword. By his very claims he must have sought to bring global division, not universal unity. Would he not set a father against son and a son against father? A mother against daughter and a daughter against mother? By the very nature of his teachings, if they were held truly by the devout, would they not cause a man's enemies to be those within his own household? Surely the king came to ignite a fire never to be doused. Let the beliefs die before being watered down to that level of compromise, diluted beyond all recognition. I can think of only two reasons for such treachery . . . for I know them well: the pride of man . . . and the fear of man.

*   *   *   *

The night before the onset of the invasion of Ultimus was spent in rare celebration. Kegs of mead were tapped, and even Apostolos—to the utter astonishment of Anthro and his men—partook of the sweet nectar, although he was sure to keep a sober spirit even in his joy.

The majority of the army simply believed their commander was strengthening their spirits before another march. But for those in Anthro's circle, it was a time of farewell. Apostolos, Harpazo, Themata, and a handful of their own selected spears would be heading south as the main army crossed the northern border. The journey was not expected to be of a great duration, but the occasion would not pass without parade.

The moon was bright as it displayed its fullness. The air had the first tastes of cooler seasons upon it. The kegs had been bled dry, the buffet of meat scraped clean. Besides the most unfortunate guardians of the camp who had drawn poor lots, only two remained awake in conversation, once more beside a smoldering blaze. A protracted lull in the varied (and unusually light) discussions had allowed for Anthro's mind to drift back into deeper waters. The tangle of his thoughts moved with a bit more freedom from the blessings of the drink. And as his thoughts consolidated, his proud tongue also worked with far more than its usual privilege.

"Apostolos, let's just say that everything you have been telling me over the last half-year is true. I'm not saying you're right, and I'm certainly not confessing your king, but . . . for . . ." Even with liquid courage he hesitated.

"For the sake of the argument." Apostolos generously gave him the words.

"Yes, for the sake of the argument, let's assume your king is true. What . . . what do you think he'd do with me? I mean, Apostolos, I've done some horrible things. I've bathed in atrocities that I don't think you can even imagine. I am a man laden with the guilt of human blood. I ought to be a fugitive until death. I've never denied my sin—my sins. You know that's not a part of my objections. But then again . . . maybe . . . just maybe . . . I don't think that I am worthy of someone like him. Of a king like him. Of a God like him." Given a million sober attempts, those words would never have escaped the prison of his mind. He remained temperate enough to feel the growing warmth in both a rising blush and an awakening stain.

Apostolos sat there quietly, his response not yet discernible, not yet assembled. The dying fire made him barely visible to Anthro. Even with this finite vision, Anthro was able to perceive Apostolos rubbing his thumb across his lower lip, back and forth, back and forth—listlessly, methodically. It was an odd gesture; the man had never done it before in Anthro's sight.

"Who could be worthy?" The words were slow. "Not I." The words were certain.

"Keta," Anthro said with a slight laugh, managing to get a

snicker from Apostolos. Anthro meant it, but he knew he was already speaking for the sake of the argument, so he continued. "How do you do it, then? I've heard your story, but if you knew mine in full, you'd think even your past sanctified by mere contrast. If you feel the conviction, how do you still approach such light?"

Another enduring hiatus. Once more that curious migration of digit across lower lip. The movement stopped abruptly, as if Apostolos only then became aware of the activity. More reserve, then finally, "By listening to him, and not to me."

"What do you mean?" Anthro's speech was a mixture of both hunger and waver.

As soon as he started to speak, though Anthro could not see it, he was certain that the frosted look that occasionally overcame Apostolos's gaze as he spoke of his king was once again present. The man's voice dripped of freedom. Anthro envied the familiarity with which Apostolos spoke.

"Come to me, all who are weary and heavy-laden, and I will give you rest. Shall the fatigued stand aloof? Shall the burdened not come forth? If anyone is thirsty, let him come to me and drink, and from his innermost being will flow rivers of living water. Shall the parched not cup their hands? Shall the barren soul not indulge a spring whose waters never fail? It is not those who are healthy who need a physician, but those who are sick; I did not come to call the righteous, but sinners. Shall the dying not seek life from such a herald of grace? Shall the sinful flee the surgeon of their soul's condition? Let you, oh prodigal, who claim unworthiness of being called a son, or a daughter, come and be given my finest clothing, my personal ring, and let us banquet together in reconciliation. Shall those in the pigsties of their rebellious ruin still wallow in their filth? Shall the wayward children not greet their Father's open arms? Anthro, shall those who feel their stains of scarlet, of crimson, of red—those who know they belong with the dead—shall men such as us not bathe in the blood that washes whiter than snow? He says come. The king says come. For me—even me—he says come. For you—even you—he says come. He is the way. You've only to go. You've only to come." If ever darkness could be relinquished by sound, the light from Apostolos's words would have accomplished the task.

Chapter XVIII

The Three in One

Though his army was still a day's march from beholding the first walls of Ultimus, the scouts had declared that the proud, wind-tossed flags of each turret had been raised inverted. The garrison flags, likewise, waved in surrender. Victory wrought by mere approach.

Too good to be true. Will it really be this easy? As the foreign menace violates your border, shall you roll over, defeated like a terrified mutt? Shall you lick the muzzle of this rabid beast at your door?

With his army now set, following the rise of the next day's sun, the capsized banners flew and the gates were raised, simply inviting invasion. There was new movement from the city that revealed a trio of horses and their riders cantering through the apparent invitation and yet, the egress was kept open; the drawbridge was not lifted even after this small cohort crossed it. The riders were on fine war horses, both man and animal were wrapped in elegant armor. However, the beasts were ready for battle while the men were coming forth only to yield.

Anthro, fully arrayed in his own armor and riding his ever-faithful warhorse of grand stature, pressed forward to meet these men of appeasement. Symmetrically strafed by ten on his left and ten on his right, Anthro approached the trio. He would demand complete surrender or total destruction. There were no other options.

Nearing a distance of where they could see the whites of each other's eyes, the parties halted. A young man, noble in the face, came forth just beyond his fellow riders. With the pride of youth and the voice of age he spoke, "Hail! General of the Army of Tenebris!"

"Hail!" His two shadows echoed.

Anthro eyed the man, boring into his determined eyes. Such confidence in resignation. The young leader was garbed in a full array of polished steel, shining with intricate craftsmanship from his flawless combed helm down to his garnished greaves. The armor of a king. Such elegance in defeat. Anthro liked him immediately. He urged his horse a few prominent steps forward. "The General greets you; for whom do you speak?"

The man raised his chin in a pompous way and delayed a response, seemingly relishing this last moment of power before giving even his title. "I am the King of Pax, sovereign district of Southern Ultimus."

"Is it a habit of your king's to ride out to terms?" Anthro's horse snorted as its wild eyes beheld those of its own four-legged foe.

"Only if in a desperate plea for mercy to be shown to his own subjects."

Wind blew across the field, the gentle bite in the air refreshing for those in the heat of armor. "Mercy is never without cost." Anthro said the words with forceful grace. This could be his brother. This could be his friend, their wildest dangers found only in competitive horse races across these arid forest lands that adorned this handsome country. In another life. In a distant dream. In a world not fallen.

"Will a king suffice for pardon?" His horse reared on two,

neighing fiercely, lamenting the words of its master.

"I will ensure that it does, Your Highness." Anthro lowered his head and stuffed the fullest amount of dignity he could supply into those final words.

"You have my most sincere gratitude, General." Then came a reciprocated bow of honor, dark hazel eyes meeting emerald death.

Companions. Devoted allies. Travel and adventure. Warm fires and deep talks. Songs and laughter. Drinks and stories. Friends and brothers.

War. Fixed enemies. Battle and surrender. Stayed arms and fire power. Victory and defeat. Hero and villain. Sacrifice and executioner.

It's never good. It's never easy.

*   *   *   *

Forty-eight thousand hooves pounded into the soil across the expansive tundra. On the distant horizon stood the city's noble walls. They would fight. This district of the north would not yield. Nor would they wait for fire to fall upon them as they cowered in their cage. They would charge. They *did* charge . . . in open combat. In one last stand.

Nevertheless, fire rained down, the craters forming open graves. Many fell. Yet still, more rode. Arrows became dark, angry clouds. More plummeted from their mounts. Hundreds were expelled to a painful death. Fewer rode. Even then, they lowered lances. Nonetheless, they jeered with reckless abandon. His army met them. Not one remained.

*   *   *   *

In just four short months, Ultimus was on the verge of complete defeat. Six states had either surrendered or been brought into a forced subjugation; only two, those western guardians of the coast, remained.

The early winter's first snow had just fallen as Anthro's army camped once more on the edge of fresh combat. Even with a continent against them, neither of the two states would freely surrender. Both would fall, but on their own terms and not those of Tenebris. However, despite the looming frustration of the needless prolonging of bloodshed, not all was winter in Anthro's heart; Apostolos had returned, and with him were the four testimonies of the King of Lux's life in the flesh.

Anthro was well aware that this was not the entire word of the king, for he had been instructed that two entire covenants comprising sixty-six books all bore witness to him. By prophetic exclamation, through a web of types and antitypes, in an assortment of lesser precursors, with pages of shadows and mysteries, with stanzas of light and clarity, an entire cannon witnessed to the coming of the King of Lux.

Then, with a new covenant having been wrought in his blood, there were additional commands, further exposition, complete fulfillment, and even more narrative of his works accomplished from his hidden throne of authority. These four books—which Apostolos now carried with him—were not superior in their proclamation nor in their authority, but they were the clearest depiction of the events that had transpired while the King of Lux walked among his own. They were the direct reports of who this man was—whatever he may be—and, if any writings could, they would shed the most light as to what to make of his death and his rising. If such a spectacular feat could be confirmed, or if it was believed in with sound reason, would not the rest of the books fall easily under the authority of such a belief? Indeed, this fact was the only one that promised such luminosity; no other defense would take its place. The direct message of this king's cross would not be made void.

And yet, Anthro could not get around one last nagging annoyance, one confounding stumbling block to his reason, before seriously approaching these books. The last several months, he had twisted his mind every which way to seek harmony with triunity, but to no avail. Therefore, at his request, he delayed, for one more night, the reading aloud of the books within the circle of his confidante.

* * * * *

Apostolos moved his hand under the log that he was sitting on, groping within it for a few seconds before taking out a wilted green plant that was soon to perish after this season's first snow. Apostolos held the clover up, displaying the varying sides, but never once looked at Anthro. The man just sat there staring at the clover, in apparent awe. It was a simple three-leafed clover, but Anthro knew that some lesson was eventually going to proceed from it.

Many of Apostolos's instructions and metaphors were drawn from nature and agriculture. To Anthro, that was just fine; he was slowly finding such exposition and analogies most helpful in gathering a better understanding of these beliefs in the things unseen. The two men were alone. The brown graveyard of fallen leaves was protected in part from the assailing white above by frosted branches of evergreen. Apostolos and Anthro were preparing to discuss the nature of God's being, and somehow they were now silently sitting together in a snow-covered forest and staring at a clover. Oddly enough, this type of thing was starting to feel normal to Anthro.

Who is this God you want me so desperately to believe in, Apostolos? Or, better yet, what is he? This only God. This God consisting of three Gods. Father, Son, Holy Spirit—three not one. Is polytheism really any more of a stretch than just plain theism? But this—this Trinity—just what is it? This bizarre belief. This three and one, one and three, three in one, one in three—this wildest of reaches for an explanation of God. I've heard nothing like it. Who would come up with such a doctrine of confusion?

I suppose that in some way, it almost feels right. It seems so utterly removed from human imagination, as if this idea itself was unlikely to arise by merely speculative human origins. And on this point, of all details, Apostolos is adamant—fanatical almost—that this is a nonnegotiable truth to affirm for anyone wishing to confess the King of Lux as Lord. In so many concepts of the man's religion he allows for charity despite disunity. Not with Trinity.

Despite his general confusion, Anthro found Apostolos to be rather consistent in holding tenaciously to the necessity of this doctrine, were it to be found true. This was an ontological confession of the one true God. Could a true worshipper of this God not be led to a correct (even if simply understood) confession of his very nature? Certainly, some lasting confusion could be understandable, but would it not be ludicrous to believe that one who actively rejected or warred against the very nature of the true God actually knew him? What would this lesson from the clover reveal? From where Anthro's conception was currently at, the clover could not do anything to hurt his actual understanding of the concept.

"Anthro, do you see this clover?" Apostolos's voice snapped Anthro out of his thoughts. "Look closely at it. Look at its formation, its structure. Never mind this one's sad appearance; think of a clover in all its summer glory! Observe how the three leaves are attached to the one steam; do you see? Three projections flowing from the one structure. Good. Now this is of the utmost importance, Anthro; God is absolutely *not* like that."

Well, that was not where I thought he was going with the analogy. God's essence is not like a clover. Got it. But what could possibly be an acceptable analogy for the three-in-one factor that Apostolos is so determined to defend? "All right, God is not like the clover. Simple enough. But then what *is* he like?"

"Patience. We must approach this slowly and tread cautiously. Do you understand, Anthro? We are talking about the very nature of the eternal and only true God. *The* creator. *The* sustainer. The only one who simply just *is*. It is in his self-sustaining nature to simply *be*. The aseity of deity. Shall we approach such a God with hasty feet? No, we dare not—not when describing who he is."

Apostolos stopped speaking for over five minutes as he simply observed the gentle brook and watched the ivory squirrels chatter among the trees. His silence was a visual reinforcement for the patience required with this subject.

"Anthro," Apostolos began.

Finally!

"We must be slow. We must be cautious." Fifteen more minutes of silence.

For the first ten minutes or so, Anthro's mind was racing as he sifted through the possibilities of who this God was and how to describe him. Finally, his mind settled as humility began to quiet his thoughts. The remaining time was one of his most peaceful moments in recent memory.

"Anthro," Apostolos said his name as if their conversion had never paused, "observe the stream. Do you see the water, how it flows? Do you see the ice, how it stands firm? Do you remember the steam rising from the melting snow by our camp? Think of those three. Ice. Water. Steam." Anthro could follow this, he could begin to see this concept of God forming within his mind.

"They are three states of one substance, are they not?" Apostolos asked and Anthro nodded vigorously. His understanding was coming together as various thoughts were harmonizing. "Good. I am glad you understand that. Now, you must know—you absolutely need to see—that God is *not* like that."

Anthro slapped his forehead. "You're killing me, Apostolos! So, not like a clover, and not like water. Got it. But how is this helping? Or, better yet, *why* don't those analogies work?"

Apostolos might have concealed a slight grin, but he spoke with his usual reverent seriousness. "The clover analogy divides God into three parts of one whole. It creates parts out of those who are completely whole. The three persons of the Trinity are not divisible from God's being, nor are they a *part* of God. We must remember the fundamental simplicity of God; he is *one*. All the while, we must keep in mind that the *persons* of the Trinity are not to be confused with *parts*. In contrast to each leaf being a part of the clover, *all* persons of the godhead are *fully* God.

"Neither are Father, Son, and Holy Spirit mere presentations of a single *person* of God. They are neither modes nor expressions of God. They are unique *persons* of *the* unique *being*. Hence, the water analogy denies the Trinity completely. Ultimately, such a view of God, when it takes a doctrinal form, rejects the core tenet of initiation into God's family; that is, being baptized in the *one name* of the Father, of the Son, and of the Holy Spirit."

Anthro rubbed his chin, trying to comprehend. "I followed half of that. But isn't all this just saying that there are three things that are fully making up themselves, and yet they all fully make up only one thing? Unless math is different in your country, isn't one plus one plus one equal to three, not one?"

"Anthro, I see your confusion, but that is not what I am articulating. It is helpful to remember that God's *three-ness* is *different* from his *one-ness*. He is three *persons* in one *being*. When we speak of the Trinity, we are referring to only one *what* and three *whos.*"

Anthro thought for several minutes, and Apostolos let his mind process. Finally, after some time, Anthro spoke. "And this is necessary to believe?"

Apostolos held a strange look in his eyes, one completely new to Anthro. "Anthro, truly I say to you, following the King of Lux is a hard road. It is a narrow path that will cost you much. You will not find the word 'Trinity' in our books, but you will see it *everywhere*. It is the very revelation of God's redeeming act and is required by an incarnate Son and an outpoured Spirit. Truly, don't waste your time trying to follow after the King of Lux if you fail to accept this doctrine. It is not against reason, but it is beyond the heights of the finite to fathom in full. Did you really expect the true and living God to be just like you?"

Anthro was silent. Despite his confusion, he could sense a compelling mystery beneath it all as if this God—and only this God—would mock and laugh at every other attempt to declare who he was. Here was a truly *godlike* God. A deity so separate from humanity . . .

And yet he claims to have come to us in his Son . . . to become like us . . . to be murdered by us. What a claim.

"Anthro, I know that the majesty and mystery of my God takes time to ponder. But do not think this is all some dry form of cold doctrine. The implications are vast!"

From there, Apostolos began to describe the wonders of what a triune God meant for the world. Not only was this triunity the secret of God's beauty, but it also showed that the creation of the world was not necessary for God but was an overflow of his eternal love! Indeed, Trinity is how God has *always* been love!

Apostolos had only just finished the last word when Anthro uttered, "That is perhaps the most terrifying concept I've ever heard of or could ever have imagined."

Apostolos looked at him, baffled beyond belief—unable to conceive of how the love of God could be terrifying. "I'm not sure I understand. I don't deny the frightening aspects of my God, but how do you see it here, of all places? As I said, God *is* love! And this love is forever exchanged and flows between the three persons of God in a relational connection that forms a radical harmony of love and beauty and doctrine. I see no terror—not here."

Anthro smirked like a witness on the stand about to shatter the court's expectations. "I guess you've only seen the beauty of such a love within God and expressed among his persons because . . . you're on the inside of it."

As if obscured by a wintry mist of dazzling attraction, Apostolos showed no signs of comprehension. "Inside of it? I'm not saying that I'm a part of my God. Don't think I'm . . ."

"You misunderstand me," Anthro interrupted, still with an almost guilty smirk on his face. "I mean, you are inside *of the love of God*. If I understand your theology correctly, the Father has bestowed the same love that he expresses toward the Son upon you and all who are like you, am I right?"

"Yes. It is a love we believers now share as his children, but only through the work of the Son." The snow from above was strengthening and starting to find its way down beyond the canopy overhead.

"Of course. But that's just it; remember, you're on the *inside*. I'm not. If you're right about my rebellion against God and the Trinity and the love that exists within God, then he who does not pay homage to the Son or the Spirit insults the Father *because* of his love *for them*, invoking not a selfish reaction of mere displeasure—even if that were warranted—but a revulsion at the dishonor shown to those whom the Father loves infinitely and eternally. It is that infinite love their triune affection shares that will—if it is anything remotely like our own finite love—ignite his jealousy and anger and rage, precisely because of the fact that God is love." Large flakes of the pure powder were now falling upon them.

Apostolos spent some time in thought, oblivious to the increasing chill. "Anthro, I've never thought of that before. Truly, there is so much I've yet to learn. But it . . . it could be. It makes sense to me. I've just never looked at God's love from that angle before."

Anthro laughed with a friendly mock, brushing off the accumulating winter on his shoulders. "Well, enjoy the view from the inside for me. I know love. I know affection. There is no more deadly alignment possible than to be against the love that one has for another. To be hostile toward this God of love that you preach is not to ignite a self-centered, focused fury; it is to come against an infinite consuming fire of relational outrage of a triune jealous love. It's a terrifying thought." Pure white snow blanketed the ground with the remnants of decaying life hidden by the reign of this infinite perfection from above.

Chapter XIX

The Revelation of God

Far in the distance trumpets sang. Off in another land there was song and dance and celebration. Over hills and beyond mountains the report of victory had spread. A single banner now cast its shadow across the land, from coast to coast, from north to south, from west to east. Tenebris had triumphed. The fires of Beelzebul's vision had been unleashed upon the world and the blaze had consumed all that it could reach. The dragon's breath could now rest having accomplished its work. The ash would settle, fertilizing the freshly plowed lands. A phoenix would rise from the earth, united, prosperous, beautiful, healthy, and strong. No knight would rise up against either beast, none would wage war against such power and authority, such wisdom and might. Beelzebul had won.

With his shoulders divided by bark once more, Anthro took in a view from another perch, his emerald eyes both haunted and hopeful. He sat alone, his thoughts as vast as the watery expanse before him. The ocean was a deep, majestic blue, and misted by a ghostly cover of fog. He looked into a sea of the unknown, contemplating a future that looked all too certain. The splendor of these waters was not lost on him, though. The ever-churning, briny movement of the liquid wilderness was a wonder and mystery that reflected a light within that could not be silenced. From this bluff he beheld only a fragment, but it spoke to him about the whole.

Endless swells were rising from dark depths and crashing against the shoreline of stone and weathered lumber long since extracted from its lofty grasp on the rigid mountainside. The roaring of the waves was both calming and disquieting with their liquid awe and raw power. Beasts of flippered feet sat haughtily along the coastline, unfazed by the mist of the surf, impervious to the inclemency of the icy waters from which new creatures were emerging. These surfacing rulers of the sea blew geysers of breath from their bodies of brilliant black and wild white. As they moved in unison, their blending forms appeared as a flowing calligraphy written upon the canvas of life. It was as if their movements, their lives, their breath, their hunger, their chase, their beauty, and their grace—as if their very beings were the penmanship of that preeminent poet of perpetual ingenuity.

Although they could hunt all within their liquid domain, this day they surrounded schools of scale and gill. Their orchestrated actions were filled with craftsmanship and complexity. Chattering above Anthro were furry creatures that bounded upon roadways of branch and needle. Soaring before him was a being of feather and talon, showboating its aeronautic abilities as it glided effortlessly along the currents of its abode. Every realm had been given both its rulers and subjects. These creatures, all of them—their patterns, their measure, their number, their order—though they spoke no words, they seemed bent upon being understood. They laughed at their contingency. They danced at their reality.

Anthro absorbed the feelings of freedom and phenomenon, knowing that his mind and heart were called to more than perpetual speculation and eternal wandering. Everywhere he had been in this world of the living, there was always this presence of ecosystem—countless ecological communities of variation and uniformity. Before his eyes, the black and white creatures were somersaulting along the edge of their prey, tightening the circular school as their comrades shot through the bountiful harvest.

What intelligence these creatures displayed. Even the actions that seemed random to Anthro were surely compatible with the animal's overarching tactics. The intricate entrapment of their prize was a work of design that would make even the most masterful of Anthro's defeated enemies envious of such tactical artistry. Intelligence. Design. Anthro saw them everywhere in nature. They were omnipresent in life.

Life itself was an overflowing composition of pervasively complex information that bore witness to its masterful informer. This development of diverse creatures defeated nature's corrupting influences at every turn. From the intricacy and delicacy of each interconnected ecosystem to the technical features inherent to all living things; from the tiniest building blocks of life itself to the mightiest beasts of land, sea, and air; each type of being was crafted for its environment with a sophistication that even the most grandiose fabrications of human engineering would covet. No amount of devolving nor degenerative activity could obscure that reality. Natural selection's true efficacy was to refine what already was, for it lay forever slave to the requirements of novel, inventive insight. Life survives, because it was *made* to be fit.

Creation.

The word thundered in his mind, echoing across every fiber of his being.

Created by . . .

a . . .

no, more than that.

the . . .

Creator.

Anthro was a theist.

There was no single proposition that tipped the scales of belief within him. No. It was the cumulative weight of thoughtful existence itself, as if ten thousand signposts had been scattered throughout human experience and observation that all pointed toward this great confession. Some were grand clues plastered upon human morality. Others were subtle signals traced through the power of beauty and through that deep longing to behold the source from whence it all came.

Yet, there were other signs that seemed as if they pointed another direction. Certainly, the greatest of these was that horror of human suffering. But then there was this King of Lux with whom Anthro had now become most acquainted. His very existence added a significant counterweight to even that wretched experience. In fact, without a God to ground human suffering, its own reality was little more than the inner workings of a heartless universe; that would not negate the possibility of such a reality, but it would mean that suffering was not at all a substantially significant reality. Despite humanity's deepest protests, it would be little more than the universe mindlessly weeding out the weak and no longer useful. With not just a God, but a God such as this King of Lux, there was at least evidence that spoke of the final conquering of this human condition. There was testimony to a time when every tear shall be dried, to a victory with no more pain and no more sorrow, to an endless age even devoid of death, with that greatest of enemies swallowed up in victory. Even more, there was a tangible hope for this material world to be made new, for even humanity to participate in this joyful renewal of all things.

Had Anthro never come across such claims, across one such as this King of Lux, he wondered if theism would ever look as plausible in light of the darkness of this contradictory world and with the perennial wintry gloom within his own heart. But with this king—with these reports of a God who enters time and space to show his love for this wretched race? The shift was possible, and the conversion to belief in God somehow more plausible with the mere existence of such a proposition.

That change in belief, in thought pattern, in intellectual alignment was awesome—and dreadful. Yet, in this moment, it was seemingly arbitrary to Anthro, for he knew what must come next. To believe in a god was one thing; to believe in the King of Lux was quite another. This king was no mere teacher of an unknowable deity, but he was the very exegesis of God. A fact that was only possible because the King of Lux claimed to be one with God. He and his followers declared that he was the only begotten Son of God, of his essence, and of his being. He was the radiance of God's glory and the exact imprint of his nature. He was the image of the invisible God and the fullness of deity in bodily form. Truly, he was declared to be the Son of God and God the Son.

One could drift with little practical change from atheism to mere theism. A deistic reality added minimal pressure on how one lived life and in what one confessed. Yet, here with this King of Lux was a God who demanded complete and holistic repentance, and who declared his sovereign reign over every minor action, trivial word, and scattered thought. This kind of theistic confession was all-encompassing. This was a confession of a living God, of an omnipotent God, of a *holy* God.

Over the last few weeks, Anthro had read the four books— the Gospels—over and over again. He had listened to them read aloud in his camp and he had read through them privately with

Apostolos, but now he was alone. They were beside him, stored in his pack. He had read them in full one more time with creation before his eyes, but he knew one could only delay so long. What was he going to do with the King of Lux?

Reading through these reports had brought up countless questions. Apostolos had answered some quite easily with robust satisfaction. Anthro was still unwilling to affirm some other explanations, but he had not let this stop him. Who was this king? What happened at and after his death? Those two questions dominated Anthro's readings. He knew that Apostolos had an epistemology filtered through this king's cross, that he worked from that presuppositional framework and within its many implications. And Anthro was not ignorant of many of his own presuppositions that he brought to the stand. He had learned long ago that, no matter the intellect, the most ignorant were always those who believed they themselves brought neither prior beliefs nor bias to the table of examination and evidence. The foolhardiest were certainly those who believed that they were able to recognize and freely suppress all competing external influences and attain perfect objectivity.

Apostolos believed things about these texts that Anthro refused to embrace, for now. *If* this king was who he said he was, *if* he genuinely rose from the dead, *if* these books were the Word of God, then Apostolos was altogether reasonable to affirm the complex harmony and truthfulness his religious scriptures attested to. Even if Apostolos was misguided in his belief of the king's resurrection, he was still reasonable for believing as he did. If the king had not risen from the dead, Apostolos was then mistaken, but not illogical. Apostolos did not primarily believe in the King of Lux *because* he believed in the inspired nature of every sentence of these texts; he believed in their inspiration *because* he believed their testimony about the King of Lux was true. One belief gave great merit to the other, but all belief rested upon the latter.

There was no escaping the fact that it kept coming back to that. This entire belief system structured itself around that one cornerstone. Even the king himself had asserted that those within his own spiritually idolatrous and sinful generation would be given no other sign of this type—that of his death, burial, and resurrection. Was this current generation of humanity any less set against the true God? Any less sinful? And more than that, Anthro had to admit that, taken on their own terms, the accounts were quite credible.

Not just one religious zealot, but four diverse individuals well acquainted with the king or in direct contact with his eyewitnesses, wrote these reports. Highly specific historical details filled the accounts with the casual style of simple witness-bearing. Subtle references were made to one another—coincidences even appeared from time to time—and yet these connections were not forced, but rather organically written into the narrative flow. Discrepancies? Surely. Contradictions? Anthro was hesitant to conclude that, despite some clear differences. He had studied culture, literature, and language enough to know its rich variances and hidden nuances. He had interviewed and interrogated enough witnesses to know that different perspectives did not equate to fallacious testimony. Nor did mention of a single person imply the absence of others.

Therefore, he was certain that it was expedient to give some allowances for nonfictional cultural quirks surrounding these writers and their own rules for what was allowable within a truthful narrative; possible chronological differences bothered him little. Lack of complete and blatant alignment bothered him even less. In all actuality, the fact that these writings even required a reader to consider these surface-level differences only added to their credibility; it would have been far more suspicious if every detail had been exactly replicated by each account. Such discrepancy hinted heavily toward general authenticity.

Furthermore, regardless of the judiciousness of such a set of interpretive moves, none of those factors held significant weight *against* the actual veracity of the king's death and rising. Anthro would not get lost in the finer details and fail to see the blatant and comprehensive whole that was laid clearly before him in these accounts. For it was all too clear that the writers were writing from a historical framework; this simply could not be denied. Obviously, there were theological concepts involved in these narratives, but only one lost in the clouds of awful quixotic theorizing would deny that these accounts claimed full historicity wrought through careful investigation into exact truth.

Another peculiar characteristic of these writers was their unabashed representation of themselves. The king's followers wrote these narratives, and still they were represented as weak, foolish, slow to believe, highly doubtful, and even disloyal. People trying to fabricate a story with the desire to have others follow their message would never be so unashamed in revealing their own failures.

More than that, the miracles they described were written in the way that anyone familiar with the standard workings of the natural world would describe such events. They told of astonishment by all, hysteria by many, greed from the crowds, ridicule by those in power, doubt in spite of sight, awe in the heart, confusion in the mind, and fear present in all.

Even more, there was that stubborn aspect of women being more faithful than the men, and even being the first witnesses to the King of Lux's rising. Why would men who wanted others to believe their accounts within a patriarchal society ever include such facts if they had not actually happened? Why not insert themselves or leave it out altogether if they were not trying to give the full truth?

One thing was for certain: these men believed that the King of Lux had physically risen from the dead. They were utterly convinced of it in spite of themselves.

But *why*? What reasonable explanation was there that could account for their unity of belief? Why suffer so greatly for something that you did not know to be true? These men were beaten, mocked, rejected, hunted, and killed. From the writings of the other scriptures that Anthro knew about, even the most radical for the king's cause had originally been the most violently set against it. No vague vision could accomplish such thorough conviction. Why did they all go to such great lengths, bleeding all the way to their deaths for this risen king, if they had not actually touched his pierced hands and put their own hands into his speared side? If they had not spoken with him? If they had not eaten with him? The body had been dead. No man could survive the torture described; that was beyond imagination. Even granting that ridiculous possibility, apart from the miraculous, no man could inspire others to go to such lengths if he had merely been a ruined cripple. Who would make this up? Who could make this all up? Why make any of it up? This was far from cleverly devised mythmaking. It was, without a doubt, historical eyewitness testimony, and quite compelling testimony at that.

But it's not only all of that. Credible witnesses, yes. Things I don't understand, absolutely. But it's not just the hard facts, is it? Ultimately, there is the actual King of Lux himself. The man . . . he is fascinating—humble and meek to the lame and poor, harsh and dangerous to the proud and hypocritical, open with his identity to the untouchable, a master of riddles to the elite. He speaks with such authoritative confidence but walks with a gentle love that weeps and bleeds. In a moment he abounds with compassion and in the next he is filled with rebuke. He calls all to come but is unafraid of total abandon. He holds power beyond imagination and grace beyond measure.

Is this really what it looks like when God comes to this world?

Is this really what it looks like when you come to this world?

I . . . want to know. But if . . . if he is who he says he is . . . then I know that I need you to show me. I don't want to follow a lie—not even a mistake. I want the truth. Whether it's oblivion or eternity. Whether it's a meaningless abstraction or grounded in this historical person. In this King of Lux. In you. If he's true, I can't come to you apart from him . . .

Is this prayer? Such an odd thing. Such a natural thing. Is this what it is like to talk to the hidden God? To the living God? I have so many doubts . . . but I guess they did too, right? Though he never praised it as a virtue, I did not once read of him turning the doubter away. Nor the confused. Not even those who nailed him to that tree. You could forgive them. Could you really forgive me? It would take this king; I know that much. It would take your Son. I understand that.

I can't help it. I find myself drawn to his majesty. He's mysterious. He's frightening. He's wonderful. He's believable . . . if I stop there, I've said nothing.

He is Lord. He is risen.

Though his thoughts were wild and his emotions a storm, there was no abrupt onset of endless tears of joy. A great lingering presence of doubt was still hanging in the air. Nothing miraculous seemed to have occurred. Even that haunting stain had not vanished, despite his hope for its complete banishment. It felt as if it had not been touched. All seemed rather ordinary, and yet, thanks to the sound teaching of Apostolos, Anthro knew the supernatural reality of what had just transpired despite its apparent simplicity. To confess the King of Lux as risen and as Lord of all, in genuine faith, was a tangible act of the power and work of the Spirit of the living God.

Faith. Years before Anthro would have mocked such a word, said that it was merely a crutch for the weak. In fact, he *had* ridiculed the word, but he could think such a thing no longer. Faith, quite literally, was to believe with confidence. To believe with assurance of things hoped for, conviction of things not yet fully seen. Faith was believing in what would be, based on what had been. It was not believing in something with fideistic expectations; it was trust in a person, in promises, and, in this case, in the one who had proved himself reliable beyond even death. Faith was a claim *on* reality. It was embracing a lens of existence in which competing views were mere counterclaims and counterfeits impinging upon the real thing. Faith, though it did not allow for full sight, worked alongside evidence and implied believing in such a way that one believes they have the truth, not that they are believing in spite of the truth.

Finally, as Tenebris claimed victory over the world, that is what Anthro believed. He believed that in this world of chaos, war, suffering, and death, he had been rescued from this domain of darkness and had been transferred into the Kingdom of Lux. He had found the way. He had been given life. He had come to the truth.

Chapter XX

The Two Become One

Clear panes of glass were filled with a flickering light from within. As a gentle heartbeat, the color steadily brightened and dimmed and brightened and dimmed. Shadows moved across the glowing frames, observed by passers-by as blurry ghosts of gray gliding beyond a veil, coming and going, leaving and returning, forever lingering, endlessly departing. Upon the street, where Anthro stood, the voices inside sounded rhythmic and unified. Even the glow of the windows matched the hum in the air. The melody spoke of freedom and motion—the light, of fluidity and transition.

Anthro pushed through the tavern door, now seeing the crowd in their true form. For hours, he had wandered aimlessly about the city, yet somehow he felt as if he had been heading here all along. Ever since he began his journey back to Josias to reunite with Diatris, she had been dominating his thoughts. With each step he had taken the image of her within his mind had grown in its sharpness, but also in its distance. He imagined her brow furrowed in judgement at his new beliefs. He could not escape the feeling that once he was before Diatris, her understanding would seem infallible, and his conclusions deranged—despite all that he gone through to come to them. This living fear of the immediate future ate at his newfound hope and had carved his aimless path. At last, with the mass of people before him that spectral image, and the thoughts that surrounded it, faded enough for his mind to focus.

The pub was filled with the sounds of laughter and dancing, eating and drinking, the joyful songs of merriment, or . . . perhaps not. Could it actually be that these were the echoes of a subconsciousness consuming a menu of medicinal distraction? Anthro, with a new way of looking at the world, marveled at the illusory atmosphere of supposed fulfillment and even now feared the power of such parodies to obscure a reality of far greater magnitude. Although he himself had gone into this pub in years past with similar motivations as those in attendance tonight, he could not help but think of the vast amount of superficiality before him.

Had such charades ever truly, or fully, satisfied him before? The drinks, the women, the pleasures of this world: Had they ever filled the hidden cluster of voids within his being that silence and stillness alone could remind him of? Or were they merely a tonic of diversion carefully crafted to keep him snared within a stupor of insignificance and held captive to a trance of vanity? Was all of this some form of opioid for a people who were being kept from knowing that there was more? That *they* were more? Before his eyes were the sighs of a race of oppressed creatures who were seeking to fill their supposedly soulless bodies with anything that would numb them to the true bitterness of their askew beliefs. An entire nation wore a mask of fictitious meaning and synthetic pleasure to obscure their ever-searching hearts filled with infinite dissatisfaction.

Anthro thought all of this as he pushed through the crowd, methodically making his way to a more secluded section of the tavern where he took a seat at the end of the bar. He felt odd no longer wearing a uniform, as he had officially retired with the end of the war. For now, Tenebris would not be sailing west. He had chosen to wear a dark, hooded cloak to ward off others and allow him to think in peace while yet in the company of the crowds. This had its intended effect, even on the barkeep, who was experienced enough to know when to simply ask a man his drink and then leave him be.

The mug was ice, the beer frothy and aromatic. Anthro took one long draught, deep as his thoughts, then leaned back and watched the bubbles rise within his glass as he began to reflect upon another counter-narrative. Anthro had begun following the King of Lux and had found a measure of simplicity in it. To a degree, obedience was clear: love God and neighbor with all one's strength and being and seek to follow the king in every area of one's life. Apostolos had been discipling him on the basics and Anthro had already learned much by simply having spent so much time with the king in his Gospels. Despite the simple aspects of following the king, there were also very profound thoughts that arose from these beliefs as well. Many of these surrounded his most dearly held carnality, his sexuality.

Neither man nor woman need travel as much of the world as Anthro had to understand sex's profound and unique power. Within it was a capacity to captivate the heart like no other indulgence in this world. Surely it held the potential to bind or to destroy, to give or to dominate. Sex had the force to drive men to war, the power to bring women to madness, and the wonder to cause life to begin. Anthro knew what a complex thing human sexuality was, and so did the King of Lux.

In the Kingdom of Tenebris, sex was in fashion. To know many sexually was the standard for both male and female. The body was seen as an instrument of self-expression; even one's biological structure was to be liberated from any form of governing order. To be free sexually was synonymous with being fully human. Human sexuality was many things in Tenebris, but with all the people's numerous adjectives of praise for it, never would a citizen of Tenebris declare sex to be truly *sacred*, as something *set apart*, as something fenced in by design and inherent function and something filled with a meaning beyond itself. But this King of Lux offered a different vision of sex's beauty, order, and mystery, without denying its goodness.

Anthro's views had been directly challenged, but the underlying depth of the king's way appealed to him even as it directly confronted him. At the most foundational level, the King of Lux had redefined Anthro's vision of human nature, thereby reshaping the moral landscape, imagination, and interpretation of any sexual behavior. One's sexual views were inseparable from the larger story of what it meant to be human. Anthro had always been taught that at its core, sex was about survival. Any deeper meaning than that had to be created by the person and was not inherent to the nature of sex or humanity. It could not be discovered, only made—thereby leaving it subjective, a fading ember swirling upon the drifting currents of an eternal night sky.

Anthro had long believed this story of sex, simply living with the inconsistencies that it created. Substantially, sex had been nothing more than a physical sensation and action, a temporal experience devoid of any transcendent truth. But when Diatris was in his arms—when any woman had been in his arms—none of this had seemed to matter. He had been able to drift along just fine within the confines of this story. He could create whatever was needed to fill the voids. Desire could be fulfilled, lust could be quenched, and the limits of love could be found within the experience. He knew that he could live it up; he just could not think it through. If she was only matter, how could it actually matter? If it was only necessary, how could it be free? If it was only about two bodies, what remained of the persons? If their desires were enslaved to survival, how could it be love?

Now a different story sat before him, inviting deeper thought and more grounded action. This story said that sex had been there from the beginning and that its meaning would reach fulfillment in the end. This counter-narrative flowed from the idea that God had declared sex to be a sacred bond that is never to be treated as a mere physical interaction between two bodies. And birthed from that core, it was a narrative that spoke of creaturely submission rather than of autonomous expression.

There was much to fathom, for these were deep waters of great significance. How easy it would be to assume the shallow, to gloss over the depth, to ignore even the implications in service of one's self. Anthro, who had spent nearly half his life feigning loyalty to royalty, was done living such a farce. He would bow to this king's law; however, he did not believe the King of Lux forbade him from seeking to understand why a command was given, as long as the search was approached with a servant's heart of submission and not a skeptic's games of avoidance.

However—and in Anthro's view, thankfully—the king did not go the way of certain ascetic cults he had come across who denied the goodness of sex or the bond of marriage; in fact, sexuality and marriage were to be understood as a metaphorical expression of the very story of God and humanity, a wedding of the self-giving power and others-centered creative love inherent to the one who fashioned and knit together both male and female. This king took the power of sex and forged it within the sacred, binding the persons engaged not just to each other, but to the true expression of their own creaturely bodies—each person a small but powerful reflection of its crafter. In a mysterious rupture against the established ideas of Tenebris, the self was not just to be expressed *through* the body, but the self *was* the body. The individual body was a poetic song of its triune creator; the bonding of two unique bodies of difference into one completed and harmonious flesh, was the chorus and climax of the created order.

Anthro took another heavy sip from his drink and looked out from the bar toward the crowds. He saw a woman still with an exterior beauty of youth, though it was a beauty fought for against the wheels of time and the trials of life. The woman danced in the arms of a man whom Anthro did not know. The woman, however, he knew. Or was "know" even the right word? Before tonight, he would not have hesitated to say that he knew this woman who, in years past—long before Diatris—he had slept with. Now he felt like that kind of knowledge was not a true knowledge of who she was. He was starting to see just how the physical power of sex had a way of fooling one with such false judgment. To recklessly take part in such a mystery with another—apparently a bond both within, among, and beyond bodies—was fuel to the emotions and blinders to the mind of what it meant to truly know someone.

Here in this old stomping ground of his and Aradis's recruit academy days, he watched the woman, remembering her name was Skia, and he felt a sudden rush of sadness and displeasure. There was no jealousy, nor even desire for her, but he felt an ache of the heart as he had never felt before with a woman in mind. He was suddenly uncomfortable in a way that only the conscience is able to make one feel. This was no mourning of the loss of the unknown or an envy of one's own youthful excursions; this was moral guilt and conviction. The king's view of sex was melding with his mind, and he knew that some part of this unease was coming from the realization of having transgressed the sacred—having trampled and taken when he should have protected and abstained. In his relationship with her, he had stolen from her future husband what was meant for that man alone. He had taken from Skia as well—taken what was not meant for him and treated her in a way that attacked her very humanity. In his lust, in his desire for conquest, in his service of self-oriented pleasure, he had disregarded her humanity. She had been a means to his end. His own humanitarian hatred for sexual violence had been undermined by his very sexual acts. He had seen her body, separated it from her person, and then taken it. Despite being consensual, when exposed to pure light, his sexual exploits were of the same dehumanizing nature of those he so vehemently decried.

These ideas hit him hard. They were heavy, nearly overbearing. His conscience fired arrows of flames at his inner man. As if by his own doing, his conscience had been seared all these years allowing him to wander in the depths of perverse sexuality, only now to be released and functioning as it ought. Still, he knew he must press on.

Skia was a woman—that is all he had ever really viewed her as—but was she more? Was her sexuality tied together with more than just her physical nature? She was a person. She was a being—not *just* a woman. There was a depth beyond the parts of difference. This was true of every woman; they were all not just women, but were—and are—so much more. Their femininity was undeniably an essential part of them, but certainly not all of them. These women, who for so long were only objects of lust to Anthro, were suddenly seen in their full humanity, their powerful dignity, and their wonderful being. This knowledge stemmed from the fact that they were crafted from a shadow, or an image, of incomprehensible splendor and unfathomable depth. They were indeed—side by side with men—image bearers of the living God—not physical representations of him, but miniature reflections of who he is. Anthro had always known that there must be some hedges of protection around sensuality, yet he had always drawn these boundaries by his own reason, being his own judge of what was good and evil. These thoughts were all new, both cutting and majestic.

He wondered more, probing deeper into the reality of sexuality. He had also taken from himself. In his greed for immediate physical gratification his sexual encounters had hidden the much deeper non-physical damage and havoc they were wreaking on his soul and mind. Fleeting pleasure had robbed him of far deeper meaning. Moments of satisfaction had stolen a lifetime of it. He had been shackled to a master who had given him no respite, no contentment, and no freedom.

Another thought came to his mind, and this one troubled his conscience in a way none of the others had. It was as if all of those thoughts pointed toward this one great reality. He had stolen from Skia. He had plundered from her husband, and he was sure, with Diatris heavily on his mind, that he had robbed even his future wife. He had even stolen from himself. But there was still one more from whom he had embezzled, still another he had transgressed with his triviality.

With this story of God and humanity woven into the created reality of sexual intimacy, there was no denying that Anthro had transgressed the God who had crafted human sexuality as well. His conscience could not stand the thought. He knew that he could not have truly faced it on the opposite side of grace. Despite his extreme failings, as a servant of the King of Lux he could look into the depths of them without fear. The king had paid whatever penalties there had been for such sins. As Anthro's knowledge of his own past wretchedness grew, so did his wonder and awe at the depth of the king's love and sacrifice. The king had not only died for him while he was sinner, but a sinner of this magnitude. Such love was stunning. The more he understood it, the more he began to understand his master's words that those who have been forgiven much, love much. He soberly chewed on the thought of those past transgressions one final time while clutching tightly to forgiveness, before setting them aside for another day in order to continue his meditations for the evening.

Despite what it was doing to his conscience, this sacred sex sounded *good* to Anthro. It sounded *right*. It provided a meaning and an ethos around sex that seemed to match its grandeur and guard its passion. Anthro took another sip from his brew, noticing the flavor, savoring the reaction it created on the senses. Sight, touch, smell and taste, were dancing together in a myriad of pleasurable sensations. The beer was good, but it likewise had to be restrained. He had seen the drink ruin men, make fools of the wise, and humble the esteemed in ways few other vices ever could. An evening that began with numerous pleasures could so quickly disintegrate into a midnight of misery. Nevertheless, this beer, in this amount, was certainly good. Here was another powerful enjoyment that thrived within its boundaries and brought sorrow outside of them.

These ideas about sexuality were not at all denying the physical goods of sex but were in fact filling them with transcendent meaning as they were married together within this truth. The physical and the transcendent were both true and good when united, but found painfully wanting when kept apart.

More and more, Anthro understood that any rules or restrictions around sex that the king demanded were designed to guard its goodness, not to prevent one from pleasure. Despite knowing what these limits around sexuality would do to his own personal life, he did not find these ideas burdensome. Where many would have seen the king restricting, he considered himself set free. The sexual morals given by the King of Lux were the very waters that made for human flourishing and happiness. He was not placing such ideals on lofty mountains to taunt his followers by denying them what they needed. There was power within this king's ways, yet there was also a great beauty in them. The king had taken Anthro, who had tasted so heavily the dryness of self-ascribed meaning, and had not just revolutionized his idea of sexuality but had resurrected it from the grave in which it had lain dormant.

What had been a concept idealized by a mere physical action and means of self-pleasure, even if shared with another, had been remade into a sublime reality of two beings becoming one flesh. In this reality, the physical and spiritual are inseparably linked together in a bond as mysterious as the act of sex itself. Human sexuality had been crafted from the dust into a dance of love like nothing this world could have fashioned on its own. Sex was now seen in its designed reality as a uniting bond for life; it was not a transient and fleeting passing of simple pleasures, nor a mere survival mechanism for the species, but a celebration of covenant. It was a poem between one man and one woman, forging them into a union of one body and giving them a taste of a tangible mystery laced with hints of eternity.

Anthro thought of how to describe his newfound wonder in this ancient reality. What words would suffice to capture it now? Sex, what was it? Human sexuality was a song of praise written with chords and harmonies only possible within the boundaries the composer had given to it. Sex was a sonnet of wonder, a melody of life, and a symbolic chorus forever echoing the story of humanity and divinity. Sex, it is the song of songs.

Chapter XXI

The Chains of Freedom

A dreary, sunless noon sky blustered overhead in a swirling mass of vapor and haze. Waves of gray and silver melded together in a sea of their own. As one they held the distant light at bay, tolerating its obscured presence but never allowing it to reign. On occasion they briefly permitted a ray to pass their blockade—a transient beam left all on its own, its warmth never to be felt and its light hardly to be seen.

A mingling and diverse crowd sat beneath this sky, forming an atmosphere all their own. The air here was comfortable, amiable, and tranquil. This mood was its own kind of light, rising from the ashes and embers that had brought it to life. It was created by those who had conquered and by those who had conformed. Tenebris's appeal for unification had not been a spurious claim. In just a few weeks the flow of troops across borders had been replaced by an exchange of trade. Culpam could continue to exist, just as long as it was willing to be remade.

On the far edge of this crowd sat Anthro and Diatris. The peace of the lower air could not invade their space. There was war still behind them. There was war right above them. There was war within and around them. Unsettling shadows moved across Diatris's keen eyes. Her ebony skin was one with the shifting light; she wore each shade with a radiant beauty. With the dimming of the sun, Anthro's stout and sandy flesh was an unsteady color as well. Through his swathe of dark curl, she was reading him. She could sense a rare disconnect between them: a disunity of spirit akin to summer and winter, one synonymous with spring and autumn.

Their reunion had not been what she had expected it to be, nor what she had hoped for. The war was over; it was all finally over. Their dreams finally had the freedom to form into reality. Yet when he had seen her face, he had only so lightly kissed her. When she had drawn him close, he had only so barely pressed her into him. There was a manifest distance between them. The tip of a knife hovered over her heart; with every beat within her breast it fell closer to its mark, not yet ready to plunge, but present, and drawing ever closer.

Her mind and emotions rushed through a maze of doubts. Was this what happened to all great men who had fulfilled their purpose? Could no woman, no love, no passion, fill the void that remains once having reached the pinnacle of success? Was this the cause for the stranger before her? Or was it worse? Had there been a woman, a love, a passion, found within the void— one that was not her? The knife lurched down, now drawing blood with every beat. Keta. The name invited more doubt and fear. No friendship of such statute could remain seamlessly platonic. No man could find such a refuge and not seek to drink his fill. No woman—not one—could hold a man at such a distance as had been Diatris's task.

"I'm sorry." He held her gaze as he said the words. Even after speaking them, he refused to look away. This did not seem possible for a man who had another woman on his heart. For the moment the doubt was quieted, yet it was far from removed. "I know I haven't been acting like myself. It's just . . ." He paused.

A distant memory flashed through Diatris's disheveled thoughts as she recalled the first time her amber eyes had looked at him in this questioning manner. "Diatris . . . I don't really know how else to say this, but do you remember the king from the parchments? Well, I've found him. Or, I guess more accurately, he's found me."

She sat there in silence for half a minute, thinking about why that would affect his behavior so greatly. The agitated sky above their open balcony was condensing into a solid mat of final winter farewell, the turbulent atmosphere refusing to yield to the approaching southern warmth.

"Anthro, what are you talking about? You've found another parchment? Found *him*? What, his grave? What . . . what do you mean?" Diatris was trying to move nonchalantly. She knew answers would come, but her heart was wild—her emotions a storm as if bound to the will of the sky above.

"Definitely not his grave. Do . . . do you remember what the parchments said?" Anthro felt his face warm up. Somehow speaking these words out loud and knowing where they were leading made everything that had transpired seem more real.

"Kind of hard to forget that message." Frustration filled her words, tempered only by her love for the brilliant fool who was on this absurd quest. That message against humanity was buried in the past, where she greatly wished it had remained.

Anthro beheld this woman of rich thought and envious form before him, and suddenly—unexpectedly—a part of him shouted within his heart to take her in a thought-suppressing grip of love once more. It shouted to let this subject rest forever, to simply split his devotion between the king and his beloved mistress without this unnecessary conflict. If he kept this belief to himself, could he not have both worlds? Enjoy each love?

A bit of sun seemed to be penetrating through the mattress

of cloud above as he felt that whisper of temptation deeply calling to him—that distraction, that desire, that drug. Already he felt the intoxication seep into his veins, pumping through his heart and arteries, even filling his hands with a pleasing warmth. Never had his stain been so silent, never had its presence seemed so far removed . . . but that thought jolted a fear into his mind, brought back his reason, and recalled his truest love. In an angry fury, his invisible scar screamed out in protest, as if being crucified itself.

"Diatris . . ." There was no going back if the next words came, and like the delayed first foliage of an overdue spring, they bloomed with vibrance and energy. "I believe it."

"What?" The word was razor sharp. "You believe that a dead king thought all his people weren't good? Anthro, why does any of that matter? I know you are interested in the history, but I don't understand why you're even still following this elusive trail." She took a deep breath, trying to calm herself. Her love for him was working against her patience.

"Well, everything hinges on that right there." His voice was deep, his tone stoic, his thoughts focusing, and his mind clearing. Everything hinged on this. How often he had thought of this, considered it, and feared it.

Diatris took another breath, closing her eyes briefly, willing herself to be long-suffering. Anthro obviously cared about this; she would let him speak as he felt he needed to. After all, he would do the same for her no matter how insane an idea she was processing. "You know you're drawing all of this out, right?" She said it playfully and with an old wink, trying to bring back the usual tempo of their conversations. Before he could respond, she continued. "And which part, may I ask, does everything hinge on? What exactly is *everything*?"

Her placating tone added a small sense of urgency to his

words. "Diatris, is the king dead? Is this just some ancient report from the past? Or does it press into the present with shocking and terrifying force?" He wanted to add more, but he knew that he had thought on these matters through countless hours of solitude. He was trying to let her process in minutes what he had been working through for over a year.

"Wait . . . Anthro, you're still not making sense. That parchment was from an ancient city called Roma, correct?" Her tempo had once again sharpened. She took a hand and brushed back her midnight black hair while drawing her fingers around her slender chin.

Anthro gave her a prolonged nod as whispering shadows added intensity to the gesture.

"Then what on earth do you mean by saying the king might not be dead? What do you mean by saying that this message might apply to the present?" She was putting some pieces together. This was no trick; she knew Anthro would never joke like this. It was hard enough to get him to joke about anything. But what exactly was he saying? What was it that he was believing in? She was growing even more concerned. Had the pressure of a life lived with relentless thought finally taken its toll on him?

"Diatris, this king—he is more than human." He could tell that he was slow to confess his beliefs in front of her. Why not just say what he believed? How strong the power of another could affect what someone believed (or, at least, what they would admit that they believed). How deeply fellow humans could influence and inhibit actual confessions of belief.

She looked away. Her eyes had failed her; she could not see through him this time. What could he mean? He was not a lunatic, so what could he possibly mean? Carefully, she considered the possibilities. Then a thought came. Yes. It was all coming together now. He had never been remotely spiritual, but maybe this was it. Finally, a way that this could make sense.

"All right, I think I'm starting to understand. More than human? I understand that."

He raised his eyebrows at her, now having flashbacks of his own of that conversation of similar magnitude held so long ago.

"No really, I'm not mocking you. I wouldn't do that. But the pieces are starting to fit. You think that this king . . . that he is some kind of abstraction—some kind of symbol and spiritual metaphor—and that his message, despite what I think of it, is still around for us to heed today? He and his message are something that can guide us to better morality? To better human flourishing? By this you mean that he is alive and more than human?" That was at least a possibility. Diatris had never been as naturalistically restricted as Anthro; she had always been open to various views as long as they were tolerant of other's beliefs and sought to further the goodness within the human race. But what else could Anthro, of all people, really believe?

Anthro leaned back. It was his time to process. These thoughts had been the first to arise within his mind as well. But he had come to know, with full clarity, that the King of Lux had come into this world to save sinners, not to deliver a mere metaphor or example. The King of Lux was not a *metaphor*, he was a *person* . . . perfectly both sinless man and awesome God. Something about this thought made him realize that he must make this *person* known. Nothing else would do.

"No, Diatris. In the fullest and most complete sense of the word, *no*. I'm talking about this king being physically alive, in the flesh, in every usual sense of the word *living*. In the beginning, he was with God and was God. All things came into being through him. Then he came to this world, not counting equality with God a thing to be held onto. He humbled himself by being made in the likeness of man. And he humbled himself even to the point of death on a cross, a death which paid the price for all those who would believe in him. The parchments are just the diagnosis. His death and resurrection are the solution. And that's just it, Diatris: he was raised from the dead, and now he is *alive*. Is there a metaphor in that? Yes. But the entire thing is worthless if it is only symbolic. The poetic and moral lessons are merely the fruit of the roots of this mysterious but historic reality."

Having initiated his confession, he could not be stopped. "Diatris, I'm talking about this king being alive and being the true ruler of this world who will come back to judge the living and the dead. I'm talking about him being fully human and fully divine. Diatris, I don't just believe in God; I believe in this king, and the King of Lux *is* God."

Her eyes had widened; for once, they looked weak. It was as if that dagger over her heart had only been present to distract from the presence of this foreign enemy, who had now driven a sword through the back of her.

"That message in the parchments wasn't just for Roma. It was for both past and present. It is a universal declaration against the human condition. It was written *for* us and it is *about* us. It is about me . . ." He held her disheartened eyes. Oh, how he loved her, but for love to be true it must speak the truth. And though it was a distant love of an offbeat type, if he could not admit this here, he would never be able to confess it as he faced those eyes of innocent blue. "And Diatris . . . it is a message about you." It stung to say those words, but there was a certain freedom in it. He believed it; why should he not say it? He loved her and she needed the same redeemer as he did; how could he not say it? Fear of what others thought had restrained him his entire life. Now, finally, there was only one whom he feared above all others, and it was not Diatris.

Her heart sank with pain and rejection. They both felt a widening gulf emerge between them. She could feel her face—her whole body—flush with indignation and dejection. About her? How dare he! Did he think that lowly of her?

"Look, Anthro, whatever you've found—whatever you think you've found—is a metaphor. Learn something from it. Take whatever good can be found from it. Apply it to *your* life as *you* see fit, but don't start thinking it applies to everyone else. Maybe it is a truth, but maybe it is a truth not worth chasing." Her eyes were watering; sadness and confusion filled her heart, but also an anger of cold steel, a burning energy of dagger and blade. Not good! Not one good! What possible good could be found in a message like that? This king was destroying the man she loved with her deepest affections, turning him into something she could not embrace.

"Diatris." He longed to reach out and touch her hand, fearing that he may never do it again. "If this king offered just *a* truth, he'd not be worth *a* thing, and I certainly would not follow him if such was the case. I don't think that he is just *a* truth, but that he is the way, and the life, and *the* truth: *singular* and *definite* truth. Objective truth, grounded outside of humanity. He is the very reason for truth and he is truth himself. Diatris, the way he talked about himself—what he is, what he came to do, what he declares about his authority; and his claims to be lord over heaven and earth, over all things visible and invisible, over all thrones, rulers, dominions, authorities . . . every single thing in complete subjection to his rule.

"There are a variety of historical reports about him, and if they capture even a shred of the real man, then there are only three options: he is either a compelling liar, a raging lunatic, or he is in fact Lord over all. Even reading the reports, it becomes clear that the diverse writers have captured a singular personality. So, there is *no* in-between in regard to the genuine claims regarding this historical person. The King of Lux made absolutely sure to remove that as a possibility." Anthro was hoping with all his heart that he would not have to choose between the king and Diatris, yet it seemed that every declaration he made about the king further extinguished the flame that tied his and Diatris's hearts together.

Still, a small fire had lit within the amber of her eyes. "Anthro, that is the most arrogant thing that I've ever heard. From you, of all people! Forget calling me a no-good sinner; you just claimed exclusivity on truth! Who do you think you are to make such a claim? As if all humans aren't entitled to their *own* truth."

The clouds thickened once more, that last affront from winter blowing in its final frigid bite. "Diatris, please, I'm not saying that *I've* created some kind of system of *my own* beliefs that are better than everyone else's. I'm saying that this *is* the system of belief that *is* tied to ultimate reality, regardless of what anyone thinks or projects. But this claim *does* invite people from every tribe, nation, and language and makes few demands on their overall cultural preferences. Despite the singularity of belief, there is vast and spectacular diversity within the community.

"And sure, if every other belief system taught that God had become incarnate in time and space to reconcile humans to himself through the sacrifice of his only Son, humans who could do absolutely nothing to merit their own salvation which they desperately need, and that God himself was a monotheistic triune being consisting of three persons in that one essence—then maybe there'd be something to what you said. But this is a *unique claim* on who God is—on what humanity is, on what the problem between the creator and creatures is, on what the solution is, and on what God did in *actual history* to accomplish that salvific work. The claim, by its very structure, is irreconcilable and incompatible with every other belief system out there."

The kindled flame within her stare grew stronger. "And *that* is cavalier and pretentious! All humans have the complete right to their own truth. No one—not even your newfound God—can stake a claim on a free-thinking sentient being. We are *human*, which means that we have power over our own free will—the will to think as we please. The will to believe as we desire and to even create our own truth. Truth comes from within, not from without. Like I said, your truth can be in this king, but get over yourself and don't try to push your views on others. And don't you *dare* try to push them on me." Her words were inferno, her eyes a raging flame.

Anthro could feel his own temper rising, though he prayed for foreign suppression. "So, everything is just relative, then? No meaning, no real truth—nothing?"

"Oh, come on! You know I don't believe that. It's like you're not even listening. I believe *in* truth. It's tied to each individual person; there may even be some wonderful universal connections, but truth itself is not defined by singularity and it is not of a definite and restricted nature." Diatris was no fool; Anthro long knew and adored the workings of her mind, yet here their views were at bitter odds.

"Diatris, I'm not trying to force you to believe anything . . ."

"Well, it sure seems like it!" Tears filled her eyes as she interrupted, a torrent of emotions within her ready to overflow. A few heads turned toward the shout, but the onlookers quickly went about their own business.

"Diatris, I would never force anyone to believe in something." Hurt filled his voice. "But I do *want* you to believe the truth."

"*Stop. Doing. That.*" Venom in every syllable. "I know you're not trying to force anything. I know." The dovelike softness returned in those last two words, but it could not continue. "But you are defining truth in a manner that I *refuse* to accept."

Anthro feared they were entering a conversational dead end, one that would not only claim the life of the conversation, but also of the relationship. He hated feeling her anger as much as he hated being the cause of it, but he would not silence his convictions—not even for her.

"Don't you think that's just dodging the word and avoiding the issue? I mean, sure, we keep defining truth differently. But ultimately, I am using the word in such a way as to make an objective claim outside of anyone's personal beliefs of what truth is, or even how it should be defined. Call it whatever you will, but if this King of Lux is who he says he is, if he is *the truth*—the singular and definite fulfillment of the reality behind what that word *meant to him*—no contrary conceptualization of the word itself could ever get around that claim without saying *that he was wrong*. Either he is that reality or he isn't. Either what he said is true for me and every other human being, no matter what any one of us chooses to believe, or the claim is, by its self-professed nature, utterly erroneous. Your concept of truth, if this king is true, is a direct assault on his very person, an attack on the very nature of the Son of God. If he is the singular, definite, and personal truth encompassing all of reality, and you claim that there is no such thing, then you are wrong, and have set your philosophy against the nature and person of God himself."

For hours they talked, debating and pleading with one another to see reason. Intelligent answers were given by both sides. As Keta excelled well beyond Anthro in morality, so Diatris—more often than not—bested him in raw intellectual might. Nonetheless, Anthro was determined to offer the best arguments he could, all the while knowing that ultimately, her acceptance of the King of Lux hinged not on a debate won or lost, nor upon the man who willed, nor upon the woman who ran, but on God who had mercy.

For God, in his destruction of the wise, in his ruin of the clever, and in his obliteration of boasting, had seen to it that his true children would not be born of natural descent, nor of human decision, nor of the will of human effort—but of God alone and by God's work alone. This true faith from above was, without exception, a miracle performed by the work of the Potter's hands as he remade each clay vessel of the regenerated human heart.

As time passed, it became clear to Diatris that the entire message of the King of Lux was foolishness. Not in its arguments, reason, or coherence, but in its content. To believe that she would have to surrender her conviction in the inherent goodness of human beings (and with it, the righteousness of her own sovereign self) was unacceptable. Furthermore, that power could only be found in weakness was repugnant to her ideals of human-led innovation and innate human progress. She hated how Tenebris had abused its power, but this king's idea of power found only in weakness was a polar extreme of similar distaste.

Diatris understood that to accept this king would be to accept not only his message of endless grace, but also his declaration of eternal wrath; not only his invitation to all, but also his rejection of many; not only his teachings of kindness and healing, but also his lordship and dominion over every fiber of her being; and not only his message of salvation, but also the bloody, violent accomplishment of it. Every image and idea related to the king's work definitively came back to that grand act of God displaying his love for the world through bloody propitiation, that fearful and awesome abating of his justified wrath through the necessary, spotless, and final sacrifice of the Son of God. Every other metaphor, symbol, idea, and theory rested upon and grew out from that work of penal substitutionary atonement. To accept any of these without that foundation was the true option of reasonless surrender or over-reasoned blunder. To accept all of them was to affirm the loss of everything that she was and wanted this world to be. She would have to lose herself to follow this God. This was the foolishness. This message about this person and his work, despite countless peripheral considerations, was the message that was laid before her. The foolishness of the crucified King of Lux—that was her rejection.

Finally, Diatris looked at him with fierce determination. This was her stance. "Anthro, I am my own. I am free. I will not be shackled down by anyone or anything. I am myself, I am human, and I—only I—may define myself." And then those vocals of songbird returned. "But all that said, I want to be free *with you*. And it's even more than that; I want *you* to be free. A mind like yours, a heart like yours—that artistry of thought within you, that poetry of imaginative expression deep inside you, Anthro—they all *deserve* to be free. *You* deserve to be free. You are worth escaping these chains that are seeking to bind you. Embrace your individuality. Express it and fulfill it. We are here to be wonderfully autonomous. Can't you taste its goodness? Anthro, be free, *with me*." Was it the gentle coo of a calling dove or the strangling slither of a sly serpent?

Anthro looked down and, for the first time, did not meet that gaze of his passion. He had only just started his service to this king and already he was being torn asunder. Would serving him always be this costly—this agonizing? Would he be forced to bear a cross daily? Somehow, despite the pain, it did not matter. This king demanded loyalty in a way that gave Anthro no other option. Loving the King of Lux meant hating all others in comparison, even oneself.

He felt his heart ripping within, but he would give up Diatris if he must. Anthro knew that aspects of the king's message were difficult, but if it was true, were such hard sayings not worth knowing? Was not the truth worth believing, regardless of how it made one feel at times? Had the king not proved that he was trustworthy even though his followers were required to confess him without having a perfect understanding? And did not this report—this message, the whole story—have a ring of truth to it like no other, as if this is what the outside observer would declare to all those lost in their fortresses of speculation, to those looking everywhere but at their own inner rebellion and utter depravity? The lengths required by the saving work of the king had sealed the proof of humanity's wretchedness. Yet, by that act of unmerited mercy, humanity was not left to itself. No, God loved the world enough to call a people out of it, to call them to the truth, to give them to his Son. Love was found in truth. Truth called through love. Could she not hear the beauty of this gospel? Could she not see the richness of the love of God displayed in such a way? His silence was telling her what she feared to hear.

Tears slowly rolled down her face, their eyes locking together—misted amber and frosted emerald.

"Anthro, I love you deeply; as I've never loved another, nor ever will. But this King of Lux, I do not. His message of sin and salvation I do not believe. Anthro, we could talk for days, weeks, and even years, but let me make one thing crystal clear: I will not follow this king with you. I cannot." Tears flowed freely from the both of them. "Anthro . . . are you sure? Are you sure that he is worth it? Are . . . are you sure that he is worth . . . me?"

Anthro stared at her, packed full of emotion. But for once, in a rare moment and at a vital time, he was devoid of any doubt. He held her sharp gaze one final time. "I love you, Diatris. You are a woman like no other, the brightest gem this world could offer me." And he meant it. "But I am *not* my own. I am a slave, but I am free. I am lost, but I am found. I am his, or I am nothing."

Anthro stood and Diatris, for once, no longer looked through him. He walked off without looking back. A rooted part of him was withering away, but fading along with it was a great darkness. From whatever remained, a new life was emerging with a gentle light shining upon it, promising lasting life if it would just carry on.

Chapter XXII

The Last Confession

Thunder rolled overhead, drowning out the noise of the crowded tavern. Another would not follow. Most of Anthro's men had returned to their families. Some had confessed their faith in the King of Lux while others had remained agnostic. Two of his men had remained with Anthro up until now; one was leaving in declared unbelief.

Harpazo stared at Themata before speaking. His wild, hot demeanor was tempered by more than a final shared brew. "It doesn't have to be like this. What a dividing wedge this king has been." His youthful, shadowed black eyes revealed their first hint of age.

Anthro looked at Harpazo with affection. In a brief moment, it was as if all of his mixed memories of and varied feelings about Aradis were intertwined within this man of kindred sinew. "We've said our peace; let us end this bond in peace." Hurt filled Anthro's eyes as he spoke, their usual vibrancy subdued.

"Here we must depart, my friend," said Themata. "Not in spite, nor anger, nor betrayal, but at a foundational disunity. If you ever have a personal need, you need not hesitate to call on me. You shall have my hammer at your side before the herald's words cease." He stood as he spoke, his stout form resolute.

Whatever those deep waters of his reasons were, the message of the King of Lux had not been enough for him. "I've other work to do. I shall continue the deeds and efforts of our years of fellowship, yet I do not desire myself—nor my methods—bound to your king."

"My brother . . ." Harpazo gripped the smaller, older soldier in a fierce embrace of bodily emotion as words failed him. Finally, they released tearfully.

Anthro drew near to the departing, a flood of memories of this other man's faithfulness before him. Taking hold of each other's forearms, with their bodies nearly pressed together, Anthro spoke thick words. "My faithful soldier. My dear friend. I am never far."

Themata firmly held together their grip. "My true leader. My intimate ally. Nor am I." Seconds passed as they maintained their physical bond. They cared deeply for one another—each would die for the other—yet both knew that their ultimate claims on reality were fundamentally contradictory. Their highest loyalties and beliefs were as far removed as lofty mountain peaks of foreign ranges.

Anthro and Harpazo watched Themata as he left the bar and departed through the shadowed, arched entryway. Heavy rain was falling. Lightning flashed across the sky as he exited, eerily revealing every etch of his form for just one moment. The darkness into which he then walked swallowed him up into the heart of every moonless night, separated wholly from light.

* * * *

Fresh paint, vibrant in the early spring light, covered the wood-paneled home before which Anthro now stood. He could hear children laughing from behind, so he made his way around to the back, knowing she would be there.

Keta was watching over a small group of young children as they played beneath the speckled shade of a freshly budding oak. Amazingly, this was to be his most difficult confession yet. More than a risen king, more than a triune God—even more than his words which had torn apart his love—this single confession would be the most strained to proceed from his lips.

How challenging it was to observe that which he was about to declare, despite the ability to see her right before his eyes. Still, he wrestled to behold how this woman of sacrifice—who bore the very scars of such service on her face—was not a good person. Stunningly, Keta believed it about herself. Anthro knew he must believe this, too. The King of Lux saw the truth far better than a feeble, finite man like himself ever could. He would not dishonor his king by failing to believe his sovereign's declarations regarding any matter, and this belief was a working assumption of his king. Furthermore, Anthro would not insult the very reason the king had come to this world, for if Keta could be found right in God's sight apart from the king's sacrifice, then the king died needlessly. Too much was at stake to refrain from confessing what his heart so labored against. Anthro would choose submission to the authority of the king, the very king who had so earned his trust despite Anthro's own hostile nature, over the persuasions of a crafty and misleading heart. The heart of man was a maze of confusion and doubt. The words of the King of Lux were true in everything he professed.

Anthro had his arms crossed and placed upon a chest-high brick wall that marked the perimeter of the orphanage. His chin was resting upon the perch of his forearms as he watched her.

Where will we go from here, Keta? Could I have made it here without you? And now, what I must confess about you. You were always—are always—better than me. That part is effortless. I've never doubted the depth

273

of my own sin. But you? It feels as if I must hate you in order to admit it, and yet love bids me on. Love and hate—dichotomized by their nature, harmonized within this confession. For my affections are beyond either of us. A love so devout that it can only make all other sentiments appear as hate by comparison, yet still love resides at both ends. I know your heart is there as well. How much easier does that make this?

Even at the word of our king, we have walked such inverse paths, following after the footsteps of our genders in relation to this king. I have been a questioner in the night; you have drunk from the well of his word and declared him true. You have washed his feet with your tears; I failed to even offer him a drink. You have anointed him with the costliest perfume, while all I could proffer were indignant remarks. You were willing to look on at the height of his sufferings, but I ran off, a coward in denial. You rose early and discovered the news; I stood still in unbelief. Perhaps there is an admirable woe within the nature of woman that holds the saying true: "Blessed are the poor in spirit, for theirs is the kingdom of heaven."

What sort of king would call two such as us? We are opposites, you and me. Yet we have both been won to the same king by the same proclamation. You, Keta—what confidence you could put in yourself. If anyone in this world might have confidence in their works of charity, you far more: born of a gentle spirit and zealous for service and acts of altruism. If there were a people who could boast about such things and in them find gain, you would surely be chief among them.

And yet . . . yet you, Keta, have counted all such things loss for the sake of the King of Lux. More than that, you have counted all things loss in view of the surpassing value of knowing him, our king and our Lord. Indeed, you count them but rubbish so that you may gain the king and be found in him. Covered in his character, you wear a righteousness not of this world but accomplished in it. By this sacrifice of self, you know him. Through this loss of identity, you have fellowship with him and find yourself. As you conform to his death, you find life and press on, forgetting what lies behind so that you may lay hold of his eternal glory. This reality achieved through the King of Lux—this is eternal life.

We are citizens of a foreign kingdom, you and me. Our minds are there. Our hearts are there. Our life is there. Our king is there. Our God is there. He has called us both. He predestined us both before the foundation of the world. He chose us all, for our family extends across any cultural walls, any barriers of language. We are all one in him. Our brothers and sisters—our fellow pilgrims on this planet—we are all a part of his present and coming kingdom, neither aspects of which we are to neglect. We are to be salt and light, here and now. We are to fix our minds and affections on what is to come. We have a bond of kindred not only with those who live, but also with those who have died—those who have paved the way for us in their service to our mutual king. Centuries and millennia of countless saints incorporate our collective family. Keta, we have hope. We have each other. We have truth. We have freedom. And, in him, we have a peace which surpasses all understanding.

Eventually, Keta looked up and noticed that ever-attentive stare from the boy on the rooftops. She glanced over, ensuring the children were occupied and accounted for, and then made her way to him as bright sunlight cascaded down beyond the reach of the oak's branches.

She stopped just short of him, curious what had brought him here and perplexed by the expression penetrating the shaggy hair that draped over his face in the fresh breeze.

"You're evil." He said it monotone without lifting his head, but while looking deeply into her azure eyes. She could see his pain within the emerald. She could see his relief beyond the ebon pits.

A crooked smile spread across Keta's face, never the same with that scar that had left a permanently squinting eye. Though somehow, with this, she was yet more beautiful. There was power within the wound. There was an artistry within the abrasion and its beauty was even deeper than mere perfection and symmetry. By fleshly raw wounds they were healed in their relationship to God through the king's many scars. This added a profound beauty to physical marks of suffering.

"I know." She said it softly, confidently. Once revealed and accepted, this had never been her struggle. "You too," she said with a truthful wink.

"I know." This caused Anthro to return the smile. It was such a strange mutual confession, one they knew was unlikely— if not impossible—to be declared if the remedy they had received was not at one's disposal. For such a declaration was only made possible by two who knew that they were no longer under any condemnation, for the king had satisfied complete propitiation for them. Their confession reflected their confidence in that reality. They were two who hated evil—two who daily waged war against the evil in the world and within the ever-present vestiges of their old selves—yet they were freed through the king's gift to admit that, apart from the King of Lux, evil was all their deeds had to offer a holy God. There was a peculiar joy in knowing that apart from him, they could do nothing.

"Took you long enough," Keta replied, resting an elbow on the wall beside him.

"I was afraid of the Light. Afraid of what the king would expose about me, this world, and most of all, about you. But Keta, I believe. Who would have thought? Not me. I believe in the King of Lux. I believe in all that he was and is and will be. A belief that will manifest its obedience in faith and action, in word and deed. Every thought will be held captive in obedience to the conviction that he is true. That he is risen. That he is Lord. That he is God."

Keta just smiled as she thought of how far they had been and of where they would go. They were brother and sister. They were friends and fellow heirs. They were servants and saints.

They were redeemed humanity. They were children of Lux.

Chapter XXIII

Behold Your King

Long weeks gave way to laborious months. With great speed and burdened delay, the months turned into years. The years faded into decades. What a different king Anthro now served. What a different life he had lived. No longer did he hold the sword of Tenebris; now he faithfully brandished the sword of Lux. He left the steel behind him and embraced a weapon of word and spirit. No longer did he bring men to death; now he sought to bring them to life. No more was he a slayer of humanity; he had become a fisher of men. He had ceased to spill the blood of others as he spent his life pouring out his own. This was the way of his savior and the call of his sovereign.

Over the years, Anthro had become convinced that no one could ever come to know this king—could ever serve him in truth—without being made into a new creation. One's initial confession was a product of a new birth, the sprouting of a watered seed planted in good soil of God-given growth. It was a tiny mustard seed of freely given faith, producing a harvest of love, joy, peace, patience, kindness, goodness, faithfulness, gentleness, and self-control. Against such things there is no law.

At times, despite Anthro's deepest protests, he felt betrayal hiding within his veins, a measure of treason in every drop of his blood. He felt that constant fear of denying his king whom he loved so deeply by either word or deed. He feared betraying him by a singular act of defiance or in outright apostasy. Never did Anthro obtain the type of faith that Apostolos had, that unwavering certainty. But faith was a gift, and Anthro was content with the measure allotted to him. Perhaps the small nature of the portion of faith he was given was itself also a gift, designed to keep him in utter weakness and total dependency.

Anthro stumbled often as he ran after his king's commands, seeking to walk in the light as the king himself is in the light, yet each time he was held fast and kept on the narrow path. Was this by his own strength? By his own doing? He would have given a hearty and deep laugh at such a thought. Not to mock—never that—but he could only find humor at the complete insanity of such an idea. Anthro saw in himself nothing but weakness; he was the weakest of all the king's servants. That would be the only boast he would make of himself. Apart from the King of Lux sustaining his faith, Anthro knew that he would depart. Apart from the King of Lux maintaining his belief, he was sure that he would deny the master who had bought him. Apart from the King of Lux, this greatest of sinners would never have taken even a single step toward his redeemer. Anthro was not left to his own will, but God's. It was God who worked in him and through him for his own divine pleasure. Some may have hated this truth, yet it was the only thing that gave Anthro rest in his doubts and eased the burden of perseverance. Nothing could snatch him from service to the King of Lux while the king still willed it, not even Anthro. What comfort lay in such power; what love in such a grip.

The king never promised him a life free of tribulation and grief. In fact, he invited Anthro into the guarantee of trouble and strife. Anthro had become well acquainted with both. Sorrow was his companion and pain his persistent mentor. Because of this king, he knew both loss of friendship and loss of love—Themata and Diatris. At times he heavily mourned their unwillingness to follow the path of Lux, but he did not falter in his duty to his king. Though friend and love should leave him, he had counted the cost. He would put nothing before his service to the King of Lux.

There was another cost in such devotion—this one even harder than the others. Daily he died to himself. Daily he denied that inner rebellion that had screamed within him from the womb. This battle was the most demanding of all; of this he was sure—so subtle was his self, so cunning, so hungry for autonomy. But daily he died, so daily he lived. Death brought forth life. Life was found only in death.

This death was not a denial of the goodness and beauty of creation that Anthro had always held to so dearly. No, it was not that type of death. The physical world never lost its luster as he died his countless deaths, and it never had to. This was a death of the abuse and misuse of every good and perfect gift that had come from above. And as he came to enjoy these gifts within their bounds, he finally had someone to thank for the fields of dance, the psalms of taste, and the rivers of meaningful thought, emotion, and sensation. This world—it was not all there was, and it was certainly not an illusion. Through humanity, the world had fallen, but it was good. It was destined to heal completely into the glory of the children of God. One day, everything would be made new, having been reconciled to and through the King of Lux.

With each new morning, the eyes of Anthro's heart were enlightened more and more by the hope of the king's calling. He ached for the riches of the glory of the king's inheritance in the saints as he came to know the surpassing greatness of the king's power toward those who believed. Anthro's deepest longings had found their sought-after promise and unfathomable hope, as if given an anchor for his soul. Such hope had been set not on a foundation of groundless desire, but on the bedrock of the Rock of Ages himself—the very sovereign who upheld the universe by the word of his power.

Though there was certain and painful loss, still more did Anthro gain. Even in this life of pilgrimage and journey he had been given one-hundred fold. More than anything, as a tangible balm for those he had lost he had gained a depth in his relationships beyond any he had been forced to relinquish. In Keta, he had found a sister, their bond and friendship beyond anything that it had been prior to their adoption as fellow children of the Kingdom of Lux. Together, they had served him as brother and sister, as fellow heirs of grace, and as fellow servants of his majesty.

In Apostolos, he had found his faithful brother. It was a love rarely seen and seldom shared between kin of gender—not a love of erotica and lust, but of a purity forged in becoming kindred of heart and mission. This was the kind of love that man was built for: a friendship that would hold to death and had a promise of true life even beyond the grave. It promised a life of fullness and all reality—both physical and spiritual—when heaven would fully come to earth. They had seen and tasted the dawning of indestructible joy, and their hunger for it only grew.

Still more did Anthro obtain in this life, for he had gained a family beyond number. It was a family that transcended race, color, sex, and status; they were all one within this kingdom. This was a family of great struggle, but also of profound peace—never perfect, but always following perfection. Many false servants came in with a guise of light, but even their infiltration could not hinder the growth of the family of Lux. Though tares did grow among the wheat, still the fields proved ripe for harvest. Wherever true belief in the essentials was found—even with the many disagreements that remained—those diverse disciples would often remember that it was under the shadow of one banner they all lived and moved and had their being. They did all these under the victorious banner of the King of Lux. All those under this standard were regarded as deceivers and yet true, were unknown yet well-known, were dying yet alive, were punished yet not put to death, were sorrowful yet always rejoicing, were poor and yet making many rich, had nothing yet possessed all things.

Anthro often reflected on these higher realities as he himself lived a far quieter life than he had led while in the service of Tenebris. Generally, the labor done for his new master was simple and unremarkable, yet every single menial task was filled with a rich, profound, and eternal meaning.

Not all was quiet, of course, for there was certainly work to be done. There was a message of reconciliation to spread—a verbal gospel declaration to proclaim. And always there were the weak, poor, and lame to be helped, fed, and cared for.

After receiving years of rigorous training at the hands of Apostolos and his people, Anthro and Harpazo—in the beginnings of what would be a leadership guided through a plurality of elders—established the first Ekklesia in Mori. Alongside them, serving as a faithful deaconess, Keta did what she was made for: serving the powerless with everything she had. And now, she had more. She had a reason for radical human dignity deeper than the shallow wells of her own feelings and the trickling streams of her own vague beliefs. Everyone she cared for—no matter their health nor their developmental stage—was a human of tremendous value and worth, not because she self-imposed that value onto them, but because each one was made as a little image of the living God. Slowly, though often unseen, more and more of Lux broke through the inner walls of Tenebris.

*   *   *   *

Now Anthro lay down underneath a grand oak of ancient birth, leaning his back one final time into living wood. His breaths came rapidly. Less and less air filled his lungs despite their increased labor. The sun was fading quickly; the air was still. His patchy gray beard and wrinkled face were contrasted by the color and vibrancy of his powerful green eyes: the color of life alive at death.

Suddenly, Anthro was standing, unmovable as a statue, like a corpse in a grave—but his heart was racing. There was nothing to see but a light of incomparable brightness surrounding him. Had the sky split? Had he heard a trumpet sound? Had he drawn his last breath? It did not seem to matter; the King of Lux was coming.

Six men were on the king's left and six on his right. They were moving closer. Anthro's surroundings were a blur. For the first time that he could ever recall, his restless mind was absolutely silent—every last thought subdued by perfect glory.

The King of Lux was coming toward him; this was all he could see, all that mattered to him in life and death. From far off, the king appeared to have no stately form or majesty that anyone should look upon him, but as he came closer to Anthro that image faded into dust. In a blinding flash the king appeared before Anthro like a Son of Man, clothed in a robe reaching to the feet and girded across his chest with a golden sash. His head and his hair were like white wool—like snow; his eyes were like a flame of fire. His feet were burnished bronze when it has been made to glow in a furnace, and his voice was like the sound of many waters. In his right hand he held seven stars and out of his mouth came a sharp two-edged sword; his face was like the sun shining in its strength. This was the first and the last, the Living One, the Alpha and Omega—the King of Lux.

The king stood still just short of him and shouted with a loud voice, a voice of thundering water that made the earth beneath him tremble.

"Anthro! Come forth!"

Anthro obeyed. He knew his shepherd's voice; another he simply would not follow. Each step was taken in awe and reverence, with fear and trembling, with great joy and thanksgiving— while owning nothing and beholding everything. Finally, after so much doubt, every other possibility was gone. He had fought the good fight. He had finished the race. He had kept the faith. Here was Truth. Here was the spring of Living Water and the source of True Bread. Here was Life Everlasting. Before him was the Conqueror of Death—the champion against its sting. For the first time since that fateful night, Anthro's hand did not burn. Not even a hint of that wretched stain was felt. It was finally and fully removed within him as far as the east is from the west. He knew that he would never think of it again.

Anthro stepped forward and fell at the king's feet like a dead man and cried out, "I am yours; save me!"

The King of Lux placed his right hand on Anthro's shoulder—firm, yet overflowing with grace—and said, "Do not be afraid. Well done, my good and faithful servant."

Acknowledgements

It's amazing to see a book like this come to life. It started off as a single image in my mind, then it turned into one over-stuffed sentence, which turned into one scene which never even made it into the final manuscript. It has had its slow-moving seasons and its many trials, but it has certainly been worth the effort to get to see the story come to life. Without a doubt, the first person to thank is the one who has read it the most, which is my sister, Lydia. Thanks for not holding back! I'm thankful to my parents John and Denise that have influenced this book in a way that only parents can, with special appreciation for my mom's continuous support of my writing. My friends, particularly Robbie and Bri Andrassy and Jon Ryan, also deserve a shout-out. True friends are indeed hard to find, but I've got some great ones. My entire family, immediate and extended, is such a blessing that I cannot help but mention them.

This book might not have ever come to life without Austin Parenti giving it a chance. Penn Street writers unite! To my two editors, Grace Alvarez and Laura Mitze, thanks for dealing with all my run-on sentences, overuse of comas, and nonsensical statements. The editing was arduous and brutal, but the book is so much better because of it. A major thanks to Joshua Griffin. He could not have done a better job with the cover design work. That process terrified me, but he captured the heart and soul of *Redeeming Royalty* in a way that I could not even imagine. I also must thank Pastor Jeremy McKeen for helping me to fully understand the depths of the gospel. As well as Pastor Patrick Lafferty for showing me in his sermons the beauty and intellectual depth of it.

A special thanks to all the Christian apologists out there who influenced so much of this book. From the classics like Blaise Pascal, G.K. Chesterton, and C.S. Lewis, to the modern voices such as Timothy Keller, Rebecca McLaughlin, C. John Collins, Gavin Ortlund, and so many others. Without your work, I genuinely do not know what I would make of the true King of Lux. Additionally, the apologists at Palm Beach Atlantic University deserve a specific thank you for their time, energy, wisdom, conversations, and friendship. Paul Gould, Paul Copan, and Brandon Rickabaugh all show that apologetics never need be separated from faithfulness, kindness, and investment in their local church.

Finally, I must thank you, my readers for thinking along with Anthro and investing your time in this book. If you've found yourself wanting to dive deeper into some of the arguments explored within *Redeeming Royalty*, the apologists and scholars mentioned in the above paragraph are my top recommendations.

www.ingramcontent.com/pod-product-compliance
Lightning Source LLC
Chambersburg PA
CBHW011140180225
22134CB00041B/653

* 9 7 9 8 9 8 6 8 0 6 9 5 2 *